Rosie Archer was born in Gosport, Hampshire, where she still lives. She has had a variety of jobs including waitress, fruit picker, barmaid, shop assistant and market trader selling second-hand books. Rosie is the author of The Munitions Girls series of Second World War novels, set in and around an armaments factory, and The Bluebird Girls series following the lives of a Gosport singing trio as they find fame and fortune, as well as several other Second World War novels.

Also by Rosie Archer

The Girls from the Local
The Ferry Girls
The Narrowboat Girls

THE MUNITIONS GIRLS SERIES
The Munitions Girls
The Canary Girls
The Factory Girls
The Gunpowder and Glory Girls

THE BLUEBIRD GIRLS SERIES
The Bluebird Girls
We'll Meet Again
The Forces' Sweethearts
Victory for the Bluebird Girls

THE CRITERION GIRLS SERIES
The Picture House Girls

ROSIE ARCHER

I'll Be Seeing You

Quercus

First published in Great Britain in 2021 by Quercus
This paperback edition published in 2021 by

Quercus Editions Ltd
Carmelite House
50 Victoria Embankment
London EC4Y 0DZ

An Hachette UK company

A CIP catalogue record for this book is available
from the British Library

PB ISBN 978 1 52940 538 5
EB ISBN 978 1 52940 536 1

10 9 8 7 6 5 4 3 2 1

Typeset by CC Book Production
Printed and bound in Great Britain by Clays Ltd, Elcograf S.p.A.

Papers used by Quercus are from well-managed forests and other responsible sources.

For Oliver Hall

Chapter One

'Is there a doctor in the house?

Please present yourself at the Criterion's foyer immediately.'

Connie Baxter looked at the enormous mound of her friend Queenie's stomach, uncovered so that Gertie, hopefully, could detect progress in the imminent birth. 'The message is on the screen, now, love,' she said.

She stepped neatly back into the soundproofed staffroom of the picture house, removed her maroon head usherette's uniform jacket, and threw it across the back of a chair. Trust Queenie's waters to break while she and Gertie were at the pictures to see the new Bette Davis film. 'And your husband's coming down from the projection room,' Connie added, trying hard not to let panic show in her voice for she was sure Queenie's baby was not due yet. 'Len says young Gary can cope with the end of the film and the national anthem.'

Queenie, on the carpeted floor, groaned. 'I don't want Len to see me like this. He's not even the father . . .' Her voice tailed off as another spasm gripped her and, automatically, she began to pant, sweat pouring from her face, heightening the scent of the Californian Poppy perfume she perpetually drenched herself with.

'Maybe not but he's a better man than the Yank that filled your belly. And he's put a wedding ring on your finger, hasn't he?' snapped grey-haired Gertie, who sat on the floor tenderly wiping Queenie's face with a damp cloth. She then asked calmly, 'How many patrons are still watching the film?'

Connie knew she really meant: what were the chances of a doctor actually coming forward? 'Only a few,' she mumbled. 'Most of them left when the siren went and the usual notice broke into the big film telling them they could stay or leave for the public shelters.'

The first bomb blast had hit seconds after Moaning Minnie began to wail and the explosion that followed caused the picture house to shudder on its foundations. Anything that wasn't nailed down had moved precariously. Gosport and the south of England were taking yet another battering from Hitler's bombs.

The film *Now, Voyager*, thought Connie, had enticed a full house, which had thinned out the moment danger became imminent.

'So even Bette Davis and Paul Henreid couldn't persuade picture-goers to stay in an air raid.' Gertie leant closer to Queenie and said softly, 'Never you mind, love. You got me and Connie.' She plucked at Queenie's flowered maternity smock, drawing it down over her body for modesty's sake.

Exhausted, Queenie cried, 'I can't do this no more!' Her bleached blonde hair clung wetly to her scalp and her face was grey with tiredness.

'Yes, you can,' said Gertie, firmly, as she stared into Queenie's blue eyes.

Queenie threw her head from side to side, took in another deep breath and paused, as if holding it could stop the torture of the approaching contraction.

What, thought Connie, if something goes wrong?

Early on in the pregnancy Queenie had allowed herself to be butchered in an attempted abortion. What if she bled to death now, as she nearly had then? What if the baby was born deformed?

Connie's panic was interrupted by the staffroom door clattering open. A small round woman, a whiff of disinfectant preceding her, called, with authority, 'What's going on here, then?'

'Edith!' cried Gertie, rising to her feet.

A tall, worried-looking curly-haired man in a yellow waistcoat followed Edith. After kicking the door closed he dropped to the floor beside Queenie. 'Oh, my love . . .' was all he managed, taking one of her hands just as a strangled scream left his wife's lips.

Edith's apple-cheeked face broke into a knowing smile at seeing Queenie. 'Stop all that racket,' she said. 'Else the patrons remaining might be listening more to you than Bette Davis!' She placed her capacious handbag on the table next to a pile of the *Portsmouth Evening News* and wriggled out of her coat, thrusting it towards Connie. At Edith's arrival, Connie breathed a huge sigh of relief and hung the coat on one of the hooks near the lockers.

From her handbag the woman produced an elongated eggcup-shaped object. She looked about her, miming washing her palms. Connie nodded towards the sink, where a bar of Wright's Coal Tar soap sat in a saucer on the draining board. Unhurriedly, Edith cleansed the item and her hands.

4

'Thank you, God, for sending us a midwife!' said Gertie, dramatically looking heavenwards.

'It's going to be all right, my love,' Len said. 'Edith's here.' He moved to allow Edith access to Queenie.

Queenie, in the throes of a splitting contraction, seemed oblivious to his words. Len's face was wreathed in anxiety.

'How did you find Edith?' Connie asked.

'I remembered her saying she wanted to see *Now, Voyager* tonight. Miraculously, as I broke into the film to put the request for a doctor on the screen, I saw her get up from her seat.'

Edith Stimson, a neighbour of Len's, had looked after Queenie when she'd been found doubled up in pain on the pavement near Old Road after her visit to the abortionist.

'I need to examine you, love,' Edith said to Queenie now. 'Let's have a bit of quiet, everyone,' she added.

'I'll put the kettle on,' Gertie whispered, staring at Connie before she slid away, muttering, 'I need a fag.'

Connie saw Queenie was doing her best to keep still while Edith pushed up her smock, bent over and listened to Queenie's belly through the little wooden contraption. A sort of hush had fallen over the room as Edith moved the object across Queenie's taut skin.

Connie, unable to bear the silence any longer and watching

Queenie's face as it screwed up with the onset of another wave of pain, asked softly, 'Is everything all right?'

Edith removed the device and smiled up at her. 'Three strong heartbeats,' she said, leaning back. 'Queenie's doing fine and so are the twins.'

Gertie spluttered smoke into the air. 'Twins?'

A stunned silence fell over the room.

'Twins?' Len's face was like parchment.

'Twins?' echoed Connie.

'Wasn't she told at the hospital?' Edith had moved along to peer between Queenie's raised knees.

'She never went to no hospital.' Gertie's voice was shaking as was her hand, which was trying to strike the Swan Vestas match to light the gas beneath the kettle on the stove. The Woodbine stuck to her lip quivered.

Connie thought about Ace Gallagher, the club owner she was engaged to. He'd said he would provide a good doctor for Queenie, but his assurance to her friend was like his promises to her: meant in the moment and easily forgotten.

'Are you sure?' The projectionist had found his voice. He was once more down on the floor beside his wife and Queenie was clutching his hand. Connie saw the moon-shaped dents in Len's hand fill with blood as Queenie's nails dug into his palm.

Sharply Edith said, 'My hearing and Pinard stethoscope never lie.' Dropping her voice, she added, 'We're coming along nicely, Queenie, love.' To Connie, she barked, 'Get some towels, and I'll have those newspapers.'

The soundproofed staffroom wasn't equipped for the delivery of babies but it had been the safest place to take Queenie when her waters had broken while she and Gertie had been watching the film. Connie yanked at the lightly soiled towel above the sink, immediately breaking the roller so it dropped from the wall. There were clean tea-towels in the cupboard below. She showed Edith her meagre offerings. Edith's face was inscrutable.

A series of gunfire strikes ricocheted across the crenellated roof of the picture house. Connie drew a sharp breath. Flakes of white paint, mottled brown by years of cigarette smoke, fell from the ceiling, like dirty snow, and she used the hand that wasn't holding tea-towels to brush the bits off her face.

Another tremendous blast wrenched open locker doors, revealing their lack of towelling. Instead she saw an umbrella, shoes, an empty brown carrier bag with string handles, and a bundle of candles. In one a first-aid box sat on a shelf. She wrenched it open to discover only a bandage and a couple of safety pins. Connie doubted the manager's office in the foyer contained anything more useful for a woman giving birth.

She tried to push away thoughts of the scenes outside the picture house where probably an inferno raged. There'd be craters where buildings had stood. Halves of houses with gaping bedrooms and furniture hanging precariously from broken flooring.

And that awful stink of cordite and burning . . .

An unearthly screech from Queenie brought Connie's thoughts back to reality.

Then Len was at her side. 'It's not going right! She's bleeding. Edith says she needs the hospital.'

'Ambulances won't come out for women in labour,' snapped Connie.

'Not with that lot going on outside.' She saw the fear in Len's eyes and knew that he, too, was remembering the botched abortion.

'I can't lose her,' he said. He looked like all the life had been leached from him.

'Nor can I,' Connie murmured, and she turned away. The last strains of 'God Save The King' were playing and the house lights were up as Connie pushed past patrons who had sat through the film until the end.

In his dark red uniform with the gold trimmings and fringed epaulettes, Commissionaire Thomas Doyle was shepherding people out of the main door, telling them to

8

keep safe on their homeward journeys. Earlier Connie had asked him to oversee the last of the usherettes going home. Normally this was the job of their new young manager, Gilbert Willard, but he wasn't in today.

'How is . . .' Doyle called. Everyone called him by his surname.

Connie left his question unanswered but she shook her head to let him know that all wasn't well. She pushed open the office door, grateful for Doyle's loyalty in caring about the correct running of the Criterion.

She grabbed the black telephone from the desk, dialled and put it to her ear.

Dead.

Slamming down the receiver, Connie ran from the office, squeezing beneath Doyle's raised arm as he was about to lock the door. 'Don't lock up. Queenie needs help,' was all she said, as she ran out into the night.

Chapter Two

I wonder if Mum still leaves the key on a string. Marlene Mullins unlocked the Alma Street door, then pushed the key back through the letterbox into its usual place.

Inside the terraced house she dumped her battered card-board suitcase tied with string onto the lino in the passage and threw her gas mask down beside it. She breathed in the aroma of polished furniture, cooking, the warmth coming from the black-leaded range in the kitchen, all overlaid with the stale smell of Woodbines, the familiar scent of home. Marlene took off her coat and hung it over the back of a kitchen chair, then went to the window and pulled the blackout curtains across. Only then did she switch on the electric light so the single bulb dangling from its cable in the centre of the ceiling lit up the room and showed her how little had changed in the time she'd been away.

She looked at the range. 'Not like you to let the fire get so low, Mum,' she surmised. 'You've been gone some time.'

Marlene used the metal lever to lift the top off the hob so she could drop in a couple of small logs from the filled scuttle. She nodded with satisfaction as bright sparks and flames welcomed the offerings.

In the scullery, having drawn the curtains on their wires across the window, she shook the kettle, making sure there was water enough for tea, then lit the gas.

She paused by the mirror hanging near the sink to smooth her blonde hair and check her make-up hadn't suffered too much in the damp air during her walk from the bus stop to the house. On the Provincial bus, when she'd powdered her nose, her compact mirror had told her she looked good, very good indeed.

Marlene yawned. She was tired.

It was less than twelve miles from Shedfield to Gosport but the inefficiency of wartime transport meant she'd spent a long time waiting for vehicles that were late or had never materialized.

It seemed funny being alone in the house. These past months in the country she'd hardly been alone at all. Alex Huggins had glued himself to her, like a verruca to a foot. She'd thought when she'd volunteered to help the young teacher look after the evacuees from the National Children's Home at Alverstoke that she'd see a bit of life. Well, she'd thought wrong, hadn't she? Shedfield didn't even possess a shop! Wickham, a nearby village, boasted a post office, a bakery, a general store, a meeting place and not much more.

Entertainment was one measly dance in the tin-hut parish hall every fortnight and was the highlight of her life there, accompanied by Alex, of course. He didn't think it seemly for her to attend alone. The lively social gathering was for the benefit of the American servicemen stationed at a nearby airbase. But now the Americans had been moved to Lee-on-the-Solent at Gosport so the dances had been abandoned.

Initially Marlene had thought to better herself by eventually becoming a teacher's wife – Alex earned good money. After meeting a few American servicemen, though, she didn't want to be anyone's wife: she wanted to have fun and Alex bored her. He'd irritated her with the constant clearing of his throat. She'd found she was on edge waiting for him to cough. It also grated on her nerves that he hesitated, then stuttered, before practically every sentence – 'Er ... Er ...'

Sharing a bedroom at the rectory where they had been billeted had been out of the question: the housekeeper had seen to that.

In the beginning Marlene had thought she could use her substantial charms to persuade Alex to propose marriage. She soon realized what a fool she was to have considered tying herself to a man who bored her rigid. All he cared about was making sure the children were happy in their new surroundings. Last night he'd said that today they would take the children on a ramble. That meant ploughing through brambles and mud looking at wild flowers and birds. Marlene had decided she'd rather stick pins in her eyes. Enough was enough.

She'd woken early after packing her belongings into her suitcase the night before. She'd already taken cash from Alex's savings, which were tied in a sock in a box at the back of his wardrobe – he really was far too trusting, she'd thought.

Before even the housekeeper was awake, she'd walked away from the rectory in search of new experiences. Marlene wasn't particularly worried about Alex coming after her because he'd have to find her first, wouldn't he? He'd never suspect she'd return to Gosport after pleading with him to take her away from the place, would he?

Marlene perched on a kitchen chair to drink her tea.

The cruet set and an ashtray full of dog ends sat, as usual, in the middle of the table, with half a bottle of milk and a glass bowl containing a spoon encrusted with tea-stained sugar granules. She looked at the clock on the mantelpiece. Next to it was a photograph of her mother with her arm around a young woman who looked uncannily like herself but was, in fact, Connie, her cousin. The background seemed to be here in Alma Street. Marlene recognised the honeysuckle bush that draped itself over the lavatory wall at the bottom of the garden next to the Anderson shelter. Connie and her mother looked contented – no, more than that, happy together. A spike of jealousy drove itself through Marlene's heart. Admittedly, though, her mother was a sucker for taking in waifs and strays, wasn't she?

Where on earth could Gertie be at eight in the evening? Had she changed her working hours at the Criterion picture house? Marlene smiled to herself. She couldn't see her mother as a torch-wielding usherette: she'd never aspire to higher things because she was a cleaner through and through. Obviously she had got herself caught up in something she considered important – she'd never normally forget to feed the fire. April was still a cold month.

In the cupboard she found half a loaf of bread. After cutting herself a chunky slice and spreading it thickly with condensed milk, she poured herself another cup of tea. Before she sat down again, she switched on the wireless.

Vera Lynn was singing 'I'll Be Seeing You'. Marlene hoped that didn't apply to her and Alex.

Did Gertie still have her other lodger? The bloke from that club in town? Marlene had never met him. She remembered her mother telling her in a letter that Ace was opening another club in Portsmouth. She didn't always read Gertie's letters properly – the only interesting things about them were the postal orders or the occasional ten-bob notes her mum enclosed.

She supposed Connie was still living here. Where else would she be after her mother had got herself blown up in Portsmouth? Marlene remembered Connie as a pathetic child who wouldn't stick up for herself. Marlene would give her Chinese burns and pinch her, knowing she was too frightened to tell on her.

She took a bite of the bread's sweetness. The way to find out who was lodging here would be to check the bedrooms. Marlene sipped her tea then yawned again. It had been a long day and the food, drink and warmth were making her sleepy.

It really was too bad of her mum not to be here to welcome her home.

Leaving the bread, condensed milk and her used crockery on the kitchen table, she walked along the hallway to inspect the sleeping arrangements. After pulling across the blackout curtains and switching on the light, Marlene saw Connie had made the front room her own domain.

A photograph of Jean, Connie's mum, sat on a small table next to the bed. Marlene remembered it being on the mantelpiece in the kitchen. Gertie would have placed it there to comfort Connie. Again, the spear of resentment cut through her heart. A folded fan-shaped newspaper in the grate told her the fire was never lit. The bed was made, and on the dressing-table there were items of make-up, a hairbrush and comb, nothing of any importance except a bottle of Evening in Paris perfume. Marlene shook the bottle and dabbed a little on her wrists, wondering who had bought it for Connie. She couldn't see her cousin paying for anything this glamorous and expensive in these days of austerity.

Clothing hung along the dado rail on hangers. Dowdy dresses that had been remade to look different. Make do and mend was definitely on Connie's agenda, Marlene thought. She recognized a couple she'd thrown out before she'd left home. Marlene fingered a woollen frock, definitely one of her cast-offs that now looked quite wearable, with its pleated front, knee-length skirt and sweetheart neckline.

She remembered her mother saying that after the bomb had decimated Auntie Jean's house, Connie had been taken in by her employers with only what she had in her handbag.

She had been at work in the Sailor's Return pub when the bomb dropped.

A well-worn flowered winceyette nightdress was draped across the bed. Marlene recognized it as belonging to her mother. She picked it up and smelt Connie's fragrance on it. She crumpled the material in her fist, then threw it back on the bed.

Marlene clattered the door shut and went upstairs.

Her mother's room was just as she remembered it. Iron-framed bed, dressing-table, chest of drawers and the smell of fags hanging over everything.

The back bedroom was more interesting, once she'd drawn the blackout curtains and switched on the light. A good-quality suit hung on the back of the door. A silk shirt dangled from a hanger on the dado rail. A new bar of Imperial Leather soap lay on a clean towel on top of the washstand. She opened the jar of Brylcreem on the chest of drawers and noticed it was missing some scoops. She sniffed the scented white cream.

Pulling back the quilt and blankets, she saw pristine white sheets and pillow-cases, in readiness for use but as yet unslept in. Everything in the room was tidy and clean. Despite the scent of lemon cologne hanging in the air the room looked unlived-in, unused.

Marlene yawned again. She kicked off her high heels, undid the button on her tight black skirt and let it drop to the rag rug covering the lino. She pulled her fluffy pink jumper over her head, climbed onto the bed, hauled up the covers, closed her eyes and slept.

Chapter Three

'Where're you off to? It's early yet.'

Ace Gallagher spun round at Jerome's words. 'Keeping tabs on me, are you, old man?' He straightened his trilby, which he'd just set on his head, and gave a wide smile. Then he picked up the glass of whisky from the shiny new bar counter and drank it in one swallow. It crossed his mind he'd had a few more drinks tonight than usual.

'Me keeping tabs on you? That'd be the day, wouldn't it?' Jerome put down the local paper he was reading and pushed his spectacles further up the bridge of his nose. A lock of grey hair fell over his forehead and, with a blue-veined hand, he smoothed it back.

'If you must know, at long last I'm finding the time to drive round to Gosport to pay a visit to my fiancée and her lovely landlady. As neither have set foot in Gosport's Four

Aces, and this second club of mine here near Southsea's South Parade pier, in Portsmouth is nearing completion, I thought they might like an invitation to see the place.'

'Never mix business with pleasure, son. They'll have forgotten what you look like.'

'I very much doubt that,' Ace said.

He glanced at himself in the mirrored wall at the rear of the bar where brightly coloured bottles on shelves were reflected. A tall, good-looking man in an expensive camel-coloured overcoat stared back. The bright chestnut colour of his hair peeked out from beneath his hat.

Ace didn't take either his looks or his wealth for granted. He remembered only too well being a snotty-nosed hungry street kid, who would have perished if Jerome hadn't taken him under his wing.

Ace had been ten years old then and cheating people of money to feed himself by playing Find the Longest Straw, a version of the card game Find the Lady. He was being pursued by an irate man he'd swindled when Jerome grabbed him by the collar, thrust him out of sight and saved him from a beating.

Billy Hill, the gangster, Jerome's mate, then employed him as a bookie's runner. Invariably on the lookout to make money, Ace didn't always hand in the pledges, especially the bets he thought had no chance of making money.

Jerome had saved his life again, after Ace had spent a punter's bet. The bloody horse had unexpectedly romped home and the man had wanted his winnings. Billy Hill, who at fourteen had murdered a man and was now much respected and feared, was none the wiser.

For once in Ace's life, he had someone to care about him and he'd never forgotten how good that felt. Now he was the owner of two gambling clubs on the south coast. He dealt in black-market goods, ran the monopoly on fruit machines in pubs and clubs the length of the country, and all because Jerome still believed in him.

'You'll be all right, won't you?' Ace turned and spoke before he reached the exit.

'I don't need babysitting,' Jerome said.

Ace nodded. A sudden noise caused him to look towards the kitchen. He heard the tap run. The late-night cleaners were about their business, he thought. He took a deep, satisfying breath of the fragrance of new paint and disinfectant before leaving, then picked up the bags of groceries and packets of Woodbines he invariably took to Gertie. On an impulse he collected a bottle of his favourite whisky from behind the bar. Gertie sometimes liked a drop 'for medicinal reasons', she said.

Once outside he looked through the darkness to where the outline of South Parade Pier loomed. He couldn't see the barbed wire on Southsea's beach, a deterrent for a possible German invasion, but he knew it was there. The sea rattled softly across the stony shoreline, surging calmly, unhurriedly. Ace pulled up his collar against the chill of the April night and walked around the corner to where his black MG VA tourer was parked and began unbuttoning the mohair hood.

Soon he was out of Portsmouth's war-scarred streets and driving across Portsdown Hill. Even high above the city, with the salt waters of the Solent below, he could still smell the scorch of Hitler's desecration. He thought there was a possibility of another raid tonight. The bloody Germans wouldn't waste a clear bright sky.

He allowed himself to think about Connie, her soul-searching green eyes, her fall of blonde hair that reminded him of film star Veronica Lake's peek-a-boo style. She was a girl in a million was Connie. When he'd told her his dream was to own four clubs on the south coast, and the premises in Southsea had come up for sale, she'd never berated him for setting aside their wedding. He'd needed every penny he could get to build the second club, and Connie had understood a fancy engagement ring was out of the question.

At Christmas, however, he'd made her a present of a solid gold bracelet. A matching chain necklace followed. Connie knew he would have showered her with expensive gifts if this second chance in a lifetime of buying and building in a prime location for the proposed Four Aces club hadn't arisen.

At first, he'd put in a temporary manager at the Four Aces club in Gosport so that he was free to oversee the building work's progress in Southsea. Of course, that had meant visits to Gosport, Connie, and his lodgings at Gertie's had been severely curtailed.

His builder in Portsmouth was A. G. Knight, a man known for his dodgy dealings, especially in obtaining planning permissions. Ace smiled to himself. Even in wartime a bit of blackmail worked wonders, but it meant he couldn't turn his back, not even for a moment.

The manager at his Gosport club was unreliable. Jerome decided he would oversee that business to take the pressure off Ace, leaving him to run the other club upon completion

Ace swore as he lurched across a pothole in the road. The blackout meant all vehicles had to have dimmed headlights.

'That'll do the car's suspension a lot of good,' he moaned. He peered through the windscreen as the light wind chilled his face.

When he reached Fareham it was easier, on the familiar road, to manoeuvre round the hazards of previous air raids. Rubble was piled at intervals along the sides of the main thoroughfare. Traffic was scarce – petrol rationing saw to that. Not that he was troubled by rationing. He had a nice little racket going with a farmer at Rowner who removed the tell-tale pink colour of agricultural fuel by straining it through bread. Black-market coupons, too, meant that Ace never went short of petrol.

On the seat beside him he had the brown carrier bags full of groceries. Bacon, a couple of pounds – what good was four ounces of bacon per person a week? That was rationing for you, he thought. The streaky would make Gertie's eyes light up. She'd appreciate the packets of tea. Good old Brooke Bond Dividend with the stamps on so Gertie could complete a card and obtain a five-shilling refund. Gertie loved her cuppas as much as her fags. He'd brought cheese, butter, eggs and tinned fruit. And, of course, there was the whisky and several packets of Woodbines. American Hershey bars and three packs of nylons would put him in Connie's good books. What was the use of contacts in the

American service stores in Southampton if you couldn't give your girl a few treats?

Ace saw Gosport had taken a right kicking since he'd last driven along Forton Road. The place had a strange air of desolation, with gaps where previously shops and houses had stood. He raised a hand and saluted men shovelling debris from the pavement into a parked lorry for removal. Even when the raids had stalled for a while, life and work, day and night, went on, he thought.

In the distance he could see the Criterion picture house. He guessed Connie would be at work inside. She'd been promoted now to head usherette. Gertie said she had been the obvious choice when Queenie, her friend, the previous head usherette, had agreed to take it easy and stay at home due to the impending birth of her baby.

The picture house would be locking its doors at about eleven o'clock, if he remembered rightly. His being at Alma Street would be a surprise for Connie when she got home. Gertie worked mornings as a cleaner and he knew she'd give him a warm welcome – after all, he'd gone on sending her his rent money even though his visits to Gosport had, of late, seldom materialized.

He turned the car into Alma Street and parked outside Gertie's front door.

The key, as usual, hung on a string behind the letterbox and after he'd let himself in, he saw the hallway light had been left on. Normally Gertie was frugal with electricity. His eyes fell on the small suitcase but he dismissed it because Gertie was always collecting odds and ends for the church jumble sale and leaving the stuff by the front door.

He frowned at seeing the brightly lit empty kitchen and hearing no movements from the lighted scullery. Not like Gertie at all, he thought, as he put the bags of food on the kitchen table. He saw a woman's coat slung across a chair. Obviously someone was around because the range had been topped up with logs. He removed his hat and left it on the table, frowning at the remains of a bread and condensed-milk sandwich. It wasn't like Gertie, or Connie, to leave food out.

In the scullery the kettle was warm to his touch. The back door was bolted from the inside so no one was in the garden.

He tapped his forehead. 'Of course,' he said, as he walked back towards the passage and knocked gently on the front-room door. Possibly Connie was in bed, asleep. After listening at the door but hearing no sound, he turned the knob. No one was in there.

Worried now that perhaps Gertie was unwell, he retraced his steps and climbed the stairs. The door to her bedroom was open, yet it was empty.

He was surprised to see the light on in his own room.

Stepping inside he saw blonde hair spread about his pillow. Childishly, irrationally, he was reminded of a sleeping princess in a fairy tale,

He thought at first it was Connie lying there. A feeling of warmth spread through his body. Ace immediately imagined her hating their separation so much that she now slept in his room to feel closer to him.

He stared down at her. The warmth inside him came to an abrupt halt as the girl turned her head and two deep blue, long-lashed eyes opened.

She wasn't Connie.

What kind of joke was this? He went on staring at her. The heat of her warm body rose and filled his nostrils.

He grinned down at her. And in the sort of voice he imagined he would use if telling a bedtime story to a small child, he asked, 'My, my, what have we here? And who's been sleeping in my bed?'

Barely a moment ticked by before she answered, 'Goldilocks.'

Chapter Four

Connie watched the German bomber caught in the search-
light before it danced safely into the dark of the night
sky. She sighed. She wished she'd grabbed her uniform
jacket before she'd run from the staffroom at the Criterion.
Despite the flames and fires she was shivering. Smoke and
brick dust caught in her throat and her eyes itched and
watered. It didn't matter how scared she was, though: her
one thought was to get help for Queenie.

Making her way across Forton Road, she saw a huge crater
where once Kellet's, the ironmongery, had traded. To the
left, ARP volunteers toiled relentlessly where number sixty-
three had been split in two. Half of the kitchen, with the
sink intact, and above, half of the bedroom, the double bed
exposed, reminded Connie of a scene from a horror film.
In the breeze a torn curtain flapped at the broken window.

Connie was sick at heart to see the desecration around her.

She lurched along the road, broken furniture and rubble tripping her. She was searching among the frightened and dazed people around her for someone in authority. But landmarks had been obliterated and it was difficult to recognize her surroundings in the dust. She twisted her fists into her eyes to remove the grit and to enable her to see more clearly. Where were the ambulance crews to help these poor people? Please, God, let most others be safely in shelters, she prayed.

Near Park Street, by the bakery, firemen were relentlessly trying to damp down a blaze. People were screaming as auxiliary workers scrabbled to move debris and shift the remains of heavy wooden joists and rafters. A van was parked, engine running, and a heavy-set man was climbing into the driver's seat.

Connie heard another shout, 'Anyone else under that lot?'

The heavy-set man yelled back, 'If there is, we're no use to them. I'll get back quick so we can move on.'

Connie grabbed at the man's arm before he had time to shut the van's door

'Hold on, missy,' he cried. 'What d'you think you're doin'?'

'My friend's in a bad way. She needs the hospital.' She could see the sweat running down the man's face.

'You've picked the wrong vehicle, love. I'm requisitioned to collect bodies for the morgue.' The man was unshaven and looked very tired. He had to bellow to be heard above the noise going on around them.

'Surely you won't let a woman die before you take her to the hospital.'

'Up the road's an ambulance. They'll get your friend to the hospital.' He pushed her away and climbed into the driver's seat. Her heart was stricken as the vehicle fired up and he drove away without another glance at her.

Connie peered along Forton Road and saw the ambulance with all its doors open. Uniformed men and women were milling about. She ran towards them, trying to shield her face from the sooty ash that fell with scorching pinpricks on her skin from the burning buildings.

'Get out the way!'

The angry voice startled her, followed by the scrape of something sharp and metallic against her leg. A hand shot out to stop her falling. Water dampened her skirt, her leg.

'You hurt?' It was a man's voice.

Connie had stumbled into a chain of people passing buckets and other containers of water along a line, trying to quench the fire. Dazedly she looked down at her leg, at her torn lisle stocking, where a line of blood now welled and was suddenly painful. A heavy cast-iron pail had bitten into her soft flesh. It was her own fault for bumping into them, she thought. She shook her head and limped on, praying the ambulance wouldn't leave before she could reach it.

The driver was starting the engine when she hammered on the window. He glared at her and wound it down.

'My friend needs the hospital. She'll bleed to death. Please come.'

'Where is she?'

'Criterion picture house.'

The woman sitting in the passenger seat stared at Connie intently. 'We can do that, Sam. It's on our way.'

Beneath her blue gaberdine coat Connie could see part of a nurse's regulation uniform. The woman leant across the man. 'Come round this side and get in with me, love. My name's Meg.'

Connie was almost overwhelmed by the woman's kindness. At last, there was hope for Queenie. When Connie was sitting next to her, Meg asked, 'Tell me about your friend.'

Just then the ambulance backfired, spluttered and stalled. The man swore, stabbed at the gears, fumbled with the key and restarted the vehicle. It jumped and flung itself along the road.

'Sorry, love. We'll get there, don't you worry,' he said, his previous glare now replaced with a smile.

Meg pulled at Connie's skirt. 'Looks as if you could do with some help, too,' she said, as she gestured at Connie's bleeding leg.

'That's nothing,' Connie said, wiping away the blood with her hand. 'It's my friend who needs help.'

'What's the story?' Meg asked.

Connie thought it better to tell her the truth. 'My friend had a botched abortion some months back and nearly bled to death then,' she said. 'The baby survived, but there's twins, apparently.' Connie paused. 'She's in labour now but there's so much blood, the midwife says she needs the hospital.' Connie suddenly dissolved into tears. Putting the seriousness of the problem into words was too much for her

Sam broke in: 'Don't you worry, girlie. We'll do our best . . . As long as she don't mind sharing the back of this ambulance with a couple of kiddies we pulled out of that rubble back there.'

'Oh, my God!' gasped Connie. She'd been so worried about securing a lift for Queenie it had never occurred to her that the ambulance had already picked up patients. 'Are they, are they . . .'

'They'll be all right,' Sam said. 'More shook up than

anything else. The only ones dug out of that mess who've made it. Brothers. Poor little mites.'

Connie's head swung towards the closed-off rear of the ambulance.

'There's one of our nurses back there with them.' Sam said, raising his voice. 'Making sure they don't get jolted about too much.' The noise coming from outside the vehicle made it difficult for her to hear. 'They're safe now,' he added.

The ambulance slowed as the picture house came into sight.

'Hold on,' cried the driver. He stamped on the brake to avoid an obstruction in the road.

Connie thrust her hands towards the dashboard to stop herself slamming into the windscreen.

The ambulance skidded, then straightened. 'That was close,' he said. 'Potholes are deadly. Sorry about that.'

'Will . . .' Connie discovered her hands were sweating with fear '. . . will the kids in the back really be all right?'

'They've been sedated, love. Sleeping and strapped in,' said Sam. 'No physical damage we could see. Trauma, though. All the same, I'd like to get your friend on board as quickly as possible, no time to waste,' he added.

The Criterion picture house was now directly ahead.

'Go round to the back,' said Connie. 'No steps to climb

and it's nearer the staffroom where I left her.' The driver steered to the rear of the picture house. 'Pull up here,' she said, and almost before the vehicle had stopped, she was out of the cab and moving towards the double exit doors.

She looked back when she caught the sound of a trolley, pulled by Sam, trundling along behind her. Meg was holding on to the rear handles. Connie took a second to breathe a sigh of relief that the picture house was still standing. But what had happened to Queenie since she'd been gone?

She pushed down on the brass bar of the door, which swung open at once, enveloping her in the stench of stale cigarette smoke. Thank God Doyle had remembered not to lock up, she thought. A blanket of darkness sucked her in.

'Power cut,' she yelled.

'Where now?' Sam asked, from behind her. He didn't seem bothered at all by the setback.

'Follow me,' Connie said, holding the door wide so they could manoeuvre the trolley inside. Then she went ahead, guiding them through inky blackness along the side aisle while trying to ignore the throbbing in her leg. At last, she pushed against the staffroom door.

As she did so, fear gripped her heart. What was she going to see inside? She couldn't bear it if anything awful . . . She swept away the negative thoughts and entered the candlelit room.

Len was holding a bloodstained bundle in a tea-towel close to his chest. His yellow waistcoat was wrapped around it to ensure extra warmth.

'A girl,' he said in a trembling voice. The tears in his eyes didn't mask the pride on his face. The baby's tiny fist rose from the bundle. He looked at it, then back at Connie, and she saw the vestiges of a smile. Her heart melted. He'll be a wonderful father, she thought.

Len's eyes fell on the trolley. 'Thank God,' he breathed. She saw him swallow and take a deep breath. 'She's really bad,' he whispered. Connie knew he was referring to Queenie.

Out of the corner of her eye she saw Gertie standing near the sink holding a glass of water. Gertie gave her a smile that came from her mouth but not her eyes. A comforting fag drooped from her lips.

Connie followed Len's gaze down to the floor where Queenie lay on a heavily soiled coat. The pallor of her body almost glowed in the candlelight.

Edith's cardigan, for warmth, was laid across Queenie. The midwife, looking up at Connie with tired eyes that nevertheless sparked with hope, said, 'Bless you, Connie.'

Then she added, 'One baby delivered. She's tiny. She needs an incubator.'

Connie interrupted, 'Queenie?'

'She's having a bit of a breather before the second baby makes its way into the world.' Connie knew Edith was trying to reassure not only her and everyone in the room but also Queenie that everything was as near normal as possible.

Meg touched Edith's arm gently. 'We'll get her and the little one to the War Memorial Hospital. The ambulance is outside.'

Edith nodded. The relief on her face was enormous.

Meg gently lifted the cardigan covering Queenie and studied her. 'We're taking you to hospital, love,' she said softly. Briskly she added, 'Come on, Sam, we've work to do. Let's get her on the trolley.'

In strong arms Queenie was transferred to it from the floor.

'Can we come with her?'

'Sorry,' said Meg to Gertie. 'We've other patients in the ambulance. There's no room. Best if we just include one family member.' Her eyes went to Len, who was holding the baby.

'Yes, you must go,' said Edith. 'She's been continually screaming out your name.'

'Mind your backs,' Sam said, as the trolley rattled towards the door. He took a blanket from a pocket beneath it and handed it to Meg, who tucked it around Queenie. 'Come along, Dad,' he said to Len. 'You might easily have another bundle to carry before we reach our destination.'

Connie mentally blessed Sam for trying to raise everyone's spirits.

He turned to her after a quick glance at the gas stove. 'If I was you, I'd make a pot of tea. You all look as though you could do with a cuppa.' Then he winked. 'We'll look after them all,' he added.

Chapter Five

'Doyle's a nice man, ain't he?'

Without pausing in her steps Connie turned to Gertie, who was trotting alongside her. 'I don't know what I'd have done without him tonight. He excelled himself while I was out looking for hospital transport for Queenie, making sure the last usherettes and patrons left the picture house without any fuss. And it couldn't have been easy for him keeping nosy-parkers away from the staffroom once they knew Queenie was in there in labour.' She skirted some debris on the pavement. The all-clear had sounded a while ago and she and Gertie were at last on their way home after clearing up at the Criterion.

'Doyle ought to have been the manager instead of that silly young bloke they've sent us. Doyle's got the experience, and experience is what counts,' said Gertie.

Connie agreed with her. But she didn't want to get into a discussion about cocksure Gilbert Willard now. There was something about the man that didn't ring true with her. The previous manager, Arthur Mangle, had been a nasty piece of work. He couldn't keep his hands to himself where women were concerned, and all the usherettes had been glad to see the back of him.

Several times lately she'd been called to Willard's office to explain discrepancies in the picture house's takings. Since Connie was well used to cashing up, both at the Criterion and in her previous job as barmaid at the Sailor's Return in Portsmouth, she had been annoyed.

After all that had happened today her head was throbbing and the pain from the leg wound was making it difficult for her to walk

Back at the picture house Gertie had washed Connie's cut leg and tied a handkerchief around it to keep it clean. She'd said the bruising would come out in the next few days. Connie was glad the bleeding had finally stopped.

'We ought to have a proper first-aid kit in the staffroom,' Gertie had observed when, finally, Queenie had gone to the hospital and the three women were left drinking tea.

'I'll speak to Gilbert Willard,' Connie had replied. Not

that she'd thought he'd do anything about it but more to pacify Gertie, who had just lit another cigarette.

'I don't think a first-aid kit would have helped much with what we've been through tonight,' Edith had said. 'That little baby girl is a tiny beauty. I just hope the twin survives. And Queenie,' she'd added.

Connie now looked up to the heavens. She could just make out the brightness of glittering stars shining through the pall of smoke drifting across the sky. It carried with it the smell of burning wood, brick dust and cordite.

Gertie said, 'I really thought we was going to lose her. How do you think she is now?'

Connie knew that the memory of Queenie's anguish would haunt her dreams. She tried to put it from her mind. 'Asleep and safely delivered, I hope.' She looked at Gertie. 'We could find out in the morning if we went up to the hospital.'

'I wouldn't expect Len to turn up for work, especially knowing his lad Gary can operate the film projector,' Gertie said.

'I'm not due in until six in the evening and most of tomorrow's chores have been done, including your collection of dog ends for Mr Mason's roll-your-own fags, so we could go to the hospital in the morning. A bit of time off will do you good, Gertie. There's no point telephoning them.

They never tell you anything over the phone,' Connie added. 'You can pop into Mason's on the way.'

One of Gertie's wartime perks was collecting the cigarette ends left in the ashtrays and on the floor of the picture house. At home she shredded away the clean loose tobacco, put it into a bag and sold it to the local tobacconist, Mr Mason, who mixed it with the shag for rolling tobacco. It was then resold.

'How long have you and Mason been conning customers that way, Gertie?'

'Since the war started and tobacco got scarce,' said Gertie.

'Doesn't it worry you that people are paying through the nose for something that's not quite . . . quite . . .' She couldn't think of the word.

'What the eye don't see the heart don't grieve over,' Gertie told her.

Connie shook her head. Gertie had an answer for everything.

'Goodnight, ladies!' A man wearing a tin hat and carrying a shovel over his shoulder was walking on the other side of the road.

Gertie giggled and called back, 'Goodnight, love.' Then she looked at Connie and said, 'Even after this pig of a night, life goes on, doesn't it, sweetheart?'

Connie realized Forton Road was now full of people, some in uniforms and tin hats, going about their business of clearing up after the air-raid. Women from the Voluntary Services had set up a table near the recreation ground and were doling out mugs of tea from urns perched in the back of a lorry. Dazed householders with blankets around their shoulders sat on the damp grass. In the distance the skies glowed orange from fires still burning further afield.

Connie's nostrils were still stinging with the soot and brick dust she had breathed in earlier while running along the streets of Gosport. A small price to pay, she thought, glad that Queenie was safe. She clung to Gertie's arm as, tiredly, they walked home.

'I hope Edith's got back all right,' Gertie said, as they turned the corner into Alma Street.

'You've forgotten Doyle was walking her to her house, haven't you?' Connie reminded her.

'And I hope my home's still standing,' Gertie added.

Connie peered along the pavement. Nothing had changed except that Ace's car sat outside Gertie's house. Waves of anticipation roiled inside her. It had been ages since they'd seen each other. She felt quite humbled that he'd come to Gosport to visit her on such a terrible night.

Gertie stopped outside her front door and nodded at

the black tourer with its hood pulled up. 'Look at what the cat's dragged in,' she said. 'His lordship's deigned to visit.' Connie knew she was joking: she loved the bones of him.

Connie watched Gertie's fingers search through the letterbox for the key on the string. Immediately after the door was open, she stepped inside and felt for the electric light switch.

'I might have guessed,' she said. 'We've got a bleedin' power cut an' all.' Then she took a couple of steps forward and swore again as she went down on the lino with some force.

Connie hauled her to her feet.

'You all right?' she asked, her eyes accustomed now to the darkness and noticing the suitcase Gertie had stumbled over.

Breathing heavily and holding onto the dado rail that ran along the hall at waist height, Gertie grumbled, 'I tripped over that damned suitcase. Surely Ace never left it there. He's usually more thoughtful.'

'More to the point, what's Ace doing with women's clothing?' broke in Connie. The string holding the case together had broken and women's knickers and frilly nightdresses were scattered about the lino.

'Oh, no!' The two words came involuntarily from Gertie's mouth. She disentangled herself from Connie's grip. 'That looks like my Marlene's stuff.' She peered at it, then nodded. 'Now there'll be no peace in this house.'

Connie's heart had dropped at Gertie's words. If that really was Marlene's clothing it meant her cousin was here now. And, of course, she'd want to stay in the house where she'd grown up. But three rooms were already used as bedrooms. Ace was paying rent for the back one, Gertie slept in the front upstairs and Connie paid to use the downstairs front room. She shivered, suddenly remembering Marlene's cruelty to her when she was younger. Stop it, she told herself. They were both adults now, both civilized people. All the same she knew there was no way she could ever share a room with her cousin.

Gertie was rubbing her knee.

'Are you hurt?' Connie asked her.

Gertie shook her head. 'Only my pride,' she said. 'A bit of light would help,' she said. 'Damn those Germans for putting us all in the dark.'

Connie made her way to the scullery while Gertie foraged in the sideboard drawer that held everything from bits of string to screwdrivers. 'At least the gas is on,' she called, and set about filling the kettle for tea. A nagging sensation was tugging at her brain. Ace's car was here and so was Marlene's suitcase. So, where were they?

Unwashed cups littered the wooden draining-board and Gertie's favourite tea-towel, the one that said, 'A Present from Southsea' with a picture of the pier on it, had been left hanging wet over the sink. Connie knew Gertie wouldn't like that so she picked it up, shook it and hung it over the plate rack on the stove where it usually lived. Connie began tidying the mess before Gertie saw it. Gertie could be a bit of a Tartar about keeping things nice. 'Cleanliness is next to godliness' was one of her favourite sayings. She had never had many nice things so she valued what she was given.

Rinsing the dirty cups, Connie realized Ace and Marlene had had tea. But where were they? She and Gertie had made enough noise coming in to wake an elephant . . .

She left the kettle to boil and went through to the kitchen. On the table was more used crockery. It was too late to hide it from Gertie, who had lit three candles and placed them around the room. A heavy torch now lay on the table.

'You can tell my daughter's home,' Gertie said. 'She never could put anything away after her.' Gertie picked up the loaf. 'Going stale already,' she muttered. 'But where the hell are the two of them?'

Connie was on her way upstairs. She didn't need the torch. She knew her way blindfolded about the small house.

Nothing was out of place in Gertie's empty room. The

door to Ace's was wide open, and as she stepped inside, she saw someone had obviously slept in the bed. 'No sign of anyone up here,' she called down to Gertie.

'Your room's empty,' Gertie shouted back at her.

In the kitchen Connie watched Gertie fill the teapot with boiling water, dragging on her fag without removing it from her lips. They looked at each other.

'So much has happened today I think we've all gone a bit doo-lally,' Connie said. 'The all-clear sounded ages ago so where on earth can Marlene and Ace be?' She watched Gertie cover the teapot with the cosy. 'If they're not in the house they must be in the—'

'Air-raid shelter!' shouted Gertie. She picked up the torch she'd taken from the kitchen drawer and, together, the two women hurried down the garden towards the Anderson.

Pushing open the unlocked door Gertie shone the torch inside, then purposefully stepped in front of Connie as she, too, tried to look around the shelter's small space.

'I knew there'd be trouble,' Gertie said, staring at Connie. Her voice dropped dramatically in volume. 'Don't look, love.'

Her warning came too late.

Connie had already noticed the top bunk had not been disturbed, but an empty whisky bottle lay on it. The bottom bunk, however, overflowed with two bodies clamped tightly together. In Ace's arms Marlene looked like a fragile doll. A doll with a smug, painted-on smile.

'Don't look!' Once more Gertie's words were useless even though she'd spat out her Woodbine onto the dirt floor of the shelter. 'At least they're both fully clothed,' she added, anger dripping from her words.

Connie had seen everything but didn't answer.

She was outside the Anderson shelter, throwing up on the honeysuckle that climbed the lavatory wall.

Chapter Six

The music halted and Tom Smith's thoughts came back to the present. He looked towards the upright piano at the far end of the stage where Shirley Allen sat glaring at him, while miming drinking a cup of tea with her little finger stuck out.

He treated her to a big smile. Sometimes he didn't know what he'd do without the woman whose ample backside practically hid the green-velvet-topped piano stool. Everything about Shirley was big, especially her heart and the way she cared about Tom. He had stopped calling himself Tommo after she had said that name didn't fit his new image.

'Twenty minutes' break for tea,' he announced. Mutterings of pleasure came from the couples on the dance floor as they disentangled themselves from each other, gathering in the distempered kitchen of the Nicholson Hall to chat, drink tea, or stand outside for a breath of fresh air on the pavement opposite the White Horse public house.

'Where were you?' Shirley asked, sidling up to him. She answered her own question: 'Not on this planet at any rate. Standing there with a daft expression on your face.'

Waves of her favourite lily-of-the-valley perfume flowed over him.

'When you play that Bing Crosby waltz, "When The Blue Of The Night", it takes me back . . .'

'Don't tell me,' she said. 'It reminds you of your nights spent as a taxi dancer for Ace Gallagher.'

At her words he could almost feel a gullible elderly woman allowing herself to nestle in his arms as he paraded her around the floor of the Four Aces. She would be smiling up at him, her over-bright false teeth unnaturally perfect in an aged face. And he would be expected to pretend she was a wonderful dancer and an alluring woman, no matter how many times she trod on his immaculately polished two-tone leather shoes. And why? Because she'd paid sixpence at the bar for a ticket to dance with him. She might hope for something more, but when their turn ended it was his job to lure her upstairs to the gaming tables to lose money.

He shuddered. He wasn't proud that he'd been a con artist. He wasn't proud that he'd taken money from women, usually well-off widows with nice homes in Alverstoke, the expensive side of Gosport, where the houses sat in acres of green gardens instead of sharing alleys and backyards.

Shirley interrupted his thoughts again by poking a bejewelled finger into his chest. Her nails were the colour of blood and long enough to dig into his skin through his cotton shirt. Sometimes he wondered how she managed to hit the right piano notes with such long talons.

'This lot pays you to teach them to dance, not daydream about the past.' She was giving him her hard-eyed flinty look. He knew that wasn't the end of her diatribe. 'Those that can, do, those that can't, teach.' She was very fond of saying that. He didn't like to remind her that he could 'do': it was the teaching part he wasn't used to. She took a deep breath. 'This is the first dancing lesson you've ever given in your life, and to make a success of this venture you've sunk all your money into, you've got to show these people that not only can you dance but you can teach them.'

He couldn't help but grin at her. She was telling him off because she cared about him and because she knew of his past.

Shirley had been a cleaner at the club overlooking the ferry in the heart of town. She'd never liked Ace's methods of fleecing people but during wartime a job was a job, so she'd worked at the Four Aces. When she'd heard what Tom intended to do with a windfall the navy had offered him she was quick off the mark in asking if he needed a pianist.

'Want me to go and get you a cuppa?' Tom now offered. Anything to stop her moaning at him! Trouble was, every word she spoke was the truth. It was no good him standing on the stage in front of a microphone telling those couples what to do: he had to get down on the floor with a partner and show them.

'Gawd, no.' Shirley shook her dyed black hair so hard that the feather in her red felt hat danced from side to side. 'You can stay out here deep in thought if you want but I'll go in the kitchen with that lot and listen to the gossip about what they think of you so far.' He watched her waddle away and caught another whiff of her lily-of-the-valley scent.

But Shirley didn't know the half of it.

As a ghost dancer, a taxi dancer, he was well aware that his blond good looks, slim body, broad shoulders and ready smile gave him the confidence to charm birds down from the trees. He had been an asset to his then boss, Ace Gallagher.

Since then a lot had happened in his life and his confidence had been sucked away, like water down a plughole, after Ace had told him he was no longer wanted at the club. He had to admit, though, Shirley was right: to make a success of these dancing classes he must show the men and women in this hall that he was an expert dancer. If he couldn't manage that, he'd lose not only his money but all faith in himself. He sighed. Shirley could be cantankerous sometimes but mostly she was his guardian angel.

And now she was coming back, swaying like a galleon in full sail with a mug of tea in one hand and a rock cake in the other. 'Get this lot down you,' she said. 'I don't know all the ins and outs of what's happened since you was the best dancer at the Four Aces – though there's a lot I do know. Maybe one day we can sit down an' you'll tell me. But you're a bit like them poor devils what's come back from the war with changed personalities. You've lost your nerve, lad, haven't you?'

She was exactly right. All the chat-up lines, the cheeky audacity he'd felt when dancing with women old enough to be his grandmother, had left him. He took a mouthful of tea. Shirley had touched a nerve so sharply he felt tears rise to his eyes. He took a deep breath and drained the mug. She was talking at him again.

'I'm telling you, lad, I've been playing for an hour now and I've not seen you put yourself out to teach anybody anything. Get down there among them couples who have paid good money for you to set their toes twinkling. Don't tell 'em what to do, show 'em! I've seen you dance and you could knock spots off Fred Astaire – an' you're better-looking than him. Give this dance class all you've got, else no one'll turn up next week.' She glared at him.

He saw her heavy mascara had settled in clumps around her sparse lashes. Somehow that endeared her to him even more.

'I gave up my cleaning job to play the piano for you, and if this class folds, I'm out of work, aren't I?'

He took a step away to stand his empty mug on top of the piano. He looked at the rock cake in his other hand. He took a tentative bite. Hard wasn't the word; Rock cake was apt. He'd felt his top front tooth move as he'd tried to bite into it. He could no more eat the gruesome thing than he could fly to the moon. He wondered if Shirley had baked it and decided she must have done. He saw her look out across the hall and slipped the rock cake into his trouser pocket. He could dispose of it later.

'I'm off to drink my own tea,' she said, picking up his empty mug. 'You think on what I've said. You've got another hour to make a success or a flop of this.' He watched as she stalked away, the feather in her hat wobbling furiously. She was right, of course she was.

When he'd returned from Scotland's Faslane naval base, his first call had been to Ace Gallagher. Ace had arranged for another man to take Tom's medical examination so he could join the Royal Navy, his lifelong ambition, and had promised him the job of manager of his new club when Tom eventually left the services. Previously Tom had been classed as unfit: he'd had rheumatic fever as a child and it had left him with a heart murmur. Surprisingly, he'd never experienced any ill effects from dancing, even though it was a strenuous activity.

In Scotland's submarine base Tom had had a heart attack after rescuing a mate from a freezing loch, which had resulted in his navy discharge. Before he'd left for Scotland Tom had met a girl who worked at the Criterion picture house. He'd fallen for her straight away and he was sure she felt the same about him. But the budding romance had come to a halt. How could he tell her he conned elderly women when she asked, as she undoubtedly would, what he did for a living?

Since then, he'd thought of her often. Thought a naval career a more fitting form of employment. He hadn't bargained on his heart attack.

Back in Gosport Ace had laughed at him when he'd asked for his promised managerial job. 'I don't want no cripple in my employ,' Ace had said

'I can still dance,' Tom had replied. He'd wondered how Ace could have had such a change of heart towards him. He'd looked upon Ace as a good friend.

'Can't you get it into your thick skull I don't want you anywhere near my clubs?' Ace's words had cut him to the bone.

Tom returned to the home he had shared with his ailing mother before she'd died. A goodwill cheque from the family of the man he'd dragged from the loch, and the sum of his naval pay had helped him decide to utilize the only real skill he had. His idea of offering classes to people who wanted to learn the range of steps from waltzes to the jitterbug was born. After all, his mother had spent a great deal of money on dancing lessons for him when he was a kid. He felt she might, at last, be proud of him.

That Ace wanted nothing to do with him was a mystery. It added to Tom's lack of confidence in himself.

Once more Shirley's voice cut in on his thoughts and he found another rock cake pressed into his hand. 'You got rid of the other one so quick I brought you another.'

'Thank you,' Tom said weakly. This time he put the heavy cake of dough and its few burnt and blackened currants on top of the piano. 'I'll eat it later,' he said, knowing it would join the other in his pocket. 'We're about to start the second half of the lesson. I can't talk with my mouth full, can I?'

'Remember what I said? Get down on that parquet flooring, pick out a partner and show your students what you can do.'

He didn't dare contradict her. For a big woman, Shirley was quick on her feet, and in next to no time she was perched back on the piano stool, waiting for him to speak to his students.

He glanced around the hall at the ten or so couples ready to dance. All were staring up at him.

'I'd like a lady to partner me, please.'

His voice was small, and he was more than surprised when a little woman, probably around fifty or so, wearing a neat skirt and jumper, sang out, 'I will!' She pushed her way towards the front and waited by the steps to the stage so Tom could walk down and meet her.

Tom's heart was beating fast. 'How's your waltz?' he asked. 'And what's your name?'

'I'm Jean,' she said. 'I'm aware it's one, two, three. But you lead and I'll follow.'

There was silence from the couples as they stepped back and sat down on the chairs arranged around the walls of the room.

Shirley began playing 'When The Blue Of The Night' again. A hush hung over the men and women sitting in the hall.

'Ready?' asked Tom, and on the beat, he stepped out with Jean, who was relaxed and happy in his arms and, he hoped, ready to follow his steps.

Tom realized she could dance a waltz very well. 'You're no beginner,' he whispered.

'I am when it comes to a quickstep,' she said 'So thank God this isn't one.'

He whirled her around, and as he moved, he felt the piano music enter his soul. He moved with the tune, his feet automatically and lightly achieving the purpose his body was made for. Tom felt himself relax physically and mentally. It was as if a curtain had been drawn back in his mind, showing him something he'd forgotten, that dancing was like making love to the girl of his dreams. Easy . . . and wonderful.

The piano music stopped.

Tom gave his partner a last twirl and whispered, 'Thank you, Jean.'

He was amazed when the people who had been sitting stood up and began clapping and stamping their feet. Some were even whistling and shouting, 'Bravo! Well done!'

Tom looked at Shirley. She was standing at her piano, cheering him on, with a huge smile that practically split her face in two.

Chapter Seven

'Drink this cup of tea, love. It'll make you feel better.'

Connie forced herself to look up at Gertie. The familiar smell of Woodbines wafted down to her. Her aunt's face, peering at her, was grey with worry, and although she'd placed the mug of tea on the small table, she hadn't moved away from the side of the bed.

Connie's first impulse was to bury herself further beneath the blankets but deep inside herself she knew that would be cowardly. Sooner or later she had to leave the safety of her bed. She hadn't been able to sleep after the shocking discovery last night of Marlene and Ace curled up asleep together on the bottom bunk in the Anderson air-raid shelter. Her cousin and her fiancé. The same cousin who had made her childhood a misery, with sly remarks, slaps and pinches that Marlene always had a ready answer for while correctly assuming Connie would be too ashamed to tell tales.

'C'mon, love.' Gertie was humouring her. 'Remember, we're going up to the War Memorial Hospital to try to see Queenie this morning.'

Connie didn't have the makings of a smile inside her but reluctantly she nodded. She looked past Gertie to the fireplace where a fan of paper sat in the grate. Bertie, the enormous cuddly bear that Ace had won for her at the fair in Southsea, stared back at her from a stool next to the fireplace. Just looking at him, and remembering, hurt.

Gertie picked up the mug and held it out. Connie was forced to move and take it from her. 'Good girl,' said Gertie. 'I've got water boiling on the stove so you can have a nice wash.'

'Where's Ace?' Connie asked. The sip of strong tea she'd taken had given her the courage to ask.

'Don't worry your head about him.'

'Did he stay here last night?' Connie's words were sharp. Her nerves were all over the place. Knowing he'd spent the rest of the night with Marlene was something she didn't think she could cope with. Her grip on the tin mug tightened as she waited for Gertie's answer – the last thing she needed was hot tea all over herself.

'No, he didn't! He rushed straight out of the house while you were still heaving over my honeysuckle.'

'I'm sorry about that,' said Connie. Relief at Gertie's answer flooded over her.

'Well, you don't have to worry. It rained in the night so the mess is all gone now.'

Connie lowered her eyes. 'Any explanations from him?' The tea was working its magic but her unhappiness was being replaced by anger.

Gertie prised her fingers from the handle of the empty mug and set it back on the bedside table. She shook her head. 'I told you he was gone before I could ask—'

'What did Marlene say?' Connie interrupted.

'Nothing. She went to bed.'

'She didn't have a bed!' Connie was practically shouting. 'She arrived yesterday with no warning!'

Gertie was getting flustered. Her forehead was a mass of frown lines. 'She went to bed in Ace's room.'

Connie's heart plummeted, like a stone down a well. Even if Ace wasn't in his bed upstairs, the thought that Marlene was sleeping there cut her to the bone.

Gertie said, 'You're not listening to me. Ace didn't hang about last night. He shot out of this house like a bat out of hell. As for Marlene, well, I was hardly going to turn my

60

own daughter out on the street in the middle of the night, was I?' Her eyes bored into Connie's.

Connie felt more tears rising. Gertie must have anticipated her feelings for she added, 'Get up out of that bed this minute and come through to the scullery. When you're washed and dressed, we'll go visiting. It's Queenie we need to worry about an' them little babies, not some sordid behaviour of a scally like Ace Gallagher and – and . . .' Gertie paused, then finished her sentence with anger in her voice '. . . my girl who has the morals of an alley cat.'

There was silence in the room while Connie blinked back her tears and digested Gertie's words. Clearly Gertie was appalled at the disruption Marlene had caused and, in her own way, was trying to tell her that she blamed her daughter for what had happened.

'And is Marlene still in bed?'

'Don't you worry about her. She sleeps like the dead. She'll still be out for the count when we get back later.' Gertie sat on the edge of the bed and picked up one of Connie's hands, smoothing the skin with her thumb. 'If you try to put what you saw last night out of your mind, if only for the time it takes to go to the hospital, you'll be able to see things in a different light later on.'

Connie saw the logic in that, but what she really wanted

to do was storm up the stairs, drag Marlene out of Ace's bed and lay into her. Except it wasn't in Connie's nature to harm anyone, least of all the daughter of the woman who had taken her in after her own mother had died in an air-raid. Besides, Marlene had to sleep somewhere if she was back home again after living at Shedfield. And with Ace spending so much time in Portsmouth at his new club, it was natural that Gertie would want her daughter under her own roof.

Connie wanted to scream and shout. Instead she took her hand from Gertie's, pushed back the covers and sat up on the edge of the bed, next to her. 'You're right,' she said. 'My head's in no state to think properly about any of this now.' She stood up, pulled her dressing-gown from the end of the bed and slid her feet into her slippers. Gertie grinned at her. Then, making sure Connie was following, she led the way down towards the kitchen where the wireless was playing Jimmy Dorsey's version of 'Tangerine'.

After a good strip wash in the scullery Connie was feeling, if not better, a bit more settled. Gertie was dressed, ready to go out, and sitting by the range smoking a cigarette.

'It won't take me long to change,' said Connie, 'but I'd not say no to another cuppa if there's one in the pot.' She pulled aside her dressing-gown and showed Gertie the cut near her knee. 'It's knitted together well but the bruising's spread. Have you got a sticking plaster?'

Gertie grinned. 'Of course I have.' She went over to the drawer that held everything except the kitchen sink and produced a packet of Elastoplast.

The smoke from Gertie's fag, which was hanging from the corner of her mouth, rose into Connie's eyes as she watched her aunt carefully dress the wound, just as yesterday she had tenderly washed and bandaged her leg. Gertie might not have been Connie's mother but she did a good job of looking after her. When Gertie had finished, she said, 'I made a fresh pot especially for you.'

Connie wondered how a mother and her daughter could have such different personalities. Love for Gertie rose inside her.

A short while later the pair of them were waiting at the bus stop for transport to the hospital. Soon a double-decker came along, stopping to allow passengers to alight and board. After the conductress had taken their fares, Connie sat looking out of the window. Last night, as she'd run through the streets, Gosport had been full of colour, lit by the red and orange of flames. Today the town was grey and overcast, with the threat of yet more rain.

Shops that had missed direct hits were now miraculously held up by makeshift wooden props. People, ever hopeful, were outside houses, cleaning windows, brushing rubble from pavements. Craters had appeared, shops had gone. Overnight, parts of Gosport had been changed beyond recognition. And yet life went on. Women were queuing outside shops, headscarves over their curlers, shopping bags adorning their arms. Feet were firmly planted on what remained of the pavements, their owners chatting easily to each other as if last night had never happened.

But last night had happened.

Never had she thought she'd go home and find the man she loved lying in a bunk with her cousin . . .

Gertie's elbow dug into her ribs. 'Stop thinking about it!'

'What are you? A mind-reader?' Connie asked.

Gertie sighed. 'Only two more stops and we'll be at the hospital,' she said.

Chapter Eight

Jerome wound the key on the tin of pilchards. As the lid came off, the fishy smell rose to greet him. 'There you are, Cat. There's your breakfast.' He forked some of the contents onto a saucer and put it on the kitchen floor. The fat black and white cat, purring loudly, ambled across the parquet flooring and began daintily to eat.

Jerome put a hand to the animal's glossy fur and smiled. As he pulled himself upright, Ace saw him flinch: the movement had caused a twinge of pain in his back. Even his limp seemed more pronounced today.

'So, you've buggered up this romance as well, have you?' Jerome said.

Ace stared through the window at the rain coming down across Southsea beach in stair-rods. It was hard to tell where the sea finished and the sky began. 'Looks like it,' he said.

'Where have you been all night, then?'

Ace's coat and trilby were slung across the back of a chair. They didn't look particularly wet, and Ace knew Jerome would notice that.

'I drove back here to Southsea from Gosport, after checking on the club, spent some time sitting in the rose gardens on the front in one of those ornamental shelters. When the downpour started coming through its roof, I sat in the car, thinking.'

'You could have come back here.'

Ace faced him. 'What? And have you giving me the third degree like you are now because I was in a mood? I needed to think, old man. I did a lot of that sitting in the car on the front watching the sea.'

'That's as may be,' said Jerome, 'but I warned you when you first started taking Connie out that she wasn't like the rest of your bits of stuff.'

'Yeah! And I heeded that advice. Well, I've messed up good and proper this time . . . and the sad thing is that in a way it wasn't my fault.'

Jerome was looking at him strangely. 'If it wasn't your fault why didn't you make it clear to Connie? She's an understanding girl.'

'Because it was easier to get the hell out of that house before I made things worse.'

Jerome gave a big sigh and shuffled over to the kettle, lit the stove and set it to boil.

Ace was reminded of how the man had aged. A sudden pain shot through his heart. Whatever would he do when Jerome. who was like a father to him, wasn't around? He didn't want to think about that.

Jerome's voice changed in tone. 'Do you want me to cook you something? Nice bit of egg and bacon?'

For a moment the two men simply stared at each other. Then Ace shook his head, used his fingers to brush his hair back from his forehead and looked towards the window, as if he expected an answer to his problem was about to write itself on the glass. All he saw was that there was no let-up in the filthy weather outside.

'Are you going to tell me what really happened last night or am I going to drag it out of you?' Jerome continued making the tea.

Ace pulled out a stool and sat down. 'When I left here, I was shattered. All I could think of was seeing Connie and having a bit of a laugh with her and Gertie, sitting in their kitchen. I let myself into the house. The place was ablaze with lights but I couldn't find neither hide nor hair of either of them. It didn't feel right. It was a bit early for the picture house to have closed but Gertie would normally be at home. She doesn't work nights. Usually she'd be listening to the wireless, or soaking her bunions in a bowl of salt water while waiting for Connie.'

Ace went on to tell Jerome how he'd found a girl asleep in his bed.

Jerome's eyes were out on stalks, as he said she could have been Connie's sister in looks but there the resemblance had ended. 'I couldn't help myself. I was giving her the sort of chat-up lines I give all the women that come in the clubs.' He looked at Jerome. 'You know the sort of rubbish. It's just a laugh, really. It makes them feel good and it doesn't mean a thing to me.'

'Oh, I know what you're like, all right. Think you're God's gift sometimes, don't you?'

Ace ignored the dig, but watched as Jerome poured the tea. He had to stop himself taking the pot out of the old man's shaking hands as tea sloshed over the cup's sides. Ace couldn't say anything because he didn't want to upset Jerome.

'If she was in your bed, this what's-her name, this girl . . .'

'Marlene,' supplied Ace. 'She's Gertie's daughter. I found out she's been living near Wickham.'

'Was she in her nightclothes? Undressed, like?'

'God, no! She was in her underwear but she soon dressed herself in a pink jumper and put her skirt on. Apparently, she'd come home to Gertie's unexpectedly, a surprise for her mum, she said. She'd found the place empty. She'd been travelling most of the day, hanging around for buses and so on, and was dead on her feet. She didn't like to sleep in either her mum's or Connie's bed. She didn't think anyone was using my room, she said.'

Jerome was staring at him. He sighed, then looked down at the floor. 'You've had your breakfast,' he said, to the cat, which was winding itself around his feet. 'What else do you want?' With difficulty he bent down and again stroked the glossy coat. He straightened and met Ace's eye. Ace knew he had decided to hear all of the story before he attempted any advice. 'Well, carry on,' Jerome said. 'That's not the end of it, is it?'

'I only wish it was,' Ace said. He took a mouthful of tea and swallowed it.

'Downstairs she found the bottle of whisky I'd brought Gertie. Gertie likes a nip now and then and, well, so do I. We sat and talked, and the siren went. It was late. She said if her mother and Connie weren't at the Criterion they were bound to be in a shelter somewhere. I thought she was probably right.'

'Well, you haven't blotted your copybook yet, so what else happened?'

'I'm getting there, aren't I?'

Jerome glared at him.

'I made my way down to the Anderson and she followed with the drink. I got on the bottom bunk and she perched on the top. I don't know what we were talking about while the bloody bombs crashed outside – her dislike of the countryside, my tiredness. The drink I'd had earlier and her pouring whisky tots caught up with me and I found myself drowsing.' He looked at Jerome. 'You know how it is.'

'Actually, I don't remember, but you're going to tell me.'

Ace ignored the barb. 'I remember her saying she was cold. Gertie's got a paraffin stove in the shelter but it was too low on paraffin to light, so I didn't bother with it.' Ace stared at Jerome. 'She's been around a bit, this Marlene, but she's not . . .' He paused, trying to think of the right words. 'Connie's a different sort of girl altogether. She's as honest as the day is long. Marlene knows what she wants and how to go about getting it. I employ girls like her all the time. Good for business and the men like them.'

'A bit like your Belle?'

'That's below the belt even for you, old man,' said Ace.

He didn't want to be reminded of his son's mother. Belle and Leon lived in Kent and Ace looked after them with money, but he drew the line at them encroaching on his life.

'Yes, she reminds me of Belle,' he admitted. He thought for a moment that Jerome was going to point out he'd not told Connie about his son. But Jerome was merely making him feel like a cheat and a liar without saying a word. He was good at that.

'Did you—'

'Put my hands on her? No, I didn't! You can believe that or not, just as you like. But I did close my eyes while she was rabbiting on about this and that and being cold. I was topped up with drink and tired . . . The next thing I knew, the shelter door was flung open. Gertie was standing there glaring at me. And for some bloody reason that girl was tucked up on the bottom bunk with me and I had my bleedin' arm around her.'

He watched Jerome push his horn-rimmed glasses back up his nose. 'I wasn't going to try to talk my way out of what Gertie and Connie must have thought, so I made a run for it. You don't blame me for that, do you?'

'One man against three inflamed females? No, I'd have run, an' all,' said Jerome.

Ace didn't like the smile that had blossomed on Jerome's

face. But he wasn't going to aggravate him by mentioning it. He was the only mate Ace had, wasn't he?

'All night I've been wondering how I can get myself out of the stupid hole I've dug myself into . . .' Jerome was openly grinning now and Ace couldn't help himself. 'Stop looking at me like that and come up with a few ideas.'

Jerome took a deep breath. 'Look, I believe you if you say you never put a finger on that girl but it's Connie who's got to believe you, not me.' He paused. 'You really do care about her, don't you?'

'Course I do. I've never asked anyone else to marry me, have I?'

'True,' Jerome said. 'But I told you in the beginning you should tell her the truth about yourself. She should know about your Leon. She should know how you make your living. I don't mean the clubs, I mean the gambling dens, the black-market, the deals you make with Billy Hill, the fixed fruit machines . . .'

'You make it sound like I'm a right toe-rag!'

Jerome didn't speak, merely rolled his eyes. Then he added, 'How do you think she's going to feel when she finds out you deliberately made it possible for young Tommo Smith, by falsifying his medical, to join the navy even though you knew his heart wasn't up to it? He wanted something better for himself than working for you as a con man. He thought that being in the services and fighting for his country was a more honourable profession and that when he'd served his time he could come home, get to know Connie and she'd be proud of him. He knew nothing about your interest in her. But you couldn't bear the thought of someone else having her, could you?'

Ace knew Jerome was waiting for him to speak, to deny the accusations. But how could he when every word spoken was the truth?

'I don't blame you for that. I was in on it, wasn't I? And it was better for him to be hundreds of miles away in Scotland. It put him out of harm's way, and out of Connie's way . . .' He took a deep breath. 'You can't go on lying to her any more, Ace. Don't let her hear from someone else what you've done.'

'How's she ever going to find out about that? Are you going to split on me?'

Ace's temper was up now. He didn't like the way this conversation was going.

'Me? You know I'll never go against you, Ace. You mean the world to me. But if you want to marry that girl, and I've said this before, you must be honest with her. Or at least honest enough . . .'

'What d'you mean, "honest enough"?'

'Tell the girl the truth. Wrap it all up in cotton-wool, so when everything starts coming undone, as one day, possibly, it might, she'll believe you before she listens to anyone else.'

Ace thought for a moment. 'If Connie knows nothing she won't be hurt.'

Jerome shook his head. 'That's not true. Lies have a way of becoming common knowledge and someone always gets hurt.'

Ace stared at him. Then he walked over to the shelf near the gas cooker, took down a bottle of whisky and poured himself a large drink, which he downed in a single swallow.

'Starting early, aren't you?' Jerome's voice had an icy edge to it.

Ace set down the empty glass. 'So what?' He took a deep breath. He was angry with himself because every word Jerome had spoken rang with the truth. He took another deep breath and said, as he poured himself another drink, 'I see where you're going with all this, old man, but it doesn't tell me how to get out of the mess I got myself into last night, does it?'

Jerome, frowning at Ace's glass, said, 'If you don't want my advice, son, don't ask me for it. But if I was you, I'd get round to Connie and show her you care. And I'd go as soon as possible,' he added. 'Then I'd shame the devil and tell the truth.'

Chapter Nine

'This corridor's endless,' Gertie said, as she stopped to put out her cigarette in the sand-filled bucket near the red fire extinguisher. She looked at the sign on the wall. 'It says "Maternity Wing",' she added, 'and the arrow points this way.'

'Let's ask this nurse,' said Connie. To her, it seemed they'd been walking around the War Memorial Hospital for hours.

Gertie piped up with her request.

'I'm sorry, you can't see Mrs Queenie Gregory,' the pretty young nurse, carrying a covered bedpan, answered. 'She's in a private room, no visitors allowed. Her husband's waiting and he's sitting in there having a cup of tea.' She nodded towards a closed door.

'Thank you,' called Gertie, sweeping into the cream-painted room, as the nurse moved on down the corridor.

Connie saw Len sitting alone in the corner. On a small table was a cup of tea, untouched but still steaming, alongside a copy of last night's *Portsmouth Evening News*. Len sat with his head in his hands but looked up expectantly, dark circles beneath his eyes, they entered immediately.

'How you can stand being in this place, I don't know,' Gertie said. 'The smell of disinfectant is enough to kill a person.'

Len tried to smile but failed miserably.

'Jesus, lad, you'd better drink that tea and see if it puts a bit of colour in your face,' Gertie added.

Connie's heart went out to him. He needed a shave, his eyes were bloodshot, and his face was the colour of parchment.

'That nurse said there's no visiting—'

She got no further for Len scrambled to his feet, took a couple of steps towards Connie and threw his arms around her. 'Thank you for what you did. But they still won't let me see her. She's so poorly.' He sobbed. Connie automatically tightened her hold on him, trying to still his shaking form as he cried like a child. She smelt the unwashed sweatiness of him as he clung to her.

'C'mon, lad,' said Gertie, in a brisk voice. 'What's the doctor said?'

'I'm so sorry,' Len mumbled, pulling away, 'I shouldn't . . .' His face was wet with tears.

Connie hugged him to her. 'Yes, you should lean on us, that's why we've come.'

'What have they said?' Gertie was insistent. She had dug in her coat's vast pocket and was holding out a none-too-clean handkerchief, waving it in front of his face so he was compelled to step away from Connie and take it. He wiped his eyes and blew his nose.

He stood up straight and gazed at Gertie.

She tried again: 'The baby? Is it all right?'

'Two,' he answered, a smile creeping over his face.

Connie pulled him onto a chair next to her and Gertie sat down as well. In a gentler tone, Gertie asked, 'How are they?'

'So tiny, so beautiful,' he said.

Relief spread over Gertie's face. 'And Queenie?'

'They had to operate after the little boy . . . little boy . . .' he sniffed back a sob '. . . Paulie, was born.'

'Paulie?' asked Gertie, frowning.

'Yes, Paulie. Her son, our son,' he said proudly 'Bette's the girl.' He gave a tiny smile. 'She wanted those names.'

'After going into labour while *Now, Voyager* was showing,' said Gertie, with a knowing look. 'Paul Henreid and Bette Davis,' she said. 'The stars of the picture.'

Len was talking again: 'They had to operate on Queenie. That bloody woman messed her insides up good and proper with the botched abortion. The surgeon said if she recovers she can't have any more kiddies.'

'But she will get over—'

'They don't know, Gertie. I just got to wait.'

Gertie put her hands to her face and began to sob. Connie picked up one of Len's hands. 'Queenie's tough, Len. She won't let go of life, not when she's got you and them tiny babies.'

Len looked into Connie's eyes. 'I can show you them, if you like?' He sounded proud and positive now. 'They're in a special room down the corridor. We can't go in but there's this big window.'

Gertie wiped her eyes. 'Can we really?'

Len nodded, slipped his hand from Connie's. 'I'll show you. But I have to get back here quickly in case there's any change. I was told to wait.'

Gertie was already on her feet and had the waiting-room door open.

He slipped through and the two women followed him into the corridor

A little way along a door bore a sign: 'Authorized Personnel Only'.

Next to it there was a large window, and through it, Connie could see five canvas cots. Inside each was a well-wrapped baby, each resembling a tiny Egyptian mummy. All were sleeping soundly.

'They're not all mine,' Len said, trying to lighten the tense atmosphere.

'You'd know it if they were,' riposted Gertie.

Connie felt a sudden lightness at her words.

Len said, 'This is the special warm room where the little ones stay until they're able to join the other new babies in the big nursery. See the cot at the side?' Len's finger tapped lightly on the glass. 'See the big label at the bottom?' Connie peered to where he was pointing. 'Gregory, Bette,' the pink tag proclaimed. The next cot had 'Gregory, Paul' on a blue one.

Connie put a hand over her mouth. Her heart was over-flowing with happiness for them, that they had survived, and Len would be the best father either child could have wished for.

'Are they . . .' Gertie seemed to find the end of her sentence difficult '. . . all right?'

'Gertie,' said Len, putting his hands on her shoulders and looking into her eyes, 'not only are they all right but they're absolutely wonderful.'

Back in the waiting room, Len sat down again. 'Thanks for coming. You've made me feel a lot happier just talking to you—'

Connie interrupted: 'Would you like to go home, get bathed, maybe have a bit of a sleep? Gertie and I can stay here.'

'Oh, no! I'm not moving until I know what's happening to my Queenie, but I'd like it if you could go to my house and bring back a few things for her.' Connie saw the look of hope in his eyes and his voice had become animated. 'Nightdresses, personal items, that sort of thing. Her make-up bag – you know how she always likes to look her best.'

It was on the tip of Connie's tongue to ask if he shouldn't wait until he knew Queenie was going to need those things but she kept quiet. Surely it was much better to look on the bright side. Besides, Gertie was frantically nodding and already accepting Len's front-door key.

Len had another request: 'Young Gary Pink can go on operating the films in the projection room. He's a marvel at the job for one so young and won't let me down. Would you let him know what's happening? I've tried phoning the Criterion but can't get through.'

Gertie chimed in: 'That ruddy manager's probably absent

again but the electricity is on in that area so the picture house will open as usual today—'

Connie cut her off: 'We can do all that, so don't worry. Do you want me to have a chat with Willard?'

'Would you?' He looked relieved.

'Of course – if he turns up.' Gertie sniffed. 'This new bloke's almost as bad as Arthur Mangle for taking time off. Now you see him, now you don't. An' that's not all. There's the money.'

'Don't start bothering Len with stuff like that. He's got enough to worry about,' snapped Connie.

Len was staring at her. 'What does Gertie mean?'

'There's bound to be a mistake somewhere,' said Connie. 'Though how, I don't know. It's nearly always me who bags up the nightly takings and they add up then. Doyle often checks my figures, so I'm not worrying too much about it.' She looked at Len, who ran his fingers through his dark curls. 'And neither should you. It's not your department and you've enough on your plate.'

Connie was on her feet and motioning to Gertie to follow her out of the hospital. At the door she turned back to Len. 'When you can talk to Queenie, tell her we love her,' she said, unable to disguise the emotion in her voice.

Chapter Ten

There was corned-beef hash waiting for her when Connie finally got home after her shift at the Criterion. She'd been wary of entering the house and seeing Marlene but Gertie was alone in the kitchen.

'You all right, love?'

Connie hadn't answered her straight away but had looked questioningly up towards the ceiling.

Gertie, ever the mind-reader, had replied, 'Marlene's out. She don't tell me where she's going, never has.' She lit a Woodbine and sat in the armchair by the window.

While she ate, Connie told her the usherettes were agog for news of Queenie and she'd set their minds at rest as best she could. 'Young Gary says he can manage as long as Len wants him to go on showing films. We've had *Spare a Copper* start today with George Formby,' she added. 'We'll play to full houses because everyone likes to see George making a fool of himself. He's like a bright light shining in the war's darkness.' She paused. 'It was all over the Pathé news about the price of drinks going up and a hundred per cent increase on luxury items. Did you hear it on the wireless?'

Gertie sniffed. 'What luxury items? I ain't seen one in ages. Have you?'

Connie smiled at her. 'Well, at least we'll be able to have the church bells ringing once more. They don't think the Germans will invade us now.' She licked her lips. Corned-beef hash was one of her favourite meals and Gertie had a way of making it really tasty. She put down her knife and fork on her empty plate.

'Lovely, that was,' she said. Then, 'I couldn't speak to Gilbert Willard. He wasn't in tonight, but Doyle checked my figures when I cashed up and couldn't find anything wrong.'

'Don't take no notice of that manager. He can't tell his arse from his elbow,' Gertie said. 'Why the people who own the Criterion keep sending us such unreliable men, I'll never know. I suppose all the decent blokes are away fighting.' Gertie used the stub of her cigarette to light another, then dumped the old one in the saucer on the arm of the chair. It was overflowing with dog ends. 'I took a clean shirt, underwear and socks for Len, and them things for Queenie to the hospital,' she said. 'But there was no change in Queenie's condition.'

Connie accepted Gertie's offer of tea but took it into her room. She was tired. The past few days had been traumatic and she wasn't ready to face Marlene yet when she came home.

Sitting in bed Connie began leafing through the scrapbook she'd started making when she'd first arrived at Gertie's house. As a child she'd loved cutting out pictures of film stars and sticking them in scrapbooks. Sadly, all those treasures had been burned in the bomb blast that wrecked her Portsmouth home. But now, turning the pages and looking at cuttings of Clark Gable, Greta Garbo and Alan Ladd calmed her. She remembered how her mother had sat beside her, knitting and chatting to her while she'd snipped photos from Photoplay and other film magazines. Now, remembering made her feel sad but it was a good sadness: it reminded her of how much her mother had loved her.

It was her mother who had instilled in her a love of films – they'd gone to the cinema whenever they could. Connie loved everything about the picture houses. Many looked like Egyptian temples, filled with gilt ornaments, the screens swathed with dusky velvet curtains. Best of all, Connie loved sitting in the dark and being drawn into the story told on the screen by the handsome actors and glamorous female stars. The warm, smoky atmosphere with the swirling dust floating in the light shining down from the projection room only enhanced the magic for her. And then there were the ice-cream girls, with their trays of succulent tubs, with little wooden spoons, and velvety choc ices that froze your fingers as you unwrapped them. She smiled, thinking of Queenie standing in the spotlight with her ice-cream tray hanging around her neck.

Connie's one ambition as a child had been to become an usherette. She had achieved that. She loved her job, and her promotion to head usherette had been a dream come true. If only her mother had been alive to see it, Connie thought, she'd have been so proud of her.

Connie was increasingly upset at the way the picture house was run. The last manager, Arthur Mangle, had been a womanizer. This manager was hardly ever found on the premises. Wouldn't it be heaven if someone was in charge who loved the films and the atmosphere of the Criterion as much as she did?

Connie had read that women were now taking more active roles in work previously done by men. Bus conductresses, drivers, engineers, armament workers in factories – just the other week she'd read of women being trained as film projectionists. Of course, she hadn't mentioned that to Len or Gary.

Some men, even those who were kind and loving to their wives and sometimes washed up the dinner plates, might never imagine women taking on jobs that demanded the strength or knowledge they thought only men possessed. Women were supposed to stay at home. They were mothers and caregivers. Men were the providers, the breadwinners.

Connie could see the war was changing the world, though it might be a while before women were paid as much as men for doing the same work. However, she believed that one day, hopefully sooner rather than later, women and men would become equals in the workplace.

As soon as Connie had stepped into the Criterion on Forton Road for the first time she'd fallen in love with the place. Opened on 8 May 1912, containing seating for more than seven hundred patrons, in 1929 a Western Electric sound system was installed. It was a haven, paradise on earth.

Outside, shiny green tiles met the crenellated roof and there were tantalizing glass-fronted cases containing still photographs that tempted the patrons with forthcoming treats. Quite often the films changed on a Monday, and again on a Thursday, with a separate showing on a Sunday.

Connie looked down at the scrapbook. Gertie had spoken the truth: thinking about something else had put out of her mind what had happened last night, if only briefly. She had been outraged and shocked by the scene she'd witnessed in the air-raid shelter. Now she was hurt, very hurt.

She had believed Ace when he told her he loved her. But in her world loving someone meant being faithful to them. Not sharing a bed with Marlene. She really wanted to believe truth was more plausible than the obvious. She remembered the empty whisky bottle. Could they have drunk all of it, rendering them senseless? There'd been none of the usual warmth from the stove coming from the shelter, and both Ace and Marlene had been clothed. Connie knew she was trying to make excuses for the man she loved. But surely, she thought, Ace must have known that her seeing him in such a compromising position would cause her pain. And if he truly loved her why did he run? Didn't he care that leaving her with unanswered questions was like sticking a knife into an open wound?

Connie slid out of the bed. She put away her scrapbook in the chest of drawers and scrabbled in one of the smaller drawers for the little box that held the expensive gold bracelet and necklace Ace had bought her. The precious pieces were cold to her touch and heavy over her fingers.

She never wore them. She appreciated them as presents from Ace but they looked out of place on her neck and wrist in her everyday life. She couldn't wear them to work. The other usherettes might feel she was showing off and pretending to be something she wasn't. Connie replaced the items and pushed the box to the back of the drawer. She wondered why she had felt it necessary to look at the gifts.

There was a gentle knock on her door. Gertie poked her head inside the room. 'I wondered if you'd like another cuppa. I'm having one before I go to bed.'

Connie looked at her aunt's kind, worn face. 'No, thanks,' she said. 'I'll be wanting a trip down the garden to the lavatory if I drink any more tea.'

Gertie sighed and made to close the door.

Connie realized she just wanted a bit of company. 'Sit with me awhile,' she said. Gertie brightened as she stepped inside, her hand immediately feeling in her pocket for her Woodbines and matches.

Connie pulled the covers up around her. The mattress creaked and sank as Gertie plonked herself on the edge of the bed.

'What happened to that good-looking blond bloke you danced with in the Swan public house the day Queenie got married?'

The question came as a surprise but Connie's mind went back to the snappy dresser in the two-tone shoes who had held her firmly yet gently during the single waltz they'd shared.

'He was the one who came to the Criterion in the afternoons just to catch a glimpse of you,' Gertie reminded her.

Connie wondered where this conversation was heading. 'I've not set eyes on him since,' she said. 'He said he was in the navy and had to report back to Gare Loch, or Faslane, in Scotland.'

'I thought you and him made a nice couple.'

'You were too drunk to think anything, if I remember correctly.' Connie smiled. Queenie's wedding had been a small affair but a gloriously happy day to remember. 'And I was glad it was a waltz because that's the only dance I know.'

Connie suddenly remembered how good it had felt in his arms. Ace had taught her the waltz steps only days before. One, two, three, ran quickly through her mind. She'd felt awkward dancing with Ace. Felt as if her feet would never do what her head asked of them.

She also remembered how on the very first time her fingers had touched the blond man's, when she'd torn his picture-house ticket in two, a feeling of being unable to wait for whatever would happen next had run through her. He, too, had felt it – she could tell by the way he had looked at her.

'Why are you talking about him?' Connie was curious. 'I thought you liked Ace.'

Gertie took a long drag on her cigarette, then pushed herself up off the bed. 'You sure you don't want another cuppa? I'm about ready for my bed now.'

Connie shook her head and Gertie continued talking. 'Oh, I do like Ace,' she said. 'I love the bleedin' bones of him. I told you once I wished I was thirty years younger. But he's a right dodgy customer and I wouldn't trust him further than I could throw him.' Gertie grinned at her and shut the door as she left the room.

Connie shivered. She felt as if someone had just walked across her grave.

Chapter Eleven

'Tom, I've brought you some home-made blackberry jam tarts. Practically straight out of the oven they are.'

He opened the front door wider and allowed Shirley to ease her bulk into the passage. His heart sank. Jam tarts. And she'd made them. Tom remembered the hard-as-iron rock cakes she had plied him with at the dance class. One had almost broken a tooth and he'd secreted them both in his trouser pocket, hoping she'd believe he'd eaten them. Later he'd thrown them into his garden, thinking the sparrows might have better luck with them than he had.

'That's kind of you,' he said. 'And you baked them?' He was keeping his fingers crossed that the answer would be 'No.'

'Oh, yes,' she said. She'd already marched through to his kitchen. 'Sugar being rationed meant I had to economize when I made the jam way back in the summer. I picked the blackberries from along the railway lines and used crushed saccharine tablets as sweetener.' She pushed the paper bag into his hands.

For a moment Tom couldn't speak. He thought quickly. 'I hope it's all right if I don't have one just at this moment. I've just eaten some bread and dripping with salt on. The dripping was a bit rich, you see.' With a bit of luck, she wouldn't see through his excuse. She was a brilliant pianist, a lovely lady with a heart as big as a house, but she couldn't cook. He opened the food cupboard, put the bag on the shelf and added, 'It's lovely of you to think of me.'

'You think nothing of it. I had to come round as I've had enquiries about the dance class. Word seems to have got about that people are enjoying it.' She ferreted in her large handbag and pulled out a folded sheet of paper. 'I've written down their names and addresses so you'll know who they are when they turn up at the Nicholson Hall.' She sat down in the armchair near the range with a big sigh. 'Good to get the weight off me feet,' she said.

Tom flattened the piece of paper. 'My God, there's loads of names here,' he said.

'It looks like those cards we stuck in shop windows are doing the trick.'

'I've had some enquiries too,' he said. About ten people had knocked on his front door asking about the classes. It had surprised him that all sorts of people seemed to want to trip the light fantastic. Women perhaps more than men, but that was to be expected with most eligible men away fighting in the services.

Shirley wriggled out of her voluminous brown wool coat, beneath which she wore a flowered dress that seemed utterly without shape. She pulled the pearl pin from her red hat and the large feather swayed in the warm air of the heat from the range. She rested it on the wide arm of the chair.

'Would you like some tea?' He was being polite because Shirley had made herself comfortable and looked as if her visit might not be as short as he'd hoped.

'You're twisting my arm,' she said. He went into the scullery and lit the gas beneath the kettle.

Shirley was still talking. 'I wondered if you might be thinking of splitting the class now it's growing.'

'You mean teach on two days instead of one?'

'Something like that. Too many people in one small hall means they can't see what the dancing master is doing.' She paused. 'And that tiny kitchen area can't cope with a lot of people fiddling about in it making tea.'

He thought for a while. God forbid he cancelled the tea

break! What she was suggesting would mean paying for the hall twice and doubling her wages. The money he had put by wouldn't last for ever, and he'd needed to buy a new suit and special soft shoes – thank God he'd had the coupons for them. It was important to look the part of a dancing tutor to make a success of the venture. But that had meant spending money before he'd earned any.

'Dancing is very popular now,' said Shirley. 'I think it's because people like watching all those musical pictures with Fred Astaire and Ginger Rogers.'

'This war makes everyone depressed,' agreed Tom. 'They see all that lovely dancing on the screen and feel better, so they want to have a go.'

'You could be right.' Shirley had a wicked glint in her eye. 'I think one of the reasons elderly men want to come along and dance is because they like the feel of a young lady in their arms!' She gave a loud guffaw and Tom laughed. In the warmth of the room her lily-of-the-valley perfume was making the kitchen smell like a flower shop.

Out in the scullery he swirled boiling water around the empty teapot to warm it, tipped it out, then spooned in two heaped teaspoons of Brooke Bond Dividend tea – he was collecting the stamps as had his mother before him. Then he stirred the pot vigorously.

After he'd set the tray of tea things on the kitchen table a sudden thought struck him. He'd offer her something to eat with the tea. 'I'm still full up but I'm sure you could manage one of your tarts with your cuppa,' he said.

'Oh, no!' she replied, 'I made them for you. I couldn't possibly!'

'I'll save them for later, then,' he said, with a sigh.

'Shall I be mother?' Shirley asked. She wriggled up from the chair. Tom grinned at her. He wondered if for the rest of his life he was to be surrounded by elderly women who wanted to take care of him.

As she handed him a cup, she said, 'Can I ask you a personal question?' She turned the full beam of her mascaraed eyes upon him. He nodded. 'Why ever did a lovely-looking talented bloke like you get mixed up with Ace Gallagher?'

Her question shook him. 'When he first opened the club near Gosport ferry, he wanted presentable male dancers. I seemed to fulfil his requirements. Ladies could buy a sixpenny ticket to dance with us. We then had to entice the old girls up to the gaming tables so they'd lose money . . .'

'Surely you could have got better work than that.'

He drank his tea and set the cup and saucer on the table. He was going to have to confess to Shirley he'd badly needed the money at that time. And that he'd had to lie to his mother about the real nature of his job. To her he'd insisted he was a 'dancer', nothing more. 'Mum had wanted to get me on the stage when I was a kiddie. You see, I loved dancing. It made me feel . . . sort of free inside and outside my body. She spent a lot of money on me with lessons, often going out cleaning to pay for them.'

Thinking about the past was making him feel sad.

'The thing was, she never asked me what I really wanted to do when I got older, which was go into the services. Gosport's a naval town, and there's navy establishments all along the south coast. I sometimes wonder if she was the one who really wanted to go on the stage. She was a pretty woman, my mum.' He went to the sideboard, opened the cupboard and brought out a photograph album. Then he moved Shirley's feathered hat from the arm of the chair and sat there. He began to point out sepia photographs fixed to the pages with transparent corner pieces.

'I see what you mean by pretty,' said Shirley. 'She looks like an older version of that child actress, Shirley Temple, don't she?'

Tom had to admit his mother looked uncannily like the great star, with her curls and dimpled smile.

'I was named after Shirley Temple, as well,' she said. 'Never looked like her, though,' she added.

He smiled at her, closed the album and put it down on the floor. 'When the war had started, I'd signed on for the navy. This was before I started working for Ace. I failed the medical. The doctor said I had a heart murmur probably left from the rheumatic fever I'd had as a kiddie. So, no navy career for me. For a while I was still chasing dancing work in the chorus and going to auditions at theatres. The money I brought home didn't keep us but Mum was still working. She kept saying my big break would come. Then I discovered she hadn't been telling me the truth about herself.'

He looked at Shirley, who was listening intently. 'Mum started coughing up blood. Consumption, you know, tuberculosis. There was no money for doctors or medicines or sending her off to the countryside for a cure. Anyway, that was when Ace offered me good money for working at the club. Soon I was getting "gifts" from the women, money that paid for a nurse to stay with Mum when she got worse.' His voice went quiet as he said, 'I never told her what I was doing.'

'I heard you got some . . . er . . . really nice presents off the old dears.'

'I make no excuses for that. I was paid "for services rendered", and you can read what you want into it.' His mouth set defiantly into a straight line before he spat out, 'I got money the best way I knew how to keep my mum alive.'

Shirley put her hand on his arm. 'She's up there looking down, proud of you for opening a dancing school. It's an honest job . . . But tell me, lad, if you failed the medical to get in the services, how come you're not long back from a stint in the navy in Scotland at Faslane?'

'You really do want to know all the ins and outs, don't you?' Tom said. 'After my mum died, I had no reason to con old ladies. I wasn't paying for doctors and medicines any more, was I? I wanted to make something of myself. Ace pulled a few strings . . .'

'He got you into the navy?'

Tom nodded.

'You don't think he had an ulterior motive in wanting you out of the way?'

Tom stared at her. What on earth was she talking about?

A red blush was rising from the neckline of her shapeless dress to creep up and over her face.

'I know that's started you thinking, Tom, but I was a cleaner at the Four Aces. Ace would talk to Jerome and forget I was there. But I listened all right.' There was a hard edge to her voice now. 'I left the Four Aces because I found out he's not the nice man people think he is. I don't agree with the way he makes his money. Profiteering, extortion, mixing with gangsters as well as having them gambling tables rigged. That meant I was being paid with dirty money and it didn't feel right to me.'

'Lots of people run black-market rackets, Shirl—'

He didn't finish what he was saying for she weighed in again: 'I found out a few things working there. He charges exorbitant rates of interest to his gamblers. One bloke got in so deep he didn't know which way to turn. His wife found him hanging from a beam in their shed. That's what a nice man Ace Gallagher is. He was no friend to you, Tom. He wanted you out of the way.'

Tom frowned. How could she say such a thing?

'That's surprised you, hasn't it?' Shirley said.

She had his full attention now.

'You met a girl, the gossip reached him and when he realized it was the girl he was determined to marry . . .'

Tom's head was swimming. Ace aiming to marry the girl working in the Criterion? The girl he'd danced with at the pub? Impossible!

'He wanted you out of the way so he killed two birds with one stone, like. You got your wish to join the navy and it got you out of his way.'

'You're making this up,' he said. But deep down he knew she wasn't. It certainly explained Ace Gallagher's peculiar treatment of him when he'd offered to work for him again. Another thought struck him. 'You know this girl?'

'I know of her. Gertie Mullins is her aunt and she lodges with Gertie. Connie's a nice girl.'

Connie, he thought. So that's her name, Connie. Even when he'd danced with her, he'd not got around to asking it.

'She and I hardly spoke,' he said. If at that time he'd had a decent job, he would have asked her out. He remembered the warmth flowing through his body from his fingertips into hers as they had touched. It was as if they had known each other for ever, which, of course, they hadn't. No, surely he couldn't believe all he was hearing. It was ridiculous. Would a man like Ace resort to such extreme tactics just to get him away from the girl he wanted?

Just for a second common sense took over. He would, if he thought he might lose her to someone like himself.

Tom realized Shirley was talking again. 'Your heart attack brought you back here a lot quicker than he expected. Didn't you ever wonder why he wouldn't give you your old job back? And I heard he'd turned you down for the manager's job in that new club of his over in Southsea. Listen to me, Tom. He just didn't want you and her to meet up again so the further away you were from her, and him, the happier he was.'

A sudden thought struck him. 'Does Connie know what's been going on?'

'Don't be daft, lad. She's the innocent in all this. She's the mushroom in the dark. Ace took her and Gertie away for Christmas, thinking he had a clear run without any obstructions. The biggest one being you.' At this her red-painted index fingernail poked him in the chest to prove her point. Tom stepped sharply away. he wanted to disbelieve Shirley's revelations.

But everything fitted together now.

There was something else he needed to know. 'I understand how you found out about all this but I'm at a loss to know why you offered to throw in your lot with me, when I've nothing to offer.'

'I chucked my job with Ace for the reasons I told you but I heard you'd need a pianist as you was thinking about teaching a dance class. I had faith in you then, like I got now. I knew you'd not be paying me much at first but I'd watched you dance at the club. You got class, Tom. I thought we could make a success of this venture, you dancing, me supplying the music.' She laughed. 'And we will, if I have anything to do with it.' She was about to prod him again but he saw it coming and moved backwards. 'We got to think about the new clients coming to Nicholson Hall. Got to arrange to work more hours and hire the hall. I've got a bit of money put by if you needs it, Tom. That's how much I believe in you.'

Tom was overwhelmed by her kindness. For a moment silence filled the kitchen. Originally Shirley had come round to his house to bring him some jam tarts. Now she'd told him of Ace's ulterior motive. It was a terrible shock but it all made sense. His first thought was to go and confront the man, get it all out in the open. But that might involve Shirley, who had spoken to him in confidence. Ace wasn't a man who liked to lose at anything, so who knew what he might do in retaliation? Best to let sleeping dogs lie, Tom decided, for now.

But was Ace really worried that Connie might favour him, in some way? He was about to ask when Shirley said, 'Actually, this cuppa's made me bit peckish, Tom. I will have one of me jam tarts now.'

He got out the bag, opening it for the first time. There were four tarts. He passed the bag to Shirl and daintily she removed one. The blackberry jam looked glossy and dark against the creamy colour of the pastry.

'Go on, join me,' she said. And bit into it.

This time he really couldn't refuse, whatever the consequences. Not after all the confidences they'd just shared.

Shirley was turning out to be a very good friend and he didn't want to hurt her feelings. He picked up a tart up and tasted it, fearing for his teeth, but when the pastry melted in his mouth and the blackberry jam, sweet yet with a saccharine tartness, hit his taste-buds, he smiled with pleasure.

He thought suddenly of the saying, 'You can't judge a book by its cover,' and realized that nothing in his life was as it had first appeared.

Chapter Twelve

Doyle was trying to hide the excitement in his voice as he pushed open the door of the Criterion's staffroom. 'You've got to come outside, Connie. Now! If you don't, he said he's marching in here and making a scene in front of everybody and he knows you won't like that.'

Connie, working out the rota for the coming week's hours for the usherettes and other staff, stared at the commissionaire in his dark red and gold-brocaded suit. She was finding it difficult enough to concentrate on shifts and wages when the gnawing pain of loss wouldn't allow her to forget that Ace, who'd professed to love her, had been cosily tucked up in bed with Marlene. She'd seen them together with her own eyes, hadn't she?

Ever since Christmas when Ace had asked her to marry him, and she'd agreed, Connie had never doubted him when days and weeks had passed without him contacting her. To her, trust went hand in hand with love. It was perfectly feasible that he'd needed time and money to get his second club up and running in Southsea.

After she'd witnessed him with Marlene, Connie wanted to believe she didn't care, that the pain in her heart wasn't real. But it was. Never before had she allowed herself to have feelings for any man until Ace Gallagher had got under her skin. Now she was suffering for it.

'Whatever are you talking about, Doyle?' she managed. His enthusiasm was exhausting. She put her hand to her leg, where the cut she'd received the night Queenie was in labour had healed to an itchy silver line.

Already Doyle was pulling at her uniform sleeve so hard she feared he might damage it, so she stood up from the table where she'd been working and allowed him to propel her towards the door.

A wave of stale cigarette smoke that had been building since the picture house had first opened its doors that afternoon hit her as she was forced into the darkness of the auditorium. 'What—'

'Sssh!' Doyle cautioned, as the staffroom door closed behind them.

Blood and Sand, the main feature, was playing: handsome

Tyrone Power was once more working his magic with the leading lady, and holding the patrons spellbound. It certainly wouldn't do to interrupt the viewers' rapt concentration just before the film ended.

'God Save The King' would come next, and the patrons would stand to attention before the Criterion closed for the night.

Connie decided it was easier to go along with whatever Doyle wanted. If she caused a fuss, young Gary Pink's attention might slide away from the projectors he was using upstairs to show the film. That was the last thing she needed when he was coping so well in Len's absence.

She hoped everyone had their eyes glued to the bull-fighting scene where Tyrone Power would afterwards die in the arms of his childhood sweetheart, played by Linda Darnell. Then they wouldn't notice what was happening with the head usherette and the commissionaire.

At least there'd be no telling off from Gilbert Willard as, once more, he was taking a night off and leaving all the work to Connie.

Doyle was dragging her away from the auditorium into the foyer where, due to the severe blackout restrictions, the glass doors were safely curtained off from Forton Road.

Doyle pulled open the main door and positioned Connie

so she could see outside. The moonlight shone on the MG tourer parked in front of the picture house and the man standing proudly next to it, wearing a suit and two-tone shoes. He ran a hand nervously through his chestnut-coloured hair and smiled at her.

Connie gasped. The hood of the car was down and the rear seating area was filled with flowers, some bunched, some loose. Wild daffodils, early forget-me-nots, primroses, late snowdrops. Doyle gently pushed her towards the car and Ace moved forward holding out to her a single daffodil.

Behind him the fragile flowers were a desert of brightness in the glistening moonlight. In the still night air, their fresh spring scent was sweeter than all the expensive perfumes she had ever known, including Evening in Paris, which, courtesy of Ace, she owned but seldom wore. To Connie the blooms' freshness seemed to eclipse the stink of burning that hung, like a shroud, in the air over Gosport.

For a moment there was stillness and silence.

Then Doyle coughed to let her know he was still there. 'I'll close up, Connie love,' he said. 'It's time you left a bit earlier for once.' And he turned away, leaving her and Ace alone, amid the bombed streets.

Connie looked at the car, resplendent with its offering,

and felt like the leading lady in a romantic film. She was speechless.

Ace stepped towards her. He waved his hand back towards his car. 'For you, Connie. Because you bring freshness into my tired life. If I could, I'd give you the world. I'd certainly bestow on you shop-bought hothouse flowers.' He smiled. 'Alas, since Digging for Victory was introduced, garden vegetables can't convey what I'm attempting to say.' He was close enough now to put his hands on her shoulders and look deeply into her eyes. She could smell whisky on his breath. And why not? she thought. It was a cold night and he must have come from one of his clubs, but he certainly wasn't drunk.

He tucked the single daffodil he was holding behind her ear.

'But where did they all come from?' She got no further for he interrupted her.

'Gathered from Gosport's fields, hedgerows and woodlands because I love you. This is an apology for the scene you witnessed that wasn't at all what it must have looked like . . .' He tailed off.

Connie felt the pain in her heart begin to ease. She'd wanted proof of his love and here it was. But there were so many flowers . . .

'Whatever shall I do with all them all?' As far as she knew Gertie didn't possess even one vase.

'That's easy,' he said. 'I'm sure the hospital, where your friend Queenie is hopefully on the mend, would take some off your hands to pretty up their wards.'

Ace gave her a smile that thawed her heart. When he pulled her into his arms, Connie couldn't help but melt into him, even though she would have preferred an explanation for his conduct with Marlene.

Then he eased her away and began kissing her gently in the warm spot where her neck met her shoulder. His lips travelled to her nose, her forehead, then came back to her lips. The familiar smell of his lemony cologne and his maleness inflamed her senses. She felt his tongue begin to explore her mouth . . . A movement from the blackout curtain caught her eye.

Connie heard giggling from the usherettes watching from behind the glass doors of the Criterion. The curtain fell as soon as the watchers realized they had been seen. Embarrassed, Connie pulled away from him.

But why did she feel embarrassed? Wasn't this what she'd wanted? An apology of sorts that would make everything return to how it was before she'd found Ace with Marlene?

Her head was reeling.

'Let them look,' he said. He let his hands drop from her body to feel in the inside pocket of his jacket. Then he was holding a small dark velvet box that he opened and turned towards her. Her eyes fell on the brightness of the central jewel encircled by a cluster of smaller stones. The setting of the ring resembled a flower.

Connie gasped. 'Are they real . . .'

'Diamonds?' he asked, a smile raising the corners of his lips. 'Of course. They're only what you deserve.'

He removed the ring from its box, picked up her hand and slipped his offering onto her finger. 'We ought to set a date for the wedding,' he said. 'I love you, Connie. You're everything I've ever wanted in a woman.'

She looked at the ring. It was beautiful. It must, she thought, have cost Ace a fortune. The pain in her heart had practically dissolved. This man loved her – no, more than loved: he obviously adored her. She looked again at the ring. Beautiful though it was she knew she could never wear it at the picture house. It had obviously cost far in excess of the wages the usherettes toiled for. To go to work with this on her finger could stir up jealousy that might alienate some of the women from her. And what if she lost it? She'd never forgive herself.

Didn't Ace understand that she wasn't the sort of girl who

needed expensive or showy gifts? The heavy gold necklace and matching bracelet he had previously given her were too ostentatious for her to wear to work, so they lay in her bedroom drawer. She had already decided the ring would have to join them.

She couldn't keep the engagement a secret, though. The girls who had peeked through the glass doors would soon spread it about the picture house.

Ace kissed her again, his arms tight around her as though he'd never let her away from him. Connie's pleasure rose like the wind before a thunderstorm. He whispered, 'You are incredible, you understand that?'

Then, taking her hand, he led her to the kerb and opened the passenger door. As Connie was stepping into the car, she suddenly remembered that, as in most romantic films, like the dumb heroine she hadn't asked a single thing but had allowed the hero to sweep her off her feet. Ace, like most romantic leads, was the strong one. He was definitely a man who spoke but didn't often listen. He was talking now.

'I'm taking you to Alma Street. We're going to Gertie's house. I've peace offerings for her in the boot of the car, groceries and cigarettes. I also want to find out just what little game your cousin Marlene is playing.'

Chapter Thirteen

The tourer drew up outside number fourteen, and in next to no time Connie had the front door open and was shouting down the hall, 'Gertie, come and look!' She took a sniff of the rich fruity aroma of fresh baking that almost but not quite eclipsed the smell of cigarettes.

And then Gertie, in metal curlers, was standing in the kitchen doorway, a fag in her mouth, her dressing-gown tied carelessly around her waist, her pom-pom slippers, with the holes cut in the sides for her bunions, on her feet.

'Whatever's the matter?' Then her eyes fell on Ace carrying the string-handled brown bags and she took the cigarette from her mouth. 'Oh, my Gawd. Look what the cat's dragged in again.'

For a moment Connie could feel an argument brewing if Ace took offence at Gertie's favourite saying of the moment, but after he'd dumped the bags on the kitchen table he stepped around Connie and swept Gertie up in his arms, as if she was a lightweight, saying, 'And how's my best girl, then? As ever, pleased to see me?'

Gertie pummelled his back. 'Put me down, you great dafty!' she cried, but Connie could see she was loving the attention. 'You could smell my bread pudding, couldn't you?'

'I thought that was your new perfume, Gertie!' Ace's eyes twinkled as he set her back on her feet and turned to Connie. 'Show her your engagement ring, my love.'

He didn't wait for Connie to gain Gertie's attention. Ace gently lifted Connie's hand and held it towards Gertie so she could stare at the glittering stones.

'Well, you'll never go short all the time you can put that in hock at the pawn shop!' Gertie gave Connie a big wink. 'And are you happy, my love?'

Connie almost got her words out but Ace beat her to it. 'Of course she is,' he said. 'Come and see how I surprised her outside the Criterion.'

Connie could see Gertie's eyes were on the carrier bags and that she was longing to look inside them but she allowed Ace to shepherd her along the passage.

Gertie put a hand to her mouth when Ace showed her

the flowers spread about the back of his car. 'Gawd! What are we going to do with that lot?' she gasped.

'Not got any empty milk bottles to put a few in, then?' Ace asked.

'Not enough for all of them.' Gertie pulled at the front door so that the light from the passage didn't shine out into the night sky. She lived in fear of the patrolling wardens fining her for ignoring the blackout safety rules.

'We could take them to the War Memorial Hospital. I was hoping to visit Queenie tomorrow,' said Connie.

Gertie was still staring at the flowers. Connie knew she was thinking how romantic Ace's gesture was.

'And how are we going to carry them? On a bus?' She turned back to Ace. 'A kindly thing to do would be for you to take them to the hospital on your way back round to Portsmouth, if that's where you're sleeping tonight, Ace Gallagher.'

Gertie laughed when she saw Ace's face fall. 'You didn't think because you put a pretty ring on Connie's finger that I was going to let you spend the night here, did you?'

For once Ace was silent.

Gertie chimed in quickly: 'Have you forgotten I've got two young ladies of marriageable age under this roof? This is no knocking shop, you know. An' I got gossipy neighbours! You don't live here no more, Ace Gallagher!'

Ace began to laugh, a rumbling sound that started in his stomach and bellowed out of his mouth. Eventually he wiped a hand across his eyes. 'There's no flies on you, are there, Gertie Mullins?' He went and stood next to her and put an arm around her shoulders. 'At least don't send me away without a cup of tea inside me. And did I hear you say there was bread pudding?'

Gertie grinned at him and pushed open the front door. 'Go on, get inside before the warden catches me, or before I change my mind about you.'

Connie stepped back over the threshold, eager to get inside out of the cold, and was met by a figure in a silky dressing-gown with frills and ruffles at the collar and cuffs.

'I've already put the kettle on,' Marlene said. She smiled at Connie, like butter wouldn't melt in her mouth, and said quietly, 'Hello, Connie, lovely to see you.' Her eyes flicked over Connie's picture-house uniform and she added, 'Just finished work?'

Connie's breath seemed stolen away from her as she stood in the passage and stared at her cousin. Even though they'd not seen a great deal of each other over the years her nemesis hadn't changed. Every sentence she spoke seemed to hold a double meaning, and each look Marlene bestowed on Connie held imaginary daggers. And hadn't that been proved when Connie had gone down to the air-raid shelter and found Marlene snuggled up with Ace?

Connie took a deep breath. 'Hello, Marlene. Did we wake you?' Her voice was calm, controlled.

Marlene pushed her hand through her blonde hair but the silky mass fell back across her face, making her seem vulnerable, childlike.

'Move out of the way, girls,' chided Gertie. 'Let's get in out of the cold.'

And then they were all in the warmth of the kitchen. Gertie went into the scullery and soon they heard the clatter of tea-making. Connie took off her jacket and hung it over the back of a kitchen chair. Caution told her perhaps she should watch Marlene and see how she interacted with Ace but it wasn't normally in her nature to be jealous and, besides, she was the one who wore Ace's ring and that had to mean something, didn't it?

She decided to ignore the strange feeling in the air.

'Want a hand out there?' Without waiting for an answer, Ace put his hands on Connie's hips and squeezed past her to join Gertie in the scullery.

As soon as the two women were left together in the kitchen, Marlene closed the distance between them. 'Let's have a look at the ring, then.' Her voice was low.

Connie's first inclination was that she didn't want Marlene looking at or touching her gift from Ace. Nevertheless she held out her hand. She could smell the sultry scent of sleep on Marlene. She tried not to think of her sleeping in Ace's bed upstairs in what had been his room.

Marlene gave a low whistle of appreciation. 'He certainly didn't buy that in Woolworth's,' she said. 'You're a very lucky girl. You do realize that?'

'I am,' Connie said, the emphasis on the first word. She stared into Marlene's face. It was almost like looking at a mirror image of herself.

'C'mon, you two, get out of my way. I need to put this on the table.'

Gertie had bustled in with cups and saucers on a tray. Ace followed, carrying the steaming teapot covered with a knitted cosy.

'Do we get some bread pudding with this?' Connie asked. She could just fancy a bite of the curranty, fragrant pudding that Gertie was famous for making.

'We have to have a little talk first,' Ace said, setting the teapot on the table. 'I'll just put these on the floor,' he added, taking the brown carrier bags by their string handles and setting them down.

'They're much appreciated,' said Gertie. 'Thanks, Ace.'

He smiled at her.

'What do you mean, "have a little talk"?' Marlene sat down on a kitchen chair and crossed one knee over her other so that her dressing-gown fell open.

'Cover yourself up!' snapped Gertie.

Marlene did as she was told but her lips fell into a sulky pout.

Connie watched as every cup was filled, milk and sugar added, and Gertie had sat down in the armchair beneath the window. She took a deep breath. 'C'mon, Marlene. What really happened the other night?'

Marlene sighed, 'You saw . . .'

Ace was staring at Marlene. 'Tell them,' he said. 'The truth, mind. Don't make anything up.'

'I don't think I want to hear this,' said Connie.

'Oh yes we do!' Gertie was adamant. She'd was stirring her tea, making a horrendous racket.

'Tell them I never so much as touched you,' said Ace.

Marlene opened her mouth, which still showed traces of lipstick, then closed it again.

'Tell them,' Ace insisted.

'I got into bed with him because I was cold,' Marlene said, in a rush.

'Go on,' said Ace. 'And the rest.'

She looked at Ace. 'When Ace arrived at the house, he'd already had a few drinks. He made me laugh and we opened the bottle of whisky he'd brought for Gertie. The siren went off so we had to go down to the Anderson. He really was the worse for drink, must have had a skinful before he got here. He kept falling asleep. I tried to keep him awake by chatting to him. That was a lot of fun, that was!' Marlene sneered. 'It was freezing and there was no paraffin for the stove.' She giggled. 'He'd have been useless at filling the damn thing anyway. Those bloody bombs wouldn't let up. They scared me. Where I was out in the country it was so quiet. Ace was on the bottom bunk snoring his head off, so I climbed in beside him. It was a tight squeeze but better to be near someone than freeze to death while that lot was coming down outside.' Marlene shook her head. 'That's it. The next thing I knew you were shouting your head off, Mum. She,' Marlene was nodding at Connie, 'was being sick and his lordship here,' she pointed at Ace, 'was scarpering up the garden path.'

Gertie picked up her packet of Woodbines from the table and lit a cigarette. 'I knows when she's lying and I knows when it's the truth. That's too ridiculous to be anything else but the honest truth.'

Marlene had picked up her cup and was drinking her tea.

Connie was staring at Ace. He shrugged. 'I was still drunk but not so far gone that I didn't know it was better to get the hell out of the way before I got myself into even more trouble.' Then he mouthed, 'I love you,' at Connie.

She gazed back at him. Gertie was right: it was all too stupid to be a lie. A smile edged its way across her lips. She could either believe what her cousin had said or . . . not. She saw relief cross Ace's face.

Connie drank her tea as though nothing had happened, then asked, trying to lighten the atmosphere, 'Can I have a bit of bread pudding now?'

Marlene grinned at Connie. 'Before he conked out, he promised me a job at the Four Aces in the town.' She looked at Ace. 'Does that still stand?'

Chapter Fourteen

'It's nice to see you wearing something different.'

Connie smiled at Gertie. Then she brushed some imaginary fluff off the shoulder of her dark grey costume. 'Well, I'm not working today, am I?'

'Fares, please.' The conductress took the exact money Connie held out. 'Where to? I'm not psychic, ducks.'

'Sorry, two to the hospital,' Connie said. The buxom woman sniffed, rotated the handle on the machine and pressed the tickets into Connie's hand, then moved further down the aisle of the Provincial bus.

'I see you're not wearing your ring.'

Connie gave a huge sigh that seemed to deflate her whole body. 'How can I wear that great big thing anywhere? It's not really me, is it?'

'You're an ungrateful bitch!'

Gertie's words stung. 'Am I? Am I really?' Connie's voice rose.

'Marlene would have worn it. She'd be wriggling her hand around so everyone could get an eyeful.'

'Yes, she certainly would. But I'm not Marlene, am I?'

After a few seconds of silence, Connie looked at Gertie, who was staring thoughtfully back at her. 'No, you're not Marlene, are you, love?'

Connie stared out of the grimy window

Her ring had joined the gold necklace and bracelet in the drawer in her room. Today was a day off for her and she intended to make the most of it. After last night, she was glad she wouldn't be at the picture house to answer all the questions she'd be asked about Ace and the flowers. Gertie, who had gone into work very early this morning, had already been bombarded with questions.

Connie was keeping her fingers crossed they'd be allowed to see Queenie.

The bus stopped to allow passengers on and off and Connie watched a group of workmen hauling wooden beams from a lorry to shore up the side of a house that was leaning crookedly. Gosport was suffering badly during the raids. Still, for a couple of nights it had been relatively quiet and she was glad of that. She didn't fancy sharing the Anderson shelter with Marlene.

'I've never set foot in his club in the town,' muttered Gertie.

Connie took her eyes away from what was going on outside the bus. 'Neither have I,' she said. 'Ace said it was the kind of place he preferred I didn't frequent.'

'Oh, la-di-da!' said Gertie. 'Full of riff-raff, then?'

'Don't be daft. Ace wouldn't own anything like that, would he?' Connie said, but in her heart, she wasn't sure of the answer. 'What kind of job does Marlene expect?'

'She said he mentioned cloakroom girl, or possibly serving drinks, and they always need dancers. Especially in the Southsea club.'

'Good for her,' said Connie, without enthusiasm.

The next stop was the hospital. 'Excuse me, excuse me,' Connie said. She was on her feet and pushing past the standing people on the bus. She stepped down onto the pavement and took a deep breath of fresh air to rid herself of the stink of sweaty bodies.

She and Gertie crossed the road and entered the War Memorial Hospital. 'Look.' She pointed to the office behind the enquiries-desk window. A small vase full of daffodils brightened the spot where a woman dressed in blue sat writing in a ledger. 'Do you think that's some of my flowers?' Connie asked Gertie.

'I don't know. One daffodil looks very like another to me.'

The woman lifted her head, adjusted her spectacles on the bridge of her nose, and asked, 'Can I help you?'

'No, thank you. We know where the maternity ward is,' Gertie said. 'We're here to visit Queenie Gregory – that's if she's allowed visitors.'

The woman picked up another ledger and scanned its pages. 'Yes, she is, and she's doing well.'

Connie's spirits rose. She was about to walk on down the corridor when she gave a little cough, then asked the woman, 'Did you bring in those daffs? They look lovely.'

The woman stared at her. 'No, but it's funny you should ask that because a well-dressed gentleman knocked on this very window at some unearthly hour this morning with bunches and bunches of assorted flowers. To brighten up the wards, he said. Such a kind thought, don't you think?'

'A lovely thing to do.' Connie smiled to herself. So Ace had done the charitable thing. She had kept the single daffodil he had tucked behind her ear. It lay in the drawer beside her gold jewellery.

Now she grabbed Gertie's arm and they sauntered down a corridor that smelt of strong disinfectant. It would take more than armfuls of spring flowers to disguise the over-powering chemical smell.

'Listen to that noise! You'd think they was having a party instead of being ill in hospital.' Gertie was grumbling at the laughter issuing from the ward to which they'd been directed. Queenie was sitting up in bed, and when she saw them a huge smile lit her face.

'You're a sight for sore eyes,' said Gertie, bending over and kissing Queenie's forehead. 'I suppose it's you making all that din.' There was a chair next to the bed and Gertie plonked herself down, then felt in the pocket of her coat for her cigarettes. Immediately she lit one, then eyed the small ward and the other women patients, who were chatting among themselves. 'Go and get that chair over there, Connie.' She pointed to a chair by the window. 'Then sit down. You're making the place look untidy.'

'Oh, it is lovely to see you both,' Queenie said. She was propped up with pillows, Connie noted. 'You'll stay and see Bette and Paulie, won't you? The nurses'll be bringing in the babies soon.'

Connie nodded. 'Try to stop us,' she said. 'Anyway, tell us how you're feeling.' It was strange looking at Queenie with her face scrubbed clean of make-up. She was pale and had dark shadows beneath her eyes, but considering that a few days ago they'd all feared for her life, she now seemed to be well on the way to recovery.

Queenie said, 'Why are you looking at me like that, Connie? I know my roots need doing.'

Connie, who until then hadn't noticed the tell-tale darkness on Queenie's scalp where her bleached hair had grown, said, quick as a flash, 'I don't care about your hair. I thought I was going to lose you. I'm just so glad you're here in one piece.'

Queenie frowned and a sigh escaped her. Her hand picked at a thread on the hospital's blue counterpane. 'That's just it, Connie. I'm not in one piece. The doctors had to operate.' Tears filled her eyes. 'They had to take my womb away.'

Gertie picked up Queenie's hand, which had now unravelled a long thread, and held it tightly. With the other, she removed her cigarette from her mouth and said, 'Oh, my love, I am sorry.'

Queenie wiped her eyes with the fingers of her free hand. 'Still, I've got two beautiful babies,' she said. 'I'm very lucky. They're worth all my pain and discomfort. But it does look like I'll be in here for a while.'

Gertie, obviously without thinking, said, 'You won't be able to give Len a kiddie of his own then, will you?'

Connie glared at her. She hoped Gertie's words hadn't

upset Queenie but if they had she knew Queenie wouldn't hold a grudge against her. That was the trouble with Gertie: sometimes she didn't think before she spoke. To defuse tension she looked at the wild flowers in a vase on top of Queenie's locker. 'Bet you don't know where those flowers came from,' she said.

'No, I don't. They were there when I woke up this morning.'

Connie went on to tell her about Ace, the flowers and the suggestion that he deliver them to the hospital as Gertie hadn't any vases for them.

Queenie laughed. 'I see you have him wrapped around your little finger, then.'

Connie felt the blush rise. 'Actually, I haven't,' she said.

Gertie broke in: 'You should see the ring he's bought her.'

Connie saw Queenie's eyes gravitate to her left hand. 'It's a bit showy for me to wear all the time. You know I don't like drawing attention to myself.'

'No, you always worry about what other people think, you do,' Queenie said good-naturedly. 'Still, when I'm out of here you can show it to me.'

Suddenly Connie wished Gertie a million miles away because she dearly wanted to talk to Queenie about everything that had gone on in her life recently. Especially about Marlene's return to the house in Alma Street and how she really felt about her cousin. But it seemed disloyal to talk with Gertie there and she didn't want to upset her. But neither did she want to worry Queenie with anything that didn't concern her. Queenie had enough problems at present and the main one was to get well and take her beautiful children home.

'When's Len coming back to work?' Another blunt question from Gertie,

Queenie answered straight away: 'Very soon. He's been a tower of strength to me,' she added. She looked at Connie. 'You know, I've had a few blokes in my time but I never knew what it was for a man to love me until Len came along.'

'You'll be saying next you worship the ground he walks on,' Gertie said, lighting another Woodbine. Connie wondered what she'd done with the dog end of the previous one – she couldn't see any ashtrays anywhere. Gertie must have caught her looking for she whispered loudly, 'I put it in here!' She waggled the green Woodbine packet at Connie.

'Actually, I do worship him,' Queenie said simply. Then she laughed. 'But I told him that as soon as I get out of here, and start feeling like my old self, I'm going to try them dancing classes everyone's talking about.'

'What dancing classes?' Gertie was all ears.

'The girls in this ward have been talking about a couple who have introduced dance classes in the Nicholson Hall. It's good fun, so I've been told.' She thought for a moment. 'I know Len wouldn't like it if I wanted to go to proper dances, like at Lee Tower Ballroom or the Connaught Hall and dance with servicemen, but a couple of hours a week spent learning new dances is a different matter. Of course me and Len couldn't go together – one of us has to stay at home with Bette and Paulie.' She grinned. 'You could come with me, Connie. Len would like that.'

'I can't dance,' she began. 'Well, I can waltz a bit.'

'That's why they're called dance lessons, you dope,' Queenie said.

'Have you forgotten tiny babies need lots of attention?' Gertie said.

'Not at all. And half an hour away from the two of them while Len spoils them silly will suit me down to the ground. He can't keep away from the nursery here,' Queenie said, with a smile that ran from ear to ear.

Just then the ward's doors opened and in came a nurse pushing a canvas cot on wheels. Another followed, again with a cot. A loud howl was issuing from this one.

'Feeding time at the zoo,' laughed Queenie. 'When all the

babies are here and they're peacefully having their milk, it'll be quiet again.'

Connie was only half listening to her for she was remembering when she and Gertie had had their noses pressed against the nursery window trying to take a peek at Bette and Paulie. She couldn't believe that in a very few moments she would be having a closer look at them. She could hardly contain her excitement.

Queenie put out a hand and touched Connie's fingers, then looked into her eyes. Connie could smell talcum powder and milk on her friend's skin and decided she liked it better than her usual Californian Poppy.

'The last time you and I spoke I was pretty well unconscious, lying on the floor of the staffroom,' Queenie said quietly. 'I didn't know then how wrong things were going for me. I only found out afterwards when I knew I wasn't going to die. Connie, you saved my life. I'll never forget you ran through Gosport's streets in spite of the bombs falling about you. You saved my life,' she repeated. 'You're a true friend and I will love you for ever.'

'Shut up, Queenie Gregory. You'd have done the same for me,' Connie said. Gertie was wiping a stray tear from her eye. 'Don't you start,' she warned her aunt.

'Ready for your babies, Mrs Gregory? Which one do

you want first, boy or girl?' A nurse stood at the foot of Queenie's bed with a cot either side of her. One had a pink label, the other a blue one.

Before Queenie had time to say anything Gertie piped up: 'Can I hold one of them?'

Queenie said, 'Gertie, of course you can, but you'd better have the one who's not screaming!'

Chapter Fifteen

Ace poured himself a whisky, then picked up one of the white cotton bar cloths and towelled his hair. The rain thrashed against the windows and he thanked God that he was once more inside Gosport's Four Aces club and not around the back humping heavy wooden crates from vehicles. He hadn't expected a delivery of bottles and cigarettes before it was light when, of course, none of his men were on the premises to help unload the lorries.

He shivered and took a gulp of the drink to warm himself. He'd need to change into some dry clothes soon. Still, he shouldn't grumble. He'd make a tidy profit on Billy Hill's black-market goods – he always did. But he never knew when a delivery was imminent. That depended on the gangster's contacts.

Ace had only just dropped off to sleep when he'd been

woken to brave the outside elements. It was a good job he was in prime condition, he thought. He could hardly wake Jerome for help.

He'd seen how the old man was trying to mask his back pain when last night, after the club had closed, he'd set off for bed. Trouble was, Ace depended on Jerome a little too much. Jerome, being Jerome, tried a little too hard to give satisfaction. He didn't want Ace to know he was getting too old to be at two different clubs each day, keeping an eye on new employees. Ace had engaged managers, one in Gosport, the other in Southsea, but as yet neither had proved their worth.

He finished his drink, poured himself another, then turned on the wireless.

His lips curved into a smile. 'Don't Sit Under The Apple Tree' cut breezily through the noise of the rain, which was still hammering impressively against the windows. It was those three Gosport girls who had done well for themselves – what were they called? The Bluebirds, yes, that was them. He'd made a note somewhere to contact their agent to hire them to perform in one or possibly both of his clubs.

Not that he needed to entice his customers in: the gambling, plus the pretty boys and glamorous girls he employed, did that. It amazed him that in this world of uncertainty, with German bombers intent on almost nightly destruction, ordinary men and women were willing to gamble away their livelihoods. But it suited him that they did: he was becoming a wealthy man because of it.

If a punter lost money and wanted credit, hoping to recoup his losses, Ace had no qualms about giving it. The interest he charged, even he affirmed, was ridiculous. But true gamblers cared little about that. They always believed their luck would change and then they could pay back what they owed.

'Miaow!'

He heard the plaintive cry of the cat in the kitchen before Jerome announced his own presence. The old man was in his pyjamas, his dressing-gown loosely tied about his thin frame. He was fiddling with a small saucepan from which already the smell of fish was overpowering. 'A whiff of that and I'll lose today's punters,' Ace said. He gave Jerome a wry smile and looked down at the black and white feline winding itself in and out of the old man's legs.

'Get off with you, lad. It's only a bit of cod.' Jerome grinned back.

'People are starving out there.' Ace waved his hand dramatically at the kitchen door, which led out into the alleyway at the back of the club and the streets of Gosport.

'They can come in and have a bit of Cat's fish, if they want.' Jerome tipped the white flesh and juice into a bowl and began to fillet it.

'Jesus! You treat that cat better than a baby.'

'That cat treats me a lot nicer than some people round here. And he's better company.' Lately, Jerome had had to work a great deal on his own initiative.

'Well, I'm here today, aren't I?' said Ace.

'So you are. And I see there's a heap of wet boxes to be sorted and their contents put away. I hope you're going to help with that.'

Ace glared at him. 'Leave it until the cleaners start coming in. There's no hurry.'

'Just where you're wrong, lad.' Jerome dug out a particularly lethal-looking fish bone and threw it into the saucepan. 'The less your workers know about what goes on here, the better. You're not so well liked that any of them would keep their mouths shut.'

'Course I'm liked.'

'Not by the wife and family of that bloke found hanging in his shed. He was so much in debt to you it was the only way out for him. But you go on thinking you're liked, Ace. Truth is, during a war, or any time come to that, no one likes anyone who seems to be doing better than they are.'

Ace lit the gas beneath the kettle to make tea for them. 'You're in a good mood today.' The moment those words were out of his mouth he wished he hadn't said them. Hadn't he seen Jerome was finding it difficult to move this morning? He tried to make amends: 'I'll get the stuff all shifted before the cleaners come in.'

Ace watched as Jerome, now satisfied there was more fish than bones, forked some of the mixture onto a clean dish he kept especially for the cat. Then he bent down gingerly and put it on the floor. Immediately, the cat began eating. 'There, you get that inside you and you'll feel better,' he said. 'Seen any more of young Connie?' he asked, removing his glasses and polishing them on a tea-towel. 'Made a date for the wedding yet? Told her anything about yourself?'

'One question at a time.' Ace reached into a cupboard, took down two clean mugs and set them on the counter. 'Yes, I've seen Connie and it was a good idea of yours to present her with those flowers – I'm surprised the cleaners managed to pick so many in Gosport. The next thing will be to talk about a wedding. Maybe with a fresh young wife at my side, the punters and others won't think I'm such a bad lot, after all.'

'You can hope for that but everyone knows leopards can't change their spots.'

When the kettle boiled, Ace made tea.

'I'll ask you again, shall I?' Jerome said. 'Have you told Connie anything of your past? Is she aware of what goes on in your clubs?'

'I'll talk to her when the time's right and then I'll tell her about my lad Leon,' he said. 'Connie's not stupid. She'll expect a man my age to have a past.' Secretly Ace was proud of Leon. He was practically a young man now, a tall, good-looking lad.

Ace made sure Belle, Leon's mother wanted for nothing. He'd settled a fair monthly allowance on her, and if she needed more, she had only to ask. It suddenly struck him that at eighteen Connie was only a year or so older than Leon. He soon swept that thought from his mind.

The sound of a plate moving on the wooden floor caught Ace's attention. The cat had licked it clean. Jerome bent down and tipped out the remainder of the fish for it.

'So, everything's back on course for you and Connie?'

Ace nodded. 'Her cousin Marlene's a bit of all right, though. They're very similar in looks, those two. But there the similarity ends. You'll find out for yourself, soon. I told her she could have a job. She's sharp, that one is. Been around a bit.' He grew thoughtful. 'Could make me a bit of money, if I play her right, Marlene could.'

Ace picked up a mug of tea and took it along to Jerome. 'You get on the outside of that. It'll make you feel better. Everything's better after a nice cuppa tea.'

He sniffed, and his forehead creased. 'What's that awful smell, old man? You been smothering yourself in that wintergreen stuff again?'

Jerome made a face at him. 'If wintergreen's been good enough for the American Indians to use for centuries, it's good enough for me. It's the only thing I can rub on my poor back that gives me any relief.'

'All right, keep your hair on!' Ace grinned. 'But you'd better keep away from my customers when we open, else it won't be the smell of the cat's fish that'll scare them away!'

Chapter Sixteen

Gilbert Willard sat on the side of the metal bed, his elbows on his knees, his chin in his hands, and sighed. The last time he'd looked at the alarm clock it had been a quarter past six. He should have been at the Criterion picture house at half past four.

His managerial shift had been due to start then.

Not that he was worried the staff wouldn't be able to cope without him – he knew they could, adequately. That Connie Baxter had them all under control. He lifted his head and looked around the room. What a dump! A single metal bed with a stained mattress, a washstand with a cracked marble top, a wooden wardrobe, the door of which had to be jammed shut with a piece of cardboard or it swung open, and a kitchen chair beside the bed pretending to be a bedside table.

Lying in bed, if he couldn't sleep, which was often, he could make out patterns on the damp and discoloured ceiling. His one sash window overlooked the fish shop so the smells alternated between rank wet fish during the day and greasy chip fat at night.

A couple of months ago he had been living in a sea-front flat over in Southsea. Nice view, affluent neighbours, good area. Credit had been easy to get. Especially with his public-school accent. For months he'd managed to stay in that flat, owing extortionate rent, until he'd got back one night to find his belongings strewn about the front garden.

He pulled his trousers from the bottom of the bed and felt in the pockets. He counted the copper and silver. Not enough. He stepped towards the wardrobe for the jacket he'd taken off several hours earlier. He fumbled in the inside pocket for his cracked leather wallet and opened it to discover a solitary pound note. A smile touched his lips. His luck was improving all the time.

Going back to the bed he threw himself down. A sleep first, a wash and shave, then a visit to the picture house. At about eleven thirty the place should be empty and locked for the night. Either his head usherette or Doyle would have cashed up, and the blue bag containing the day's takings would be in the safe. As manager, he had a key to the picture house and knew the combination of the safe. He'd need only a few pounds. Nobody would ever suspect him of creaming a few quid from the takings. Why, he'd hidden his tracks by talking to the head usherette and accusing Doyle, hadn't he?

He could feel his winning streak already itching in his fingertips. It had been bound to return sooner or later, hadn't it? And here it was! He flexed his hands and stretched out his fingers. Tonight he'd make enough at the tables to pay Ace Gallagher some of what he owed him.

He sat up, pulled the pillow from behind him and thumped it with his fists to make it more comfortable, then slid back down on the bed.

His room was three floors above a café that seemed never to close and music blared up from the Wurlitzer jukebox. 'In The Mood' was the popular record of the moment and he hated that almost as much as he loathed his room. All he needed was one big win. Then he could forget this run-down place and the job that his dear father had wangled for him at the picture house.

His father had been owed a favour by the owner of the small chain of picture houses that included the Criterion. The last manager had been sacked for molesting young women, which had left an opening that needed to be filled. 'You'll take this job and you'll find yourself somewhere else to live,' his father had said. Gilbert had known immediately he'd miss his parents' Alverstoke address, which was welcomed by moneylenders. His father wouldn't miss the unsavoury men who'd come calling to collect their dues.

'Darling, Daddy says you're lowering the tone and we really can't have this happening,' his tearful mother had protested, adding, 'And Daddy has said I'm not to give you money.' That had annoyed him because in the past his mother had always helped him when he'd needed a handout. What mother can deny her only son's big blue eyes opening wide enough to show a tear forming as he begged, 'Please, Mother?'

Eventually he had visited his father's friends' homes pleading for a quick and necessary loan. Those friends, wanting to help and thinking they'd curry favour with his father, handed him money, which, of course, had ended up on the gaming tables and was never returned. Then one friend had told his father what was going on.

'Daddy's appalled,' said his mother. 'You're lucky it didn't bring on one of his attacks. How could you do this?'

And he was advised to leave the Alverstoke house.

Previously his mother and father had welcomed him back with open arms from the army, after his fall from a horse that had left him with a damaged knee. There'd never been any need for him to tell his parents that he had engineered the fall so he could leave a profession he found abhorrent. After taking to heart the Mexican proverb, 'It's not enough to know how to ride: you must know how to fall', he had provoked his horse to rear and had struck the ground, knowing his injury wouldn't be fatal but would be severe enough to discharge him from the forces. Who, in their right mind, wanted to go abroad to be shot at, blown up and killed?

No one close to him understood his need to bet on anything that moved. He had once given himself odds on which fly in the room would land on the windowpane first.

It was difficult to explain the feeling of excitement betting engendered.

When had he begun to gamble? That was a tough question. One might ask when he had begun to breathe. As a child he had spent a great deal of time alone. Poking around in a kitchen cabinet one day he'd come across a pack of cards. He'd discovered them while hiding from his nurse. He seldom saw his parents. Sometimes they would come into the nursery to say goodnight. He was boarded at a Winchester school aged seven and learnt subservience to the older boys. And found he could charm the masters because he knew how to concoct the most marvellous and outlandish stories, lies actually, when he needed to escape awkward situations.

At university, along with his fellows, he played cards and the high he experienced from winning, sometimes by stealth, sometimes by luck, made him feel superior. It wasn't necessarily the amount of money he collected from the tables but the excitement that came when a final card was placed.

Alas, since leaving the security of the army and his childhood home, his finances were taking a downward spiral. If he could have waved a wand and said, 'I'll stop,' it would have made him happy. But it was too late. When that excitement entered his heart, his soul, his being, it was like an itch that begged to be scratched.

Often, he wondered what his life would have been like if he'd acquiesced to his parents' wishes and stayed in the army, married the girl they'd hoped he might . . .

Gilbert stared at the ceiling. The large patch of damp near the bare electric bulb looked like the side of a mountain. Halfway down there were blotches of brown that looked like figures, monks perhaps, climbing upwards to a monastery . . .

Tonight, it was possible, no, definite, that his big win would change his life.

Chapter Seventeen

Bing Crosby was singing 'Moonlight Becomes You', his velvet tones making Marlene want to snuggle closer to the man she was dancing with. Already she could feel his hand creeping down to her lower back. Henry Atkins was, she guessed, a good twenty years older than her, but who was counting the years? If she made the best of this opportunity, he would hand over a lovely tip to her for services rendered before he went home to his wife.

'You're my lucky charm, you do know that,' he whispered. 'Without you I'd never have won at the tables tonight.' His breath smelt like three-day-old cod.

Marlene curved her body around his paunch. 'It's your skill, nothing to do with me,' she said. And, she thought, but wasn't going to articulate, you are winning at cards because the croupier is priming you, lulling you into a false sense of security so you'll spend more money until the night of your final game when he'll take you for practically everything you own.

Marlene looked across the sea of people dancing in Gosport's Four Aces club and saw that Ace was standing at the bar with a drink in his hand. She inclined her head towards the exit doors and waited until he gave a small nod that meant permission to leave the club, taking a punter with her. Both Ace and Marlene knew Henry Atkins never stayed late – his shrew of a wife thought he was at a council meeting. She kept him on a short leash, or believed she did. But Henry liked to slip his collar.

In the time Marlene had been working for Ace as one of his ghost dancers she had made more money than she'd ever thought possible. The men who came alone to the club and who wanted to hold a lithe young female in their arms paid for a ticket then chose the girl they desired. Sixpence a dance. Not much for an elderly man to fork out when at home he likely had a nag of a wife who no longer wanted him near her.

Marlene had long ago decided that while cloakroom girls and barmaids received tips, the amount she'd get in one of those jobs would pale in comparison to the earnings she could make from being especially nice to her customers as a dance hostess.

'You can be as accommodating as you like to your customer as long as you make sure he sits upstairs at the gaming tables beforehand. You get my meaning?'

She'd nodded when Jerome had added, 'And, of course, there's to be no hanky-panky anywhere on the club's premises. Understand?' He had explained how the club worked and he'd ended his lecture, saying, 'A lovely-looking intelligent woman like you should make a lot of money.'

A one-off loan and clothing coupons supplied by the club had enabled Marlene to buy several dresses of a sort she'd never dreamt of owning. After that, she was in business, not just for Ace Gallagher but for herself.

It hadn't taken her mother long to see that Marlene had come into money. 'Now you're working you'll have to pay me some rent. And that club must pay blinkin' good wages, the way you been splashing the dosh about! I'll ask no questions 'cos I don't want to listen to no lies. But I'll have my eye on you, my girl. I can't afford to keep you for nothing, now I don't always get regular money from Ace. He don't live here any more, an' you do.'

Gertie didn't add that every time Ace arrived at Alma Street to see Connie he brought bags of food and cigarettes far in excess of what his rent had been.

The small amount her mother expected didn't make much

of a dent in Marlene's earnings. Of course she never told Gertie what she really did for her money.

'I dance with the customers, Mum. That's all there is to it.' Marlene knew that neither Gertie nor Connie had ever stepped inside the club perched on the corner opposite the bus station facing the ferry, so they were never likely to find out if she was telling the truth or not.

And now Marlene bent her head to whisper in Henry's ear, practically gagging at the smell of his liberally applied cologne, which reminded her of camphorated oil: 'I know you don't like to be too late getting home. I'll walk a little way with you, if you like.'

'I would,' he said.

'I'll just get my wrap,' she said, and walked towards the stool at the bar, near Ace, where she had left her bag and cape.

'Don't spend all night about it,' Ace said, so only she could hear. 'Other punters have bought tickets,' he added. Then he gave her a smile that made her heart beat fast as he handed her the wrap and bag.

She'd already made a vow to herself that one day, in the not so far-off future, she would make him forget all about her insipid cousin, Connie. She'd show him what a real woman was and she'd accept the gifts he'd buy her. Unlike

Connie she wouldn't keep such treasures wrapped up inside a drawer, never seeing the light of day.

Marlene wasn't sure what love was but she knew she wanted the chestnut-haired man who dressed in expensive suits, wore two-tone shoes and could afford whatever he wanted. It mattered not a jot that he intended some day to marry her cousin. In her heart she knew that would never happen. After all, whatever Marlene wanted, eventually Marlene got. She couldn't care less that she might hurt Connie – after all, she'd done that enough as a kid, hadn't she? Connie was a fool. All she cared about was the Criterion and the films shown on the screen there. Her cousin needed to grow up, not spend her spare time cutting out film stars' pictures from magazines and sticking them in that scrapbook. Connie said it was therapeutic and reminded her of being with her mother. Yes, the girl definitely needed to grow up.

'See you later,' Marlene said, with a smile. Ace gave her a broad wink and her heart turned a somersault.

Henry was waiting for her on the steps. He took her wrap from her and placed it about her shoulders. 'I don't want my lucky charm to get a chill. Summertime might be on the way but these nights can be cold.'

Before taking any more steps away from the club he asked, 'Have you got your handbag with you, dear?'

'Of course. A girl never knows when she might need to powder her nose.' She gave a little giggle. This was how it worked with Henry. She opened her beaded clutch bag and, under cover of the blackout, he slipped a couple of notes inside.

'You are a sweetie to want to share your winnings with little old me,' Marlene simpered, as she snapped her bag shut.

He was now guiding her across the road, and over the lawns of the ferry gardens past the bus station where, lined up like soldiers, the green Provincial buses spent their nights.

Marlene could hear the sea washing against the wooden jetty and the moored ferryboats bumping together as they bobbed up and down on the small stretch of sea between Gosport and Portsmouth.

When they reached the bench, Henry took a large hand-kerchief from his pocket and wiped the seat's dampness so they could sit down together. He started to unbutton his flies. Marlene saw he was struggling with his clothing. His erection was making it difficult for him to set himself free.

'I can see you're ready for me, you naughty boy,' said Marlene.

Long and thin, it burst from the confines of his trousers. He used a hand to push it down but it bobbed up expectantly once more. He was breathing heavily. Gazing into her face, he slipped his hand into the top of her dress and quickly found her breast. He began kneading her plump flesh as if it were a lump of dough and all the while he was making peculiar little sounds of, Marlene supposed, happiness.

He kissed her behind her ear and Marlene, under cover of the darkness engulfing them, screwed up her eyes with distaste. Inside her head she was telling herself that this was a job to be done and thank God she could get it over quickly.

Her fingers felt for his erection, which hadn't diminished but seemed to thicken in her hand. Marlene could tell he was extremely pleased by her action as he murmured, 'Oh, Marlene, that's right, you know what to do.'

She hated the feel of the thing. It seemed to have a life of its own, undulating as her hand moved over it. His fingers had removed themselves from inside the top of her dress and he was now intent on her hand movements.

'Yes, yes!'

And then it was all over and he was using the same handkerchief to wipe his trousers. Seconds later, when he had buttoned himself up again, he put his arms around her and whispered, 'Oh, Marlene, I don't know what I'd do if I didn't have my little lucky charm.'

Chapter Eighteen

'Will you answer that door!'

Connie heard Queenie's voice raised above Gene Autry's loud singing of 'Deep In The Heart Of Texas'. There was sudden silence. Presumably, she thought, the wireless had been turned off. Then there were footsteps on the lino in the passage and the front door swung open to reveal midwife Edith Stimson with an opened canister of national dried milk in her hand.

'Have I called at the wrong time?' Connie asked. A strong smell of talcum powder and milk came wafting through the front door at her.

Edith's round face broke into a wide smile. 'No, it's just the usual madhouse in here.' A sudden cry from somewhere in the house started low and grew louder, then became a double act in strength as two babies were screaming. Edith was looking at Connie's hands. 'I see you're not wearing that ring everyone's been gossiping about.' She sniffed.

'No,' said Connie. Then, 'Oh, dear . . .'

Queenie stood at the end of the hall in the doorway to the kitchen, clutching a crying bundle. Connie walked towards her.

'Thank God it's only you,' Queenie said. Her freshly bleached hair was a mess and her face was bereft of make-up but her grin was genuine and, despite her untidy appearance, she looked absolutely marvellous, thought Connie.

'Would you mind if the wireless was turned back on?' Queenie gave a gentle rocking motion to the precious bundle in her arms, which did nothing to quieten the child. 'These two seem to like the music as loud as it will go. The noise will send them off to sleep in next to no time.' She looked imploringly at Connie.

'Course not! And, yes, it's only me!'

Connie glanced around the kitchen. A lusty cry was coming from a carry-cot on the large sofa. She wanted to go and look, or maybe pick up the baby inside it who seemed to have lungs of steel. She resisted, knowing instinctively that, although the kitchen looked like a bomb had hit it, Queenie and Edith had everything under control.

Edith squeezed past Connie, went to the wireless on

the sideboard and turned the volume up again. Gene Autry continued belting out his song.

With her free hand, Queenie beckoned Connie to her. 'Thank God it's you, is what I should have said. Here, take her for a moment, while I help Edith prepare their feeds.'

And before Connie could say a word the red-faced screaming baby was placed in her arms. And Queenie disappeared into the scullery. Connie was panicking. What was she supposed to do with this tiny screaming person?

"'Stars at night . . .'" sang Gene Autry . . .

Connie stared down at her charge. The baby hiccuped.

"'Deep in the heart of . . .'"

The tiny mouth was still open but the heartrending cries had miraculously ceased. Connie pulled aside the thin pink sheet the baby was swaddled in and looked into the little face. Two huge blue eyes stared back at her. And went on staring. A smile burst over Connie's lips. Her heart melted, like one of the ice creams Queenie used to sell in the Criterion.

'You little darling,' Connie murmured. The blue eyes closed, like two tiny pink petals, thought Connie. Her heart was full of love for the baby in her arms.

"'Are big and bright . . .'" sang Gene.

And Connie realized his voice was now the only one

she could hear. She looked across at Queenie who, while Connie had been in thrall with Bette, had returned from the scullery and had removed her son from the carry-cot and was holding him so that his body lay against her chest. He, too, was no longer crying.

After a while Queenie gently set Paulie down. The tiny boy relaxed on the white sheet. 'Now put Bette down.' Queenie nodded to an identical cot next to Paulie's. Connie took a tentative step forward, scared she might drop her precious cargo, and breathed a sigh of relief as she released the little girl.

As Connie stretched upright, Queenie said, 'You're a natural with a baby. Maybe you should have one of your own.'

Gene Autry had now been replaced by Kay Kyser singing, 'Jingle Jangle Jingle'. Connie gestured towards the wireless. The music really was very loud.

'I think I'll wait awhile,' Queenie said, 'before switching off.'

'How long before we can hear ourselves speak?' Connie asked

'Another couple of minutes and they'll be out like lights.' Queenie giggled again. 'For some reason both of them settle down with loud music. They love noise.'

Connie smiled. Despite the music, she could actually hear what was going on in the scullery now. 'Is Edith making tea?'

'And preparing dried-milk feeds for later,' she said. 'Both babies are right little guzzlers, so I'm giving them bottles as well as my own milk. And thank God I've got Edith. She comes along to help me most days.'

Connie was glad Queenie had found another good friend in the retired midwife.

Ace's promise to Connie when Queenie had nearly died after the botched abortion that he would send round a doctor had never materialized. Maybe a doctor's investigation could have foretold a possible difficulty she might encounter during delivery. Information she was carrying two babies and not one would also have been welcomed. A fine friend he'd turned out to be. Not for the first time she realized Ace often conveniently 'forgot' promises unless there was some gain in it for him.

Connie, suddenly ashamed she was thinking ill of Ace, dismissed the thought. Hadn't he been good to her and Gertie?

'Sit down,' said Queenie, brushing her hair away from her eyes. 'You make the place look untidy.'

The room couldn't possibly be any less tidy, Connie thought. But it had a comforting feel about it, despite the babies' detritus everywhere.

'Let's have a cuppa,' said Edith, coming in from the

scullery with a filled tray. She put it on the table, pushing aside a pile of fresh white nappies. Then, with a quick hand movement, she switched off the wireless and everything was quiet.

The sudden silence hurt Connie's ears.

'Quick!' said Queenie. 'Start talking, as loudly as you like. I don't want these two little so-and-sos waking up again until I've had my tea. Sing, shout, do anything you like!'

Connie began laughing. Oh, it was good to see her friend so well and happy.

'Come on, Connie, tell me some news!' insisted Queenie. Again, she pushed her hair out of her eyes.

'You've had your roots done,' Connie said.

Queenie was now stirring her tea, which Edith had poured out. 'Courtesy of my lovely husband, Len,' she said. 'He's a dab hand with the peroxide and ammonia.'

'One of these days it'll all fall out—' began Edith.

'Don't listen to her,' broke in Queenie. 'I shall be a bleached blonde when I'm eighty years old,' she said. 'Anyway, I've got to keep meself looking nice for when we go dancing, Connie, haven't I?'

Connie had forgotten her promise to go to the Nicholson Hall classes. 'So, when d'you think that'll be?'

A frown crossed Queenie's face. 'Not for a while yet. I've

got to get my figure back, haven't I?' She put her cup on the saucer, jumped up from the kitchen chair she'd made herself comfortable on and threw out her arms dramatically. 'But I'm getting there – look at me!'

'Handsome is as handsome does!' said Edith, frowning.

'I'm a fine figure of a woman, says my Len,' Queenie insisted. She bent and grabbed Connie's hand. Her closeness and the warmth in the room sent Connie's senses reeling as she caught the smell of California Poppy, Queenie's favourite perfume. 'Come with me and don't take any notice of Edith. She's upset because her favourite film star, Leslie Howard, was in a plane that went missing over the Bay of Biscay. Alvar Liddell announced it on the wireless. Since she saw him in *Gone with the Wind*, Edith hasn't stopped talking about him.'

Connie, too, had heard the sad news about the blond actor.

She allowed Queenie to drag her out of the kitchen and up the wooden stairs to the bedroom. At the wardrobe door, Queenie paused. She turned to Connie. 'All the time I was big and fat, carrying my babies, I longed for the day to come when I could wear pretty things again.' Connie could see tears in her eyes. 'It wasn't just for my own selfishness,' she said. 'Len asked me to marry him when I was already pregnant . . . You know, we've never even been on a proper date together. So, I want to make the best of myself, dress in pretty clothes again and be the girl I should have been for the man I love with all my heart.'

As she finished speaking, she opened the wardrobe door, poked about at the back and brought out a shiny gold satin evening dress that was the colour of her platinum hair.

Connie gasped. She could never imagine owning such a beautiful thing, let alone wearing it.

'I didn't buy it new,' said Queenie. 'I could never afford something like this, especially now we're managing on Len's money as I'm not working. Besides, just think of the coupons something like this would cost. I got it at a jumble sale,' she added proudly. 'And these.'

After replacing the dress, she held out a pair of shoes. Glittery, high-heeled, peep-toed evening pumps.

Connie could see they had already been worn by the tiny scuff marks on one sole. Queenie, her slippers kicked off, now stood proudly in the dainty shoes. Her red nail polish glittered on her toes.

'Another jumble sale,' Queenie said. 'I'm getting very good at flexing my elbows to push my way through for the best stuff. Len doesn't know I'm collecting all these beautiful things. But the very first time he and I can go out, when I've got my figure back,' she said, her eyes glistening, 'I'm going to come down the stairs dressed up to the nines especially for him and knock his socks off.'

'You really do love him, don't you?' Connie said, as Queenie was tucking the shoes away in the bottom of the wardrobe.

'Love him? I adore that man,' Queenie said, and Connie's heart constricted.

Did Ace feel that way about her? Did she love him like that?

Connie told herself there were many different ways to love people.

Chapter Nineteen

James Cagney was running up the stage wall, tap-dancing, in the film *Yankee Doodle Dandy* and Connie, lost in the magical autobiographical story of George M. Cohan, the legendary Broadway showman, was marvelling at Cagney's athletic skill when the manager, Gilbert Willard, tapped her on the shoulder. 'Please leave that picture-house seat, Miss Baxter, and make your way to the staffroom.'

Without waiting for an answer, he strode away through the dark and smoky atmosphere of the auditorium. Her heart plummeted. What could he possibly want with her now? She had seen neither hide nor hair of him for days as he hadn't been in to work at the Criterion.

She rose from her staff seat, trying hard not to disturb patrons sitting around her, and began walking after him down the aisle.

Pushing open the staffroom door she saw he was standing with his back to the sink, waiting for her to arrive. He looked grim. 'Sit down,' he said, motioning to the chairs around the small table.

Connie did as he asked. She was worried now. What on earth could he want with her this time? It seemed to Connie that the only time he wanted to talk to her was because he had a complaint of some kind. Usually about something that could have been avoided had he himself been in the Criterion at the time.

The manager rocked on his heels. Then he took a deep breath and said, in his plummy way of speaking, 'I have in the office the money I was about to deposit today in the bank. I decided to count it. Of late there have been discrepancies in the amount calculated by ticket sales in the ledger and the actual sum in the blue bank bag.' He paused. 'I'd like to ask if you have anything to add to my findings.'

Connie stared at him. It took her a while to grasp the full meaning of what he'd said. He was asking her if she knew anything about the missing money. He'd mentioned this before and she'd denied it. Surely he wasn't asking her again because he disbelieved her. Anger rose. 'Are you suggesting . . .'

'I'm suggesting nothing, Miss Baxter, merely asking if you have any idea how once again there is a shortfall.'

She took a deep breath. 'Do you mean that the bulk of the takings is still in the blue bag?'

He nodded.

Who would take only some of the money? It didn't make sense. 'I pride myself on my calculation skills,' Connie said. 'I do not make mistakes.' She stated this clearly and was about to add that not only were her figures correct but Doyle, as often as not, checked them to make doubly sure. But she said nothing of this because she didn't want to implicate Doyle in any way. Gilbert Willard's questions, which he was quick to point out weren't accusations, stung.

Connie knew Doyle was no more a thief than she was.

She was thinking so hard she almost missed Gilbert Willard's next words.

'Who, may I ask, has keys to the premises?'

'You, as manager, Doyle, and there are spares in your office, sir, for emergencies,' she answered, realizing that by being truthful she could be implicating Doyle by admitting he had keys. This was necessary as he was the first person to arrive in the mornings to open up for the cleaners and the last to leave after locking the doors at night.

Connie had a sinking feeling that the manager was about to pin the theft either on her, as she cashed up at night, or Doyle.

Doyle was a lynchpin of the picture house. He loved his job and it most certainly wasn't in his nature to steal anything.

Connie waited for him to ask more questions but he suddenly said in a cool, calm voice, 'Very well, Miss Baxter, that will be all.'

Gilbert Willard swept past her but before closing the staffroom door behind him, he added, 'I shall cash up the takings tonight, Miss Baxter. No need for you to worry about doing it.'

Connie sat without moving for a long time, thinking about what had just happened. Gilbert Willard was sharp-witted. None of the spare keys were missing because that would have come to her attention before now. Neither had Willard stated that the owners of the picture house had been informed. Why not? Willard was up to something, Connie was sure of it.

She glanced at the clock on the wall and saw the film had nearly finished.

Duty called. She stood in front of the mirror, made sure her hat was on straight, took a deep breath and went out into the auditorium to join the other usherettes in seeing the audience left the premises safely after the national anthem had been played.

She wasn't happy. Doyle was no thief. He'd be upset when she told him of the conversation she'd had with the manager. And, unfortunately, she would have to share that conversation. She wouldn't tell Gertie, even though she longed to confide in someone. Gertie was her aunt and a good friend but she couldn't keep a secret. And this further development needed to be kept under wraps until she could find out what was going on.

The only possible explanation of how a thief could enter the picture house was to let themselves in with a key. But who would take only some of the money? Surely a bona-fide thief would steal all of the day's takings.

She went about her business with a heavy heart. Oh, how she wished Queenie still worked alongside her. Len was back, but Connie saw little of him tucked away high in the projection room.

As soon as the auditorium was empty Connie, with several of the usherettes, went along the rows flipping up the seats to make it easier for the cleaners to do their work the following morning. She thought about Queenie, how much in love and happy she was with her husband, Len.

It had been quite some time since Connie had been out with, or even seen, Ace. Of course, he was a busy man and running two clubs wasn't easy for him. She knew he was working hard so she could have the best life he could provide. He'd told her that. When she'd explained ages ago, that she was content simply to be with him, he'd changed the subject. It had been different when he'd lodged at Alma Street: she seen him practically every day. She missed him teasing her. She thought back to Christmas time when he'd taken her and Gertie to Devon for a short break. How they'd walked along the cliff tops hand in hand. How their eyes had met across the bar and it felt like the two of them were the only people in the world who knew what it was like to care about each other.

Where had that closeness between them gone?

After the staff had left and Connie had completed the usual checks in the picture house to make sure it was safe for Doyle to lock up, he caught her as she was leaving the staffroom.

'The manager is cashing up tonight,' he said. His homely face broke into a wide smile. He was married to a lovely woman: Jilly had borne him three sons and he would often chat about his family to Connie. He also had an allotment on Whitworth Road at Daisy Lane. Gardening was his pride and joy. He spent his free time there with Jilly, and during the growing season he would often bring in fresh vegetables for Gertie. Runner beans were his speciality, and even Connie had to admit they were the sweetest she'd ever tasted.

'Well, it makes it easier for us,' she said, and smiled at him. 'Less work for us to do.' Connie thought perhaps this might be the perfect time to talk to Doyle but didn't feel she could say anything to him while she felt as low as she did. All she wanted to do was get home and go to bed. Whether she would sleep or not with everything going around and around in her head was another matter.

Because the manager was on the premises Connie and Doyle left the Criterion together. Doyle, taking a fatherly interest in her wellbeing, didn't like her walking home alone in the darkness. Then at Inverness Street he cut through by the almshouses to continue on his normal route to his own home.

There was still warmth in the air from the fine summer's day. Connie made an effort to chat about inconsequential things until they reached Alma Street when Doyle pulled on her arm, causing her to face him.

'I can always tell when there's something worrying you,' he said. She stared at him. His kind brown eyes searched her face in the moonlight. He tightened the belt on his mackintosh and pushed back the brim of his trilby hat. 'You can talk to me,' he said. 'Me and Gertie go back a long way. Is it that scallywag Marlene that's upsetting you?' Gertie had obviously been gossiping.

Connie felt tears rise but she pushed them back. She shook her head. 'I hardly see her,' she said. 'When I get up, she's asleep and when I arrive home at night, she's still at work.' Then she blurted, 'She's working at Ace's club.' She couldn't hold back her feelings any longer: the tears fell.

'Sssh!' he said, pulling her comfortingly close. 'If it's a bit of jealousy you're feeling you got nothing to fear from her. You two might look alike but there the resemblance ends. I've known her since she was a kid and she was a selfish little baggage even then.'

'But she sees him more than I do,' Connie wailed.

He pushed her to arm's length. 'Do something about it, then.'

Connie tried unsuccessfully to wipe away her tears. Her forehead creased to a deep frown. 'How? We both work such long hours and there's no time left.'

'Make time,' he said. 'He took the time to fill the back of his car with flowers for you and it was a lovely surprise. Surprise him,' Doyle said.

'I'm not so sure about that.' All her life she'd been led to believe it was up to the man to make the moves, especially in such important things as love. Asking a girl out was the prerogative of a man. For a woman to do the asking made her look 'fast', a tart. Women just didn't take the initiative.

'Connie, there's a war on,' he insisted. 'Women are taking the lead in all sorts of ways. They go into pubs by themselves, they drive lorries, they work at jobs that were considered a man's domain before the war. Don't moan because Marlene sees more of your man than you do. Rearrange your days or nights and see more of him.' Doyle looked at his watch. Then he smiled down at her. 'Get yourself indoors,' he said, glancing up the street. 'No doubt Gertie's kept something hot for you to eat. Then get to bed and decide how you can surprise Ace. Go and fight for him, love.' He looked at his watch again. 'I'd better get home,' he said, 'else my Jilly will have my guts for garters for being late.'

Chapter Twenty

Gertie gently wiped her bunions dry with the old piece of terry-towelling and put her slippers back on. Her feet always felt better after a good soak and that was exactly what they'd had. In a minute she'd take out the bowl of water and throw it down the sink but first she needed a fag. Now, where did she put her Woodbines?

'Ah! There you are, my little beauties,' she said, catching sight of the green packet on the kitchen table where she'd forgotten she'd left it earlier. After lighting up she drew into her lungs the blessed relief a cigarette gave her.

Her stomach growled. The meaty smell from the oatmeal sausages she'd made earlier and covered with a plate was making her feel hungry. They were Connie's favourites. 'Poor little devil,' she muttered, without removing the cigarette. It seemed to her that Connie wasn't herself lately. Maybe it was because Marlene had come home to live – she and Connie were chalk and cheese – or maybe it was because she missed working with her friend Queenie, who had no intention of coming back as an usherette to the Criterion, now she had her lovely twins to consider. Queenie and Len could live quite well on his wages as a projectionist, couldn't they?

She had the wireless on and Glenn Miller's band was playing 'Kalamazoo'. Damned shame about that plane going down. The band leader's lovely music helped make this war just a bit more bearable, she thought, feeling under the tea-cosy that covered the brown pot that sat beside her fags on the table. It was too cool to pour out, but she'd be making fresh in a little while, Gertie consoled herself, as soon as Connie came home.

She ought to be getting a move on. The remains of the onions she'd cut up still lay on the round bread board she used for chopping, and the bowl of dripping needed to be put back in the cupboard. She hadn't even closed the bag of oatmeal, but when she got an idea in her head and wanted to do something nice for someone, she just had to get on with it. Connie needed cheering up and if oatmeal sausages, made with bacon, did the trick, well, that could only be a good thing.

The grey ash fell from the end of her cigarette to her skirt and she rubbed it into the material until it disappeared.

The couple of baking potatoes she'd put into the oven were giving out a nice smell. The range hadn't been lit for a while – it was supposed to be summer but last night it had rained and today had been miserable. She thought the warmth might cheer up Connie, and Gertie just fancied a bit of a fire heating the house. Gertie looked at the plate covering the eight fat sausages she'd rolled up ready to fry when Connie came in and a contented smile moved her lips.

She pushed herself out of the chair and began gathering the used cooking utensils. 'Get on with it,' she said to herself, trying to ignore her aching knees.

She wanted to talk to Connie about some other business to do with the picture house. She didn't think her niece could do anything about it but, after all, she was the head usherette. She wanted to tell Connie that the manager wasn't pulling his weight. He was a young bloke and probably didn't understand some of the duties he was supposed to perform. Gertie had noticed Em Hardwaite wasn't cleaning the men's urinals properly. Gertie had gone behind her back and mopped the floor when one of the patrons had complained at the first picture showing of the day that the place hadn't been cleaned.

The patron had been hovering outside the staffroom, looking awkward, when Gertie, knowing Willard hadn't come in yet and that Connie was taking the ticket money, asked him what he wanted.

When Gertie had challenged Em all she'd got in return was a shrug of Em's shoulders as she said, 'That Gilbert Willard ain't bothered, so why should I be?'

That had set her thinking. Even the previous manager had performed a daily roll call when he strutted in front of his staff checking their uniforms were clean and tidy and making sure they knew what was expected of them. Gilbert Willard didn't seem to worry about any of that. Gertie wondered whether he'd even notice if one of the usherettes turned up to work in a jumper and skirt. It would be just as likely he wouldn't be there to see it, the amount of time he took off.

Maybe she wouldn't talk to Connie about that, not tonight. It would probably make her unhappier than she already was, and Gertie didn't want that.

Out in the scullery Gertie put the dirty pots on the draining board, ready for washing up, then went back into the kitchen for the bowl of water she'd soaked her feet in.

Connie wasn't happy about Marlene working at the Four Aces. Neither was Gertie, if the truth be known. But Marlene paid her for bed and board regularly every Friday and was clever enough to keep out of any trouble – even if she wasn't, Gertie would always be there for her.

Gertie thought about Ace, his swagger and chat-up lines he'd used on the girls he'd been out with before Connie had come on the scene. Oh, yes, she'd heard all about his antics. But then she remembered the holiday they'd been on, the three of them, last Christmas. Love had shone out of his eyes every time they'd clapped on Connie. She thought about the incident in the air-raid shelter and immediately pushed it from her mind. Ace wouldn't be daft enough to play around with Marlene, would he? Marlene might fancy Ace, he was a good-looking bloke, but surely he had more sense. Of course he did. It wasn't long ago that he'd filled the back of his car with flowers for Connie and set that expensive engagement ring on her finger. No, Ace loved her, she was sure of it.

Connie lay tucked up in bed waiting for the sleep that was evading her. She'd eaten as much of the oatmeal sausage and baked potato as she could. Gertie, bless her, had made it because she knew it was one of her favourite meals.

They'd not spoken much while they'd sat together at the kitchen table. The wireless had been on, with Alvar Liddell bringing them up to date on the war.

Listening to the news took her mind off her worries. Clothes rationing had saved the country £600 million so far, according to the authorities. Rationing, in force now for two years, had saved the country half a million tons of shipping and released thousands of people for work in war factories. Before the war people had spent approximately twenty pounds each on clothes per year and now it had gone down to around seven pounds ten shillings per person. Connie wasn't sure how she was supposed to feel about this. She was fed up with making do and mending, and finding nothing decent to buy in the shops. But her heart ached even more for the deaths of innocent people and the destruction of businesses and homes, which was still happening here in England. She wondered if two wrongs really did make a right. Alvar Liddell described the new phosphorus incendiary bombs that created such terrific heat that Germany's burning streets looked like rivers of fire.

'We don't want to listen to any more of that, do we?' Without waiting for Connie to reply, Gertie had turned off the wireless. Connie hadn't minded, and definitely didn't want to discuss any of the news with her aunt.

She'd helped Gertie wash up, and as she'd already had a strip wash in the scullery before they had eaten, had kissed her aunt goodnight and come to bed.

The huge teddy-bear they'd named Bertie, which Ace had won for her at the fair in Southsea, sat opposite her bed on his chair and reminded her of happier times. Ace had taught her to waltz that day, the first time she'd ever danced in her life. The second time she'd waltzed had been in the White Swan, the night Gertie and she had been guests at Queenie's marriage to Len.

Her heart fluttered as she remembered the well-dressed blond young man who had asked her to dance. She wondered where he was now, if life and the war were being kind to him. She felt the smile rise to her lips and the warmth deep inside her that followed as she thought of him . . .

The White Swan had been crowded and because of the noise they'd barely spoken while dancing. He'd had to leave early and sadly she'd not set eyes on him again. Neither of them had needed words to understand that something extraordinary had happened to them.

But why was she reminiscing about a man she had briefly met? She should be thinking about the one who'd put a ring on her finger and asked her to marry him.

Doyle was right. She should make a special effort to rekindle the happiness she and Ace had shared in Devon.

But how to go about it? He wouldn't like it if she appeared alone unexpectedly at either of his clubs. She smiled: he was being old-fashioned, making sure her reputation remained unsullied, wasn't he?

There was nothing to stop her phoning him. She'd ring tomorrow, suggest they meet. They could walk along Stokes Bay beach in the moonlight and simply talk. And kiss. She'd make it a night he would remember.

Doyle was right: it wasn't always up to the man to make the first moves. Excitement coursed through her. Ace would be surprised, but in a good way because it would show she thought about him, cared about him, loved him. Yes, she'd phone him tomorrow and arrange everything for tomorrow night.

But then another thought took over, what was to stop her going to the phone box on the corner and ringing him now? She knew he was either at his club in Gosport or at the one in Southsea. If she waited until the morning, she might not be able to reach him.

Connie slipped out of bed and threw on her coat. She didn't need to get dressed – no one would see her in the dark, would they? And the phone box was only a short walk away, past the alley that led to the recreation ground. She could be gone and back in five minutes or so. And if she was extra quiet, she wouldn't disturb Gertie.

A light wind ruffled her hair. She thought how nice it would be if the warm weather held for tomorrow night.

She wasn't frightened of the night – after all, she walked

home from work in the dark – but the noises surprised her. There were rustlings alongside the road in the piles of rubbish and bricks still not cleared away after the previous raid. Mice, she supposed, or rats, not that she intended to investigate. Trees cast giant shadows in the moonlight.

There was no traffic. Out of force of habit she had slung her gas mask in its container over her shoulder and it slapped against her hip as she walked. In her hand, tightly held, were the coppers for the call.

Ahead she could make out the red phone box. Once she was inside it, she tried to ignore the unpleasant smell. She lifted the handset to check the phone was working. After inserting the coins and dialling the Gosport club she waited a long time for someone to answer. Connie wondered if she'd made a mistake, dialled the wrong number. She pressed button B, and after her coins had been returned she tried again. Then Jerome answered. She wondered if he'd been hurrying – he was breathing heavily.

'It's Connie here, Jerome. Can I speak to Ace?' She was glad she had enough pennies, if she had to wait for Jerome to call Ace over.

'Ace can't come to the phone just now, Connie love, but tell me what you want and I'll make sure he gets your message.'

Connie's spirits fell. She wanted to hear Ace's voice.

'I'll tell him. You can be sure of that,' Jerome urged.

She consoled herself that Jerome would surely pass on her message. She explained where and when she needed to see Ace. Foster Gardens, a place they were both familiar with.

Jerome repeated her request. 'Leave this to me, Connie. No problem, he's here in Gosport tomorrow night. Ten in the evening at Foster Gardens. He'll be there. Lovely to hear from you, Connie.'

Connie replaced the receiver. She trusted Jerome to pass on her message.

Feeling much lighter, she left the phone box.

Immediately her thoughts ran ahead of her. She would leave the Criterion earlier tomorrow night to wash her hair and dress in something nice. She'd take care with her make-up and wear the Evening in Paris perfume he'd bought for her and the jewellery. Then she'd walk to the venue. Foster Gardens was not only a special place where they'd met before: it was also a convenient equal distance between Alma Street and Ace's club.

Jerome had sounded breathless. But he wasn't a well man, was he? She imagined the club as a hive of activity with Ace as the front man busily talking to patrons. Somewhere perhaps she'd feel uncomfortable to be. In films, clubs really did look like places she'd rather not enter. Besides, she had no wish to bump into Marlene.

She walked quickly, eager to be indoors. She didn't feel quite right wandering along Forton Road in her nightwear. Though no one could possibly know with her coat over the top.

When she reached the alley next to Spragg's bicycle shop, a noise, a deep whispered voice, made her jump. It was quickly followed by a giggle. Connie, her heart pumping fast, could just make out the outline of a soldier's uniform pressed tightly against a girl's body. She breathed a sigh of relief. It was only a couple kissing, taking advantage of the dark. She smiled. Tomorrow, she and Ace would be doing that too.

Chapter Twenty-one

'So, this is the big secret you wouldn't tell me about, is it? I been wondering what you've been up to, sneaking off to practise whatever it is you been practising!'

Shirley filled the kettle from the tap in Tom Smith's scullery and set it on the gas to boil. He kept the place remarkably clean and tidy, for a bloke, she thought. She was about to go back into the kitchen when Tom yelled, 'No, don't come in yet, I'm not ready. I got to pin on my badge.'

She smiled to herself, but she turned from the doorway and busied herself finding the wooden tray and gathering cups and saucers for the tea she was about to make.

After a few seconds he shouted, 'You can come in now. What d'you think?'

'Well I never!' Shirley had to put the tray on the table before it slipped from her hands and fell on the floor. She was suddenly struck dumb as she stared at the navy-blue battledress jacket done up to the neck, navy trousers, steel helmet with a W on it, and the badge Tom had pinned on the front pocket of his jerkin with the letters proclaiming ARP. Over his shoulder he'd slung his gas mask in its case.

'Well I never!' she said again. She looked at his thick-soled boots and said, with a laugh, 'You can't dance in them, lad.'

His blond hair, not anchored by the helmet, fell against his forehead as he glanced down at his boots. 'No, I can't. But I can help dig out people that are buried beneath rubble without burning my feet.' He stood on one leg to show her the tough leather and sturdy sole. 'I had to wait a long time to get hold of these.' He put his foot down again. 'I still haven't got the proper trousers – there's shortages of everything,' he said. 'Another member's wife dyed these flannel ones.'

'Tucked into your boots, no one would ever know,' Shirley said. Her eyes were smarting with tears. 'I'm ever so proud of you,' she said. She knew she could never tell him so but she looked on Tom as the son she'd never had. She sniffed, pulled a handkerchief from her sleeve and wiped her eyes. 'Air Raid Precautions,' she said, fingering his badge.

'Well, the navy won't let me fight for my country but my heart's strong enough to earn a living by dancing, which is pretty strenuous. So, I thought, Why don't I volunteer to help win this war any way I can?'

'Does that mean you'll get paid?' Shirley asked, before she disappeared back into the scullery. She could hear the kettle boiling and decided it was time to make the tea.

Tom had followed her. He stood in the doorway. Shirley rinsed the teapot with boiling water, emptied it, then spooned in tealeaves and poured on the boiling water.

'If I did it full time, I'd get three quid a week, but as I'm only part time I won't get paid. Not that I worry about that because it means I can teach dancing and still do something for my country.'

Shirley gave the pot a stir, put the lid on and, walking around Tom, went into the kitchen. She placed the teapot on the tray. 'Thank God you'll still need me to play the piano,' she said. 'I thought because you're now an air-raid warden I might be out of job. Anyway, where did you find out about this?'

'I saw the poster in a shop window,' he said. 'So, if I come round your street you'd better make sure there's no chinks of light showing through your black-out curtains. I don't want to have to report you to the authorities!'

'Your duties involve more than that,' Shirley said.

'Of course. I'll be guiding people to shelters. I've got

a wooden rattle to warn everyone if there's been a gas attack. I'll also be putting out incendiaries with asbestos bomb snuffers, helping people who've been bombed out, making sure the firemen and the ambulances get to injured people . . .'

'All right, all right, I get the idea,' Shirley said. 'So, all this is what you been practising in that building along Forton Road?' She'd known the wooden hut was being used for something special as she'd often seen the bicycles piled up alongside and men of all ages going in and out of the building.

'Yes, but that's only part of it, Shirl. I've had to learn about first aid. I'll have a kit of my own . . .'

Shirley turned his words over in her mind as she poured the tea and watched him leave the kitchen to change back into his everyday clothes. His excitement and his talk were too much for her to take in but she admired him for wanting to prove to himself he could be useful. She knew how much it had hurt him to leave the services on medical grounds. But now she had something else to worry about. What if Tom got hurt?

She didn't want to think about that. Since she'd got to know him she'd begun to realize what a special young man he was. She knew now she was right to suggest he take on these dance classes. If that Ace Gallagher had kept him on at the Four Aces he'd soon have had him slipping back into all kinds of unsavoury business. She looked at him standing in his new uniform, telling her what he hoped he could achieve by helping others, and felt as proud as if he was her own son. Except she'd never have a son now, would she? Or a husband.

Her Albert had joined up in Lord Kitchener's army soon after war had been declared in 1914. She'd waved goodbye to him from Portsmouth railway station with tears in her eyes. His mum and dad hadn't gone to see him off because they said, at seventeen, he was too young to join up. But Shirley had since learnt of youngsters of twelve and thirteen obeying the demand that their country needed them. Recruitment officers rarely questioned the ages of lads wanting to leave home to travel and see the world. Albert had wanted to get away from his strict churchgoing parents.

'The war won't last,' he'd told sixteen-year-old Shirley. 'I'll come back with money in my pockets and we'll get married.'

Albert was her first love, and her last. He'd died at the Somme. He'd been her golden boy with his blond hair, blue eyes and ever-smiling mouth. She'd promised to wait for Albert. Now she knew she'd wait until her dying day when at last they'd be reunited. Other men, when she was younger, had asked her out but she knew she could never allow herself even to think about another man taking Albert's place. If Albert had come home to her, she might have had children and grandchildren. Instead, she'd become a music teacher, sharing her life with other people's little ones. She'd stopped teaching when the school closed because the children had been evacuated.

Shirley didn't want to look around for work at another school in these uncertain times so she took any work she could find to keep money coming in. Cleaning for Ace Gallagher paid reasonably well, until she'd learnt enough about his work ethics to mistrust and dislike him. Mostly she'd worked daytimes but sometimes Jerome had requested extra night duties and, with no one to question her comings and goings, she'd never minded.

The smart young man who'd modelled himself on Ace Gallagher had reminded her of Albert. Or, to be precise, Tom Smith might have been the son of her Albert. And to watch him dance filled her heart with joy. Of course Tom didn't even know of her existence – why should he? Why should anyone? Shirley was well aware she was instantly forgettable – the fat cleaner in the funny hat.

Shirley was much affected by Tom's love for his ailing mother. She understood why he sometimes bent the rules:

he needed money for doctors, for medicine. She liked to think that if she'd had a son he would have done exactly the same for her. So, being Tom's pianist and helpmate gave Shirley great pleasure. As did the fact that people were enjoying the dancing classes and the escape from mundanity that moving to music provided. She liked cooking occasionally for Tom. She knew her baking was pretty hit and miss but she believed it was the thought that counted. She dearly hoped one day he'd find the girl who would love him as she'd loved her Albert.

Shirley sipped her tea. Tom entered the kitchen. He gave her a smile that would have melted any mother's heart.

Chapter Twenty-two

Jerome set the receiver back on its cradle, then took off his coat and hung it on a hook on the kitchen door. He'd entered through the back doors of the Four Aces to the insistent ringing of the telephone. The club was noisy tonight and it was late, but he was annoyed that no one else had answered the phone's shrill tones. There were two other phones in the Four Aces: one in Ace's office and one behind the downstairs bar. Surely the club wasn't so busy that no receiver could be picked up.

The loud purring of the black and white cat twining itself around his ankles calmed him. 'I'll see to you when I've passed on the message,' he said, bending down and tickling the animal just behind its ear.

Jerome was tired. It had been a long day at Ace's club on the sea-front at Southsea but initially he'd thought a change of scene might do him good. The weather had been fine and sunny, heralding a warm day, as he'd boarded the ferry to Portsmouth and he'd enjoyed the short walk past the naval barracks at *HMS Nelson*.

Jerome had volunteered to sort out the firm of plumbers who weren't pulling their weight doing repair work after a brawl at the club. Ace had a short fuse, and if he blew up at the men they might walk off the job. That Jerome would have to return to Southsea early tomorrow didn't please him, either.

He left the kitchen and made his way upstairs to the gambling tables where he expected to find Ace keeping an eagle eye on the punters. He nodded to the croupiers and recognized some of the men sitting at the tables. After the fresh, salty air he'd soaked up on the short ferry ride back to Gosport the thick stench of stale cigarette smoke and body odour that greeted him made him shudder as he scanned the large room.

Many of the regulars, especially those in debt to Ace, were at the tables. The young bloke, new to the club but already owing quite a tab, Gilbert Willard, didn't look too pleased with the hand dealt to him. But if the fool wanted to spend time losing money it wasn't any business of Jerome's, was it? Jerome didn't mind Ace losing his temper when debts owed weren't paid promptly. That was justified, wasn't it?

A few of the men had girls from downstairs draped over them. If there was one thing he could give credit to Ace for it was employing good-looking women who knew how to fleece blokes. Jerome wandered over to the upstairs bar. Ace clearly wasn't here. It was time to go downstairs. He put his hand to the base of his spine. He'd liked the exercise today but it hadn't liked him.

He held on to the brass stair rail going down to the dance floor. He was still irritated that with all these people around, many of them employed by Ace, it had been left up to him to pick up the phone. Hadn't Ace been anywhere near his office or the bar?

The glass drops on the big chandelier twinkled like stars. It gave the club class, he thought. Made it look like the war wasn't happening. The flock wallpaper, gold paint and mirrored backdrops reeked of glamour. He looked towards the bar. Big Mo was on duty tonight and inclined his head towards one of the small wrought-iron tables in an alcove.

Ace sat with a bottle in front of him. Jerome could tell by his movements he'd been drinking steadily. Jerome didn't worry about the whisky – Ace could mostly hold his drink – but his anger rose at the sight of the girl he was drinking with. Her face was mere inches away from Ace's. She was pretty enough, that was the trouble, but Marlene reminded him of too many other women who'd brought men to their knees. Hadn't his mate Billy Hill married one similar? A cheap gold-digger? She'd tried to take the gangster for everything he'd had, and it was only the intervention of a clever solicitor and a hit-and-run accident that had saved Hill's finances.

Jerome watched Ace for a few moments, then stood at the table in front of him. 'Had a good day, son?' he asked amiably. After all, Jerome knew you caught more flies with honey than with vinegar. It wouldn't do any good if he went in with all guns blazing at what could be a perfectly innocent chat between boss and employee. Not that he believed that for a moment. The girl was trouble.

Jerome stared at Marlene. He could see the attraction. A dead ringer for Connie. But the resemblance ended with her looks. He'd met Marlene's type so many times and knew her inside out. He moved his head, pushed his glasses further up the bridge of his nose and stared at her.

She took the hint. Her chair scraped back on the parquet flooring and she rose without a word, but with a face as grey as thunder. Jerome watched her pert behind wiggle off towards the bar.

'You're back, then?' Ace motioned towards the whisky and Jerome shook his head. Ace nodded towards the seat

Marlene had vacated, inviting him to sit. Again, Jerome shook his head.

'I've got another early start tomorrow,' he said.

'Is it sorted?' Ace asked.

Jerome nodded. He knew what Ace meant. 'They'll be paid off tomorrow, job done.'

Jerome could instantly tell by the careful way Ace was forming his sentences that he was more drunk than he had at first thought. 'You should answer your phone more often,' he said. 'Or at least make sure someone's near it to give you messages.'

'I think the bar's been busy,' Ace said.

As if that explained everything, thought Jerome, but Ace hadn't finished.

'I've not been in the office,' he said, careful of his enunciation.

Jerome pushed the whisky bottle further along the glass-topped table and sat down next to Ace. 'No, I can see that,' he said. 'Well, listen to me. By the time you get up tomorrow morning, I'll be over in Southsea. You've had a phone call from your Connie . . .' After he'd finished relaying the message, Jerome made Ace repeat what he'd said. Which Ace did, with just a little hesitation in his voice.

Satisfied that Ace was aware of what Connie wanted,

Jerome rose from the chair. He looked pointedly at the whisky bottle. 'I'm not telling you what to do, son, but there's only unhappiness at the bottom of every one of those.'

Ace narrowed his eyes, dropped his smile. 'Then don't tell me what to do, old man.'

Jerome felt the chill in Ace's words. The raucous noise of the punters in the bar area and the dance music from the tired-looking band providing background sound paled against the heaviness of the silence between the two men.

Jerome rose, pushed back his chair and stood over Ace. 'Just remember the message I've passed on to you from Connie.'

He turned towards the bar where a greasy-looking tall man was pressing a dance ticket into Marlene's hands. Then he looked down at Ace. Sometimes he had to remember this auburn-haired man wasn't still the freckle-faced kid he'd saved from a savage beating. He made a move to go, but couldn't resist adding, 'Don't lose Connie because of that little tramp.'

He began pushing his way through the sweaty couples on the dance floor. He heard liquid splashing into a glass, but didn't look back. Out in the kitchen, a cat needed feeding.

Chapter Twenty-three

Connie felt as if she could dance along the pavement just like Judy Garland in *Me and My Gal*. But she didn't want other people to think she was mad so she simply walked more quickly, eager to get home and make herself beautiful before she went to meet Ace.

Gene Kelly had been in that film. He was a terrific dancer and so handsome. She tried to imagine her and Ace moving to the music, like the two stars in the film.

Gilbert Willard hadn't been in tonight so Doyle was going to cash up and Connie had every faith in him. She couldn't be sure an air-raid wouldn't happen but that was beyond her control.

All day long she'd been thinking about meeting Ace, looking forward to what she'd say to him and, of course, what she'd wear. Finally, she'd decided on her blue linen

dress with the box pleats in the skirt's centre. It had a white
Peter Pan collar and white cuffs around the elbow-length
sleeves. Her high-heeled black shoes would match her black
handbag. And she'd decided to wear her engagement ring.
She would hate it if Ace asked her where it was and she
had to confess that most of the time it sat in her chest
of drawers because she was too worried about losing it.
And didn't want the girls at the Criterion to think she was
showing off. Oh, how she wished he'd bought her something that didn't stand out so much.

Gertie would be in when she got home and she'd promised to have hot water on the stove ready for Connie to have
a strip wash. 'I'll tong your hair for you,' Gertie had promised. To be honest, Connie would have preferred to heat the
curling tongs over the gas stove and tong her own hair. She
didn't relish going out with the ends smelling singed because
Gertie had left the tongs on the flame too long.

'You can bring him back here after – I could make you
both a bite to eat,' Gertie had said. Connie had shaken
her head at that suggestion. It wasn't that she didn't want
Gertie to see Ace: it was because she preferred to be with
Ace without Marlene coming home to spoil things. Marlene
probably saw more of Ace than Connie did anyway.

*

'Well, you've got a lovely evening for a walk along the sea-front,' said Gertie. Connie blinked away the smoke from Gertie's fag that went into her eyes as her aunt bent over her, rolling up her hair. 'It's been a glorious day,' continued Gertie. 'Shame about the barbed wire on the beaches. The sea might have been warm enough for you to paddle. Mind you, we need some rain for gardens—'

'Ow!' Connie yelled. 'You've let those tongs burn my head!'

'I'm sure you only think I have,' said Gertie, and went on mumbling while Connie was trapped on the kitchen chair.

Connie tuned out and listened to the wireless, with Bing Crosby singing 'I Don't Want To Walk Without You'. She couldn't always ignore Gertie's voice and again it broke into her thoughts.

'There, that's all the curling done,' said Gertie. 'I'll just put this out on the draining board to cool down.'

While Gertie was in the scullery, Connie felt the warm sausage-like curls on her head. The curling process had taken longer than she'd expected because every few minutes Gertie had had to reheat the tongs over the gas flames – the heat soon went out of them. Connie remembered her mother once saying to her, 'Pride's painful,' when she'd begun to use mascara on her lashes and had accidentally poked the little blue brush into her eye.

Connie had already put on her make-up. She didn't like powder on her skin but made up her eyes with loads of mascara and a dash of Vaseline on the lids to make them glossy. Red lipstick, the one Ace had given her, came next and Evening in Paris perfume behind her ears and on her wrists. As she'd dabbed on the perfume, she saw the bottle wasn't as full as she'd thought it was. She'd heard that perfume evaporated if left in the light so she'd make sure in future that she tucked it away in the depths of a drawer. Her engagement ring glittered on her finger.

Gertie came bustling in waving her hairbrush and promptly began brushing out Connie's hair. 'It's cool enough not to lose its curl now,' she said.

'Can I look?' Connie asked, wincing at Gertie's brisk technique. Wouldn't brushing that hard take out all the curl?

'You can look in a minute. I'm aiming for Veronica Lake's peek-a-boo style,' Gertie said.

'Are you sure you haven't burnt my ends?' Connie moaned. 'I think I can smell singed hair.'

'It's your imagination!'

Connie felt Gertie smooth her hands down her hair. Out of the corner of her eye she could see strands of her blonde tresses against her cheek. Automatically she used her hand to brush them aside and heard Gertie exclaim, 'Will you leave it be! Veronica Lake has her hair almost covering one side of her face.'

'I want to be able to see where I'm going!' snapped Connie.

For a moment there was stillness and silence. Connie heard Gertie take a deep breath and let it out slowly. Connie sat quite still on the kitchen chair in front of the unlit range and hardly dared move her head or her body. She heard Gertie fiddle with something on the table followed by the strike of a match and the smell of phosphorus as it ignited. Gertie took a deep drag on her cigarette, then sighed theatrically.

'You can look now,' she said.

Connie took in the familiar Woodbine smell. Then she stood up, and her eyes flew towards the looking glass hanging above the range over the mantelpiece. She gasped. A beautiful woman gazed back at her. Dance music was playing on the wireless. Connie finally said, 'Is that really me?'

Her blonde hair tipped her shoulders, curled under in a pageboy style, but her long fringe was swept to one side, joining a wave that tumbled down across the side of her face. Her eyes smarted with tears. She looked so glamorous!

'Don't you dare start crying or you'll spoil your face. Then what will Ace think?' Gertie warned.

Connie took a deep breath. 'Thank you,' she said. She turned and enfolded Gertie in her arms.

'Oi! Mind me fag!' said Gertie. She smiled at Connie. 'You better get off if you're going to meet him at ten. You don't want to keep him waiting,' she added. Then, 'Take a coat, it might rain.'

'It won't. It's been sunny all day. I don't want a coat but my white cardigan will keep me warm if it gets chilly.'

Gertie nodded. 'Go on then! Get out of my sight! Give Ace my love.' She stood looking at Connie, then added, 'You can move your head, you know. Your hair won't fall out if you shake it.'

Connie laughed, kissed her cheek, picked up her handbag and the cardigan that lay folded on the sideboard. Minutes later, she was walking down the road to meet Ace.

She didn't put her cardigan over her shoulders as the heat was still in the air from earlier. She looked at her watch: twenty to ten. Now she could catch sly glimpses of herself in the shop windows as she walked along the pavement. She allowed her heart to swell with joy when two young men waltzed out of the fish-and-chip shop, greasy newspaper parcels in their hands, and wolf-whistled at her. Connie had to admit to herself that Gertie had made a marvellous job of her hair.

The first raindrop pierced the humid evening air and fell on her just as she crossed the road near the Thorngate Hall. It was used for dances and wedding receptions but was closed at present due to bomb damage making the premises unsafe. Barbed wire surrounded the building and there was a notice saying 'Keep Out!' The few enormous houses in this area of Gosport were in large gardens hidden behind high walls, which also signified 'Keep Out!'

Connie ran across Bury Road to the shelter of tall trees at the entrance to Green Lane. She looked again at her watch. It was ten to ten. She decided to stay in the relative shelter for a while as the place she had arranged to meet Ace was just around the corner. She slipped her cardigan about her shoulders. Already the cold rain was causing her to shiver. She wished now that she had asked Ace to collect her in his car from Alma Street. The previous few days of hot weather had lulled her into a false sense of security. Gertie had been right in telling her to take her coat.

The rain had made puddles on the road now. She glanced at her watch. It was a few minutes to ten. Now the chestnut trees she stood beneath gave little shelter. Raindrops were being forced from the laden leaves and her dress was getting soaked.

Anything was better than standing there like a drowned

rat, Connie thought. She had visions of running along by Foster Gardens and Ace pulling up alongside her, opening the car door to save her.

Connie clutched her bag tightly and ran.

There was no black car waiting at the entrance to Foster Gardens.

The metal gates dripped with rain.

She moved her head quickly to see if Ace had parked further along the road. There was no traffic, no people.

Why hadn't he come?

Ace could have telephoned the picture house to let her know if there was some problem, a reason he couldn't meet her.

Her dripping hair whipped wetly against her cheek. She thought of all the time Gertie had spent on it with the tongs.

There was no shelter.

At twenty past ten Connie trudged home.

Her tears mingled with the rain on her face and the water dripping from the rat-tails of her hair.

Chapter Twenty-four

It was an automatic response for his body to react the way it did. The sinuous way she was sliding against him. Her hips grinding against his, making him engorged. How could he not go for what she was offering?

Common sense took over. He'd had too much to drink and it would render him useless. His body was telling him one thing, his brain another.

Still, this was why he employed her, wasn't it? To lull his male customers into a false sense of security that they'd receive more from her after a seat at the casino's tables. If they won a few quid, Marlene would make sure she got what was owed to her. How she did this, as long as it was away from his casino, was up to her

He'd made it a rule never to dance with any of his girls in either of his clubs. She had pulled him onto the floor when the small orchestra had started playing, and he hadn't had the willpower to tear himself away from her. So, now he wasn't surprised to find himself dancing to Al Goodman's 'That Naughty Waltz' with Marlene.

He was becoming lost in the music, her body and even her perfume. He could have sworn it was Evening in Paris. Unconsciously a smile curved his lips.

The only time he'd danced with Connie he'd had to teach her the steps to a waltz. Connie had been unsure of herself, hesitant and awkward. None of that applied to Marlene. Though even her hair, smelling of Amami shampoo, reminded him of Connie.

The rain hitting the windows with such force made him feel content, relaxed. No doubt the whisky helped with that as well.

He really should go upstairs and see what that young fool Willard was doing.

He owed a great deal of money and the stakes he was bringing in were pitifully low. Ace wanted paying, in full and soon.

'What the hell are you doing?'

A hard body pushed him and Marlene apart.

'Oi!' the girl said, but quickly disentangled herself from

Ace's arms and, in the blink of an eye, had disappeared into the crush of people surrounding the bar.

Ace focused on the interloper. 'What the f—' he began.

Jerome was standing before him. The old man was furious. 'Why are you here?' He pushed his face up close to Ace's, and Ace could tell he'd not long come inside out of the deluge. Jerome's skin was brushed pink by the wind and rain. He'd combed back his sparse hair but droplets of water still clung to it.

Ace frowned. 'What's the matter?' he slurred.

'Where's Connie?'

Ace laughed. 'How the hell should I know? Picture house probably.'

Customers were now watching them.

Jerome pulled Ace, who was unsteady on his feet, from the floor and over towards the table where an opened bottle of whisky stood by a glass and where Ace had been sitting. 'You were supposed to be with her tonight!'

Jerome was staring into Ace's eyes and, as if a bolt of lightning had struck him, Ace clapped a hand to his forehead. 'Jesus! I forgot!' The wind swept another gust of rain against the windows. 'If I leave now—'

'She wanted you to meet her at ten. It's gone twelve. You seriously think she's going to wait two hours in this deluge?'

Jerome swept his arm towards the downpour hammering against the glass.

Ace pushed him aside, almost overbalancing. 'I'll drive to Foster Gardens first, then go to Gertie's.'

Jerome held on to his arm. 'I'll give you three reasons why you shouldn't. One, you can't even stand up straight, let alone drive a car. Two, Gertie wouldn't let you see her. And three, you stink of perfume. If you've got any sense at all you'll let me attend to the casino and you'll stop showing yourself up. Get out of here and sober up.'

Jerome moved away, disgusted. He began climbing the wrought-iron stairs that led up to the casino. Once upon a time he could have taken them at a run. Not any more. He was getting old and he knew it.

When he reached the carpeted top floor, he looked back down to the bar and the dance floor. He gazed at it for a long time while the cigarette smoke swirled about him. The stink of stale beer and sweat rose and clung, like a shroud.

He couldn't see Ace. Maybe the silly bugger had taken his advice and gone through the kitchens to bed. He shook his head disconsolately. If Ace was hoping to build bridges with Connie he was certainly going the wrong way about it. It was the drink, wasn't it? That was what happened when the spirits crept up on a person. Ace was a sharp, money-making machine. But he was allowing the drink to take him over. Well, he'd do everything he could to put an end to Ace's drinking.

With Connie, he had the means to show Gosport he wasn't the bad man everyone thought he was. News had got about how Connie had saved her friend's life by running through the streets of Gosport to find hospital transport, with bombs falling about her. Marrying Connie could be the making of Ace. Jerome loved him, but he could only justify Connie taking on the liability Ace was fast becoming if he cut back on the drink. Hadn't he told Ace he should start being honest with her? He didn't have to tell her the plain unvarnished truth, that would be stupid, just sufficient for her to know he loved her enough to confide in her. A woman in love could forgive all manner of past transgressions if she was kept sweet. To the outward eye Ace had to be cleaner than a washerwoman's Monday laundry and he could achieve that by marrying Connie. Why, it only needed his old mate Billy Hill even to think Ace was in a downward spiral and the doors would close on the black-market and the gambling cons quicker than Ace could down a whisky.

Down on the dance floor he could see Marlene wrapped in someone's arms, dancing as if he was the only man in her life. Well, he was at that moment. Jerome wished Ace had never employed the girl. She was trouble through and through. She was another Belle. And look how long it had taken Jerome to banish that mistake in Ace's life to Kent. Shame about the lad, though. Jerome had to admit the boy, Leon, showed promise.

Willard was at the tables. He was on a winning streak, by the chips piled in front of him. Jerome looked at the croupier, who glanced at him and cleared his throat to let him know he would do whatever Jerome asked of him.

So, Gilbert Willard, loser, winner and heavily in debt to the Four Aces, was on another winning streak and likely to pocket a nice little cache of money, and all because Ace had been downstairs with that trollop instead of up here giving the nod to the croupier that Willard had to lose at the table. Jerome sighed. He coughed into his hand. The croupier didn't bat an eyelid. But Jerome knew he would make sure Willard lost any further bets. The only way Willard, owing the club money, could leave with winnings was if he cashed in his chips immediately and walked out of the door.

Maybe he would. But Jerome knew his habit was too strong, and when he started losing, his belief in yet another winning streak would grab him and the balance of power would once again be with the Four Aces.

Jerome had done his homework on Willard. He liked to know all about his high rollers who became creditors. Willard, ex-army, came from a distinguished family. The money was there but he'd been ostracized by his well-to-do relatives. A typical black sheep. But they'd willingly pay up rather than lose face by having the family name attached to scandal. In the meantime, the errant son had a piddling job managing a Gosport picture house. Where he was getting his stake money was anybody's guess but, to the best of Jerome's knowledge, there were only three picture houses in Gosport: the Ritz, the Forum and the one where young Connie worked, the Criterion. Woe betide Willard if he was making trouble for Connie.

Jerome pushed his spectacles back up his nose then began making his way downstairs. It wouldn't be too long before the club closed for the night.

The Southsea club was running well. His business with the plumbers had worked out to his satisfaction. He was tired. A nice cup of tea and bed with an Agatha Christie book should sort him out. He waved to Maurice, the orchestra's conductor, and mouthed goodnight: they were packing away their instruments. No doubt Cat would be in bed already. He smiled to himself. You could trust cats. You always knew where you were with them, selfish little monsters.

Chapter Twenty-five

Bang! Bang! Bang!

Connie tried to ignore the noise that had woken her. The banging stopped and the front door opened. Laughter and talking became so loud she couldn't possibly keep her eyes closed. And now, to her horror, her bedroom door clattered open.

'Come on, lazybones! I've walked all this way pushing a pram so you and me can spend the day together, so get up!' Queenie, hair freshly bleached, stood beside the bed smelling of Californian Poppy and dressed in a blue cotton outfit with puffed sleeves and shoulder pads. Her cheeks positively glowed and she had a smile a mile wide. She'd also brought in with her the tempting warmth of the summer sun. Gertie, metal curlers in her hair and fag in hand, stood behind her.

Connie groaned. 'Go away!'

After getting drenched last night when Ace hadn't turned up to meet her, she'd spent so long crying she hadn't been able to sleep. All she wanted to do today until it was time to get up and go into work was hide.

With one fell swoop Queenie wrenched the covers from Connie's bed leaving her in her nightdress, exposed not only to Queenie's sight but to Gertie's.

Gertie pulled a face and said, 'I'll put the kettle on!'

'Get up!' Queenie barked.

Connie pulled her nightdress about her to cover her modesty and sat up.

'I suppose she told you,' Connie muttered. She nodded towards the doorway where she could hear Gertie clattering up the passage.

'Told me what?' Queenie perched her bottom on the edge of the bed.

'That I was stood up last night.'

Queenie frowned. 'Look, I've no idea what you're talking about. But at five o'clock this morning when the sun was warming up nicely and I'd just got Tweedle-dum and Tweedle-dee fed and changed, I went out into the back garden in my nightie, with a fag in one hand and a cuppa in the other, and thought, What a lovely day to push the pram and go for a walk with my best friend.'

And that was when Connie burst into tears. But she managed to ask, 'Where are Bette and Paulie now?'

'Outside your front door with the pram hood up to keep the sun off and they're both fast asleep. I think you'd better get out of that pit, come in the kitchen and tell me all about it.'

A while later she was sitting at the kitchen table with Queenie and Gertie drinking tea. Fag smoke swirled in the air and Connie was telling Queenie what a fool she'd felt walking home in the rain the previous night with her hopes of time spent with Ace dashed.

'Maybe Jerome forgot to pass your message on,' said Queenie, ever the peace-maker.

Connie shook her head. She pulled her dressing-gown belt tighter around her waist. 'He promised. Jerome don't promise things lightly.'

'You should have seen her when she left here,' put in Gertie. 'Looked like a film star, she did, her hair all tonged like Veronica Lake's.'

'Maybe something unexpected came up,' said Queenie. She handed Connie her handkerchief, which she'd pulled from her pocket.

None of the excuses Queenie offered were making Connie feel better but it was so good to talk. Much better than lying in bed, worrying.

'I'll get washed and we can go out with the babies,' she said gratefully to Queenie.

'You don't know how much I've missed gossiping with you two,' Queenie said.

'Don't you talk to Len?' Gertie was lighting another Woodbine.

Queenie let out a guffaw of laughter. 'Talk? My Len never stops talking, usually about film projectors and it bores me silly! It's nice when Edith pops in, which she does most mornings. But you and me, we're pals, aren't we, Con?'

Connie could feel her intense gaze.

Queenie's voice grew serious. 'And because we're pals, I think you should tell me what else is making you feel bad. My Len says at work you've lost your sparkle.'

Connie stared at her. 'What d'you mean?'

'He says when you was first made up to head usherette, you was like a chirpy sparrow, always had a smile and a good word for everyone, but lately it's like somebody died.'

'He's right, you know,' Gertie said. 'She's been so miserable she hasn't cut out and stuck in any film stars' photographs in her scrapbook for ages. I bought her this month's *Photoplay* film magazine and she's not even looked at it.'

Connie glared at her. She so wanted to talk to Queenie about the other thing that was worrying her, the missing money, but how could she when Gertie, who never missed a trick, would no doubt tell everyone when she went into work again? Connie didn't want the other Criterion employees discussing it until she'd talked to Doyle.

Gertie got up from the kitchen chair she was sitting on. 'I'm going down the garden to the lavatory. I need to put some more squares of the *Daily Mirror* on the string. It's not nice to find there's no paper when you need it. But before I do, I'll peek at the twins outside the front door to make sure they're all right.'

Connie put a hand to her forehead and sighed.

Moments later, Gertie returned. 'They're flat out asleep,' she said, 'and the pram's still in the shade.' She picked up the newspaper, then disappeared into the scullery. The back door opened and closed behind her.

'I'll fill the teapot,' said Connie, rising from her chair.

'No!' Queenie said. 'Now we're on our own for five minutes, you can tell me why Ace isn't the only thing on your mind.'

Connie went over to the door separating the kitchen from the passage and stairs. She closed the door, put a finger to her lips and pointed heavenwards to remind Queenie that another person, Marlene, was upstairs and she didn't want her to overhear.

'This is just between us two.' Connie made herself comfortable on a chair again.

'Between us two,' agreed Queenie. Her hand snaked across the table, her fingers closing over Connie's.

Connie took a deep breath and spoke quietly. 'Someone's stealing money from the nightly takings. The manager insists it's Doyle.'

'Don't be daft!' Connie knew Queenie couldn't help spitting the words out.

'I agree, Queenie. Doyle would rather cut off his hands than steal anything. But the truth is, money is going missing and it points to either Doyle, me or Gilbert Willard himself.' She shrugged. 'It can't be him because he's the one who's discovered the money's missing.'

Queenie stared at her. 'That's the oldest trick in the book, Connie. He's the thief! Accusing everyone else so nobody will think it's him!'

Connie's mouth fell open. Then she said, 'Oh, my God! Of course! How clever of him!'

Queenie squeezed her hand. 'Doyle values his job, and I don't know about you but I'd trust him with my life, wouldn't you?'

'Yes, that's why I haven't been able to tell him the manager is pointing the finger at him.'

'We must keep an eye on that slippery Willard devil,' Queenie said. 'Len can't stand the bloke. He says he's more useless than Arthur Mangle was.'

'He's right!' Connie agreed. 'You won't let slip I've told you this, will you?'

'I'm telling Len!'

Connie gasped. 'But I don't want everyone knowing!'

'Len won't say anything but he will help us.'

'Us?' asked Connie.

'Yes, us. If anything upsets you, it upsets me,' Queenie said. 'But it'll go no further and don't breathe a word to Gertie. She means well but she couldn't keep a secret if her life depended on it. No wonder you've been upset lately. And you've kept all this to yourself?'

Connie nodded. She allowed Queenie, who was obviously distressed, to cross-examine her.

'Have the owners of the picture house asked about the missing money?'

'I don't think he's told them, Queenie. I'm sure if he

had, we'd have had someone down from head office.' She thought for a moment. 'Or maybe he's hoping it won't be discovered until the books are audited.'

'All the more reason to believe this is all down to Gilbert Willard, then.'

Connie could see that Queenie was making sense. 'I'm so glad I've shared this with you,' she said, disentangling her hand from Queenie's to wipe away a couple of tears that had trickled down her cheeks.

'Who else would you share it with?' asked Queenie. 'And if I know my Len he'll come up with a plan to expose that rat Willard.' For a moment she was quiet. Then she asked, 'Would you be willing to do anything my Len suggests to stop the manager trying to get you and Doyle sacked for something you haven't done?'

Connie just had time to breathe, 'Anything.'

The latch on the back door clicked up and Gertie trotted in.

Queenie and Connie shared a smile, then Connie rose. 'I'll have a quick wash in the scullery, get dressed and then we'll go out for that walk, shall we?'

Gertie looked at Connie, then nodded towards Queenie. 'I must say since her ladyship's come visiting you look a lot better than you did first thing this morning.'

'I feel it as well,' said Connie, stepping past her into the scullery.

'Even so, you shouldn't be going out with nothing inside you. Let me make you some toast – I think there's some bread left.' Gertie looked worried.

'Thanks, but I don't want anything to eat,' called Connie, turning on the tap and allowing cold water to pour into the sink. 'More tea would be nice, though.' She hastily scrubbed her face and neck with the flannel and the chunk of soap on its dish. Later, before she got ready for work at the Criterion, she'd have a strip wash. Now all she needed was a lick and a promise, to get dressed and take a lovely walk in the sunshine with her friend and the two gorgeous babies.

'I could do with a cup an' all,' came Marlene's voice.

Connie, scrubbing her skin with the hard towel, popped her head around the scullery door into the kitchen. Just what she needed, she thought, Marlene pushing her nose in where it wasn't wanted. Then she scolded herself for thinking nasty thoughts. After all, Marlene lived in this house as well and she was allowed to wake up and drift downstairs like anyone else, wasn't she? To make amends she said, 'Morning, Marlene.'

Queenie gave Marlene a half-hearted smile

'Hello, love,' said Gertie, to her daughter.

Connie took in the satin dressing-gown edged with marabou feathers and the wedge-heeled fluffy slippers.

Marlene didn't bother to acknowledge anyone. Instead, she said, 'Had a bad night, Connie? You look awful.' She flopped down on a kitchen chair.

Connie returned to the scullery sink and picked up her toothbrush. She had nothing to add to Marlene's comment, well aware that her tearful night had done little for her appearance.

Gertie came bustling into the scullery, shook the kettle to see if it contained sufficient water, then lit the gas beneath it. 'Don't take too much notice of what Marlene says. You know she could start a fight in an empty room,' whispered Gertie. Connie rinsed her mouth and smiled at her. They went back into the kitchen together.

Marlene stared at Connie, then said, 'I've got some blue eye-shadow you can borrow, if you like. Might disguise the bags underneath your eyes. It's good stuff, got it off an American in the club.'

'Leave her alone, Marlene. Connie's had a bad night because she was supposed to see Ace and there was a mistake.' Connie knew Gertie was trying to smooth over any bad feeling between the cousins but was unaware she was making things worse.

Connie was about to tell Marlene she didn't like blue eye-shadow because her eyes were green, when Marlene added, 'If you were looking for Ace you should have come down the club. He was dancing with me until late last night.'

Connie stared at her.

There was a sudden squeal of chair legs on lino as Queenie shot up, grabbed Connie's arm, and propelled her towards the passage and her bedroom. 'C'mon, Connie, I'll help you get dressed.'

Chapter Twenty-six

'I'm having a telephone installed sometime this week,' Tom said.

He stared at Alan Crosby, his ARP mate, with whom he'd been paired for this unexpected shift and who had been knocking at his house for ages.

'That'll make things easier,' Alan said. 'When you're needed, we can phone instead of banging your door down.'

Tom was beginning to feel the effects of the nightly bombing raids and the endless sirens. What wouldn't he give for a night of uninterrupted sleep, he thought, instead of dozing at the bottom of his garden in the Anderson shelter on a rickety camp bed?

Alan changed gear in his works van, which proclaimed on its sides 'Alan Crosby, Painter and Decorator, Work Guaranteed, Free Estimates'.

High in the sky searchlights criss-crossed, hunting for enemy bombers. The sound of exploding bombs distorted the men's voices and the noise of the van's engine. Occasional flares lit the road brighter than pre-blackout streetlamps.

Tom knew he had a lot to be thankful for: a house of his own and, despite rationing, food in the cupboard. His afternoon dance classes were extremely popular and his new telephone would be a big help with running them. No longer would he need to put his address on the postcards he stuck in shop windows. A telephone number would be more professional. He was earning money doing work he enjoyed, and he had no one to answer to, except Shirley. Not that he minded that: it was nice to feel cared about.

He quite liked the bachelor's life, though sometimes it was lonely.

Between shifts, chatting in the ARP hut, some of the men would moan about their wives. Not Alan Crosby: he was one of the more settled blokes. Maybe the men regretted the wives they'd married. Tom had met some of the couples together at various venues and they'd seemed perfectly suited, happy even. What other people saw in a marriage was not what really went on behind closed doors, though, was it?

Tom knew he'd never settle for less than the girl who had taken his fancy at the Criterion picture house. He'd looked into her green eyes, realizing she too had experienced the amazing feeling that the world around them had vanished.

He had immediately thought of new beginnings, but had had nothing to offer her then. He'd despised himself for who he was.

And now? Slowly, he was building a new life. A life that was without shame. And he believed, although his transformation was in its infancy, that written in the stars, they'd be together eventually.

But meeting her again wasn't something to be manufactured. It wouldn't work that way. There was also Ace Gallagher: what if he was still on the scene?

'Hold tight!'

The van swerved as Alan swung the steering wheel to avoid a fox that materialized from nowhere and ran across the road near the Criterion picture house. Tom heard and felt the cans of paint shift in the rear of the van.

'Phew!' said Alan. 'I wouldn't have liked to hit it. Got a right to live, just as we have. You all right?'

'Yes,' said Tom. He liked Alan Crosby. He was a good man.

Always the vehicle smelt of white spirit and putty, and Tom's footwell was awash with brown-paper bags that had once contained sandwiches Alan's wife had prepared.

The van slowed, then suddenly turned left, without a gear change, into a side road. Alan slammed on the brakes and Tom's hands braced themselves against the dashboard to stop him hitting the windscreen.

'Sorry,' Alan said.

'No need for Hitler to send bombs,' said Tom, 'not with your driving.'

Ahead they saw the smoking ruin of what had once been a large house. Now the vehicle was stationary, Alan pulled on the handbrake.

A rescue party, in blue dungarees and tin hats, was already shifting joists and bricks, using shovels but mostly hands. Tom recognized the Imperial Guest House. Last night when the emergency accommodation in an empty school had become filled to bursting point, after the whole of Bedford Street had gone up in flames, Tom had been ordered to find transport for two dazed families with nowhere to sleep. Four adults, an elderly man and three kiddies. They had been sent to the Imperial to join guests already lodging there.

He tried not to think of those men, women and children, who might have been, might still be, beneath that blackened hell.

Jamming his tin hat over his fair hair he jumped from the

van. When he reached the smoking ruin, he could already feel the heat in the soil and rubble through the thick leather of his boots. The acrid smoke made his eyes sting.

'Three not accounted for,' shouted one of the men. 'No survivors so far.'

Tom couldn't hear his voice but he read his lips. The sound of water dashing against burnt timber and glowing bricks issued noisily from the firemen's pumping machine, destroying all normal sounds. Tom began lifting, sifting, watching, listening until he felt he must have been born with intense weariness. Eventually three more corpses joined the rest of the tarpaulined bodies.

Four hours later five men and Bessie, Mrs Elizabeth Edwards, to be correct, were drinking tea as black as tar while sitting in the wooden hut that was their ARP head-quarters on Forton Road.

'Tough one tonight, Bessie,' said Alan.

Tom looked at the big woman searching for Nice biscuits in the cupboard next to the sink. He hadn't the heart to tell her Alan had finished the packet last night.

He didn't feel like talking anyway. All he kept thinking about was himself sending people, last night, to certain death. It would always be part of him. In the van on the way back here to the hut, he'd cried like a baby.

'You only did as you were ordered to do,' Alan said. 'If it's meant to be, no intervention can stop Fate.'

He knew he'd have to go on remembering those words. And take them to heart, because it was the truth. Fate was everything.

Tom swigged his tea.

Bessie slammed the cupboard door. 'You've eaten 'em, haven't you?' She kicked Alan's foot. Then she stood in front of him. He was lounging in an old armchair saved from the dump, its stuffing shedding on the floor. 'Well, you can get us another packet. That one was half full, greedy guts!'

Alan moved his foot but didn't get up. 'Cor! D'you go on at your old man, like that, Bessie?'

'No, because he's not a guts-ache where biscuits are concerned, not like you.'

Tom licked his lips. The tea was remarkably sweet. The sugar had been finished and Bessie had brought in a tin of golden syrup.

Alan and Bessie were always sparring. Bessie was the only woman attached to their group. During the day she was a full-time ambulance driver but managed three or four evenings a week as a warden.

This winding-down tea break helped to keep people sane, and Tom could see they all needed it. He never talked to

Shirley about the things he witnessed while on duty. It wasn't that he could go home and shut out the horrors. He just preferred not to share them.

Connie tried hard to concentrate on *Random Harvest*. Normally she had only to hear Ronald Colman's voice magnified by the sound system in the auditorium and she'd feel her knees grow weak. The story of Greer Garson as Paula, in love with the amnesiac Charles Ranier, played by Colman, was a tale that would normally have made her weep. Now the story-line seemed hackneyed against the real-life turmoil going on in her head.

Just like the British film she'd watched a couple of days ago. That B picture, a melodrama, was just as improbable, she thought, with James Mason as a blackguard making out he was in love with two women. Anyone with an ounce of sense could have worked out he loved himself more than anyone else. The women were at war with each other, which resulted in Susan Shaw's character, Maisie, attempting suicide by sticking her head in the gas oven – this was implied but, of course, due to censorship, not shown on screen. James Mason saved her, and they got married. The other girl, played by Jessie Matthews, went on to become a famous dancer.

It was a silly film, Connie decided. Not at all like real life. And what woman as beautiful as Susan Shaw would give a fig about James Mason two-timing her?

Today's offering of *Random Harvest* did a magnificent job of highlighting shell-shock, which Connie knew had mostly been ignored by filmmakers. And Ronald Colman, with his glorious voice, was always worth buying a ticket for.

She thought back to earlier that day.

'You take the pram,' Queenie had said. 'It'll concentrate your thoughts on what's going on around us, not what went on back in Gertie's house.'

So, Connie had wheeled the Pedigree pram, taking care when pushing up and down pavements not to wake the twins. She was aware Queenie had practically forced her from the house because her friend had guessed that, at any moment, she might launch herself at Marlene and tear her hair out.

It had taken Queenie moments to propel her into her bedroom and insist she throw on the blue spotted button-through dress with the white collar that was hanging from the dado rail. And after she had raked a brush through Connie's hair the two of them were out in the sunshine.

'I could kill her.' Connie sighed.

'Fat lot of good that would do,' Queenie said. 'That

witch knows how to upset you and you fall for it every time.' Queenie had paused at the entrance to the recreation ground. Connie began manoeuvring the pram down the steps and into the cool leafiness. Without preamble Queenie collapsed onto the sweet-smelling, freshly mown grass. Connie stared at her, then back at the pram.

'Don't they need feeding or changing or something?' she asked, dropping down beside her friend.

Queenie pointed to the metal tray beneath the pram. 'There's bottles and nappies all ready in that bag,' she said. 'I've learnt from Edith that all the while Bette and Paulie are asleep they're growing and less trouble. Let sleeping dogs and babies lie. Who am I to argue with an ex-midwife?'

Connie nodded. What did she know about babies?

'Marlene dancing with Ace isn't important, you know.' Queenie propped herself up on one elbow. 'It could have happened for any number of reasons.' She paused. 'If it happened at all.'

Connie stared at her. 'You mean she could be lying?'

Queenie merely shrugged.

'That still doesn't answer the question of why Ace never turned up,' said Connie. 'I felt angry and foolish walking home in the rain. I cried all the way.'

'There could be a hundred and one reasons why he let you down. But if you don't trust him, I think you should reconsider your promise to marry him.'

Two sparrows were flapping about, hopping around, examining the grass cuttings for insects. Connie watched them. 'You're right,' she said. 'When I first met him, I thought I knew what kind of man he was . . .'

Queenie sighed. 'No one knows what people are really like. Sometimes they don't even know themselves . . . You got a lot on your plate at present, what with Gilbert Willard trying to convince you Doyle's stealing—'

'No! Doyle wouldn't!'

'Of course he wouldn't,' said Queenie. 'We've already been over that. You're sure Willard hasn't said anything to the Criterion's owners about the stolen money?'

Connie shook her head. 'I'm sure he would have said.'

'That's to our advantage and could work to Willard's disadvantage,' Queenie said thoughtfully.

But her words were almost obliterated by the wail that came from the pram, which was immediately replicated by a second. Both cries grew steadily stronger.

Queenie rose from the grass, went over to the pram and pulled out a bag from beneath it. She took out two small terry-towelling wrapped bundles. She handed one to Connie. 'This milk's still warm. Who do you want? Bette or Paulie? Bottles first, I think, and bums second . . .'

Connie had loved being with Queenie and the twins.

Now she watched as Ronald Colman, lying beneath a tree next to a stream, pulled Greer Garson into his arms, after asking her to marry him, and kissed her.

Why, oh, why did life always seem so much easier in the pictures?

Chapter Twenty-seven

As Connie and Doyle were walking home together, she thought about what an extraordinary man he was. Not only had he worked at the Criterion for many years, with diligence and efficiency so that the staff looked up to him, but he had shown her great empathy too. She decided that Gilbert Willard's little speech about the theft from the picture-house takings was no longer something she could keep a secret.

All the staff had thought when the last manager was sacked that Doyle would take over. But it hadn't happened.

'I don't think he's after pinning the thefts on you, Connie. I believe it's me he wants to blame. He wants me out of the picture house, I'm sure of it.'

Like Qucenie, Doyle thought Willard was trying to absolve himself by bringing the pilfering to her notice.

'I'm only sorry I wasn't with you when he decided to

tell you about this, Connie,' he said. 'I'd have liked him to answer a few of my questions . . .'

She could tell he was upset when he added, 'Nothing like this has ever happened before at the Criterion in all the time I've worked there.'

'Len's planning a trap that I hope Willard will fall into and show him up for the blackguard he is,' she said. 'But I need you to be on board with all this . . .'

'Connie love, anything you decide that will stop that man treating people badly and destroying the Criterion's good name . . .' he stopped walking and faced her '. . . is more than all right by me.'

Connie smiled and nodded her thanks. Relief flooded her now that Doyle knew everything. No matter how clever Gilbert Willard thought he was, he didn't have right on his side, did he?

Walking homewards, she and Doyle had further discussed Willard's uncaring attitude to patrons. Earlier this afternoon after he'd arrived late, looking as if he'd been up all night, an irate woman had barged into Willard's office. At the metal filing cabinet sorting through invoices from the ice-cream manufacturers, Connie had been caught in the disturbance.

'What are you going to do about this sort of thing?' The woman, with a scowl, stalked up to Willard and glared into his face. Her headscarf had slipped, showing rag curlers. Connie had been mesmerized.

'Madam!' Willard managed to gather himself together.

'Madam, nothing! My girl, Maggie, was sitting in 'ere watching Ronald Colman when the bugger next to her put his hand on her knee.'

'Were you with her, madam?' Willard was smirking.

The woman looked affronted. 'Didn't need to be. It's a U rating.'

'These things happen.' He shook his head dismissively.

'Not to my Maggie they don't. She's twelve and she's been crying all night.'

'I suggest you don't allow her to come to the pictures alone in the future.'

Connie had to step in. She knew that if she didn't Willard's unfeeling attitude could harm the Criterion's reputation. She grasped the woman's sleeve and led her towards the door. 'I'm really sorry, Mrs . . .?'

'Rawlins,' said the woman. 'He's an arrogant sod!' She jerked a thumb towards Willard, who was disinterestedly peering out of the window.

Once they were in the foyer, where the manager couldn't hear, Connie said, 'You're not the only one who thinks so.'

'It's not a nice thing to happen to a young girl.'

'Did anything else happen?'

'No, because Maggie changed her seat.'

'Good,' said Connie. 'She's a clever girl.' Mrs Rawlins liked that. Connie went on, 'Trouble is, these dirty old men try to take advantage of innocent young girls, and unless the girl tells an usherette immediately, it's difficult to catch them.' She had put her arm round Mrs Rawlins's shoulders and walked her towards the glass exit door.

Doyle had been alone in the foyer. He'd looked anxiously at Connie and the woman. Connie had shaken her head, telling him not to worry and that she could handle things.

'Don't stop your daughter enjoying the pictures.' Connie lowered her voice, as if she was sharing a secret. 'That happened to me when I was ten years old and living in Portsmouth. But I was prepared. My mum gave me a sharp hatpin and I kept it in my pocket when I went to the pictures. One afternoon when a Laurel and Hardy film was on, this smelly old man came and sat next to me. After a while he began to fiddle about with his clothing. Then he got hold of my hand. I felt sick, I can tell you.' Connie shuddered. 'But I got the hatpin and I jabbed it hard where he was trying to put my hand.' Connie started to giggle. 'You should have heard him scream! He jumped out of his seat and practically ran out of the Odeon.'

Mrs Rawlins's mouth was open. She closed it and asked, 'What happened then?'

Connie could see she'd won over the angry woman. 'Nothing happened to me. I watched the film in peace. But I bet the dirty sod didn't do that again for a while!'

Mrs Rawlins gave Connie a small smile. 'Thanks, love,' she said. 'I won't forget what you've told me and it was kind of you to listen to me.' She stepped out into the sunshine. 'Not like that manager in there.' She tossed her head back towards the closed door of the office, and Connie breathed a sigh of relief that a nasty situation had been averted. If Mrs Rawlins cared to write and complain to the owners of the picture house that was her prerogative.

At number fourteen Connie pulled the key from the letterbox and let herself into the silent, darkened house. It would be nice to be on her own for a while, she thought.

Gertie had gone up to Queenie's to sit and listen to a play on the wireless. Valentine Dyall was in a horror series – the Man in Black, he was called. Queenie liked to listen but the stories scared her silly. She locked all the doors and usually Edith Stimson, who lived up the road, came to sit with her. But Edith was visiting a friend and Gertie had been roped in instead. As Len didn't get home from work until late she was going to stay the night.

Connie was weary. Her head was full of nonsensical storylines from films.

She thought the pictures should mirror real-life instead of making out that everything always turned out right for the main star. True life endings weren't always happy, were they?

In the kitchen she put another log in the range and watched as the flames licked around the dry wooden bark, then flared up. Satisfied, she kicked off her shoes and went through to the scullery to put the kettle on. Not like Gertie to light the range when the days were warm, but if the nights were cold and she had fuel she didn't like Connie to come home to a cold house.

The film-makers were always skipping over the bits that showed how disturbing the truth really was. Ronald Colman's lost memory was nothing like Percy Almond's lost memory. Percy was looked after by his wife and they lived at the top end of Alma Street. He'd been in the first war, the Great War. They'd sent him home from France with shell-shock and injuries. Eventually, after being in hospital for a long time, the doctors allowed him to go home to his wife, Emily. He'd lost an arm and had facial scarring but he still didn't know who he was. Or who Emily was. The slightest loud noise sent him cowering beneath the table, crying and screaming. This second war had taken its toll on Emily.

From a pretty woman she was now a skinny bag of bones. The hard work and worry of looking after Percy was killing her. Percy didn't sit on any riverbank in the sunshine, like Ronald Colman, kissing the woman he loved.

Connie lit the gas beneath the kettle and thought about the picture where the woman had stuck her head in the gas oven. Was that an easy way to die?

Looking at the gap between the bottom of the step and the wooden back door, Connie thought it would be impossible for enough gas to build up in Gertie's scullery. Weren't towels tucked into the gap to stop the unlit gas escaping? She wondered if it actually made a difference. She grabbed a towel from the hook and stuffed it tightly along the gap.

Connie bent down on her hands and knees and put her cheek next to the towel. Moving slowly along the width of the door she could still feel a draught. A strong one! She'd proved a point, hadn't she? A room would have to be airtight for that kind of suicide to work.

The kettle was boiling now. Connie got up, dusted the grit from the floor off her knees, turned off the gas and made a pot of tea. She was looking forward to a cuppa. Were there any carrot cookies left? she wondered. Gertie had used the oven to make a batch yesterday.

She opened the oven door and groaned at the greasy,

smelly space. Taking out the blackened rack and still thinking of Susan Shaw's character's grim decision to use the oven to kill herself, she saw there probably was enough room inside. But who in their right mind would put their head in that horrible, food-encrusted space? It'd make a person's hair filthy, wouldn't it? Definitely not a nice way to go. Susan Shaw's character must have been distraught.

She stood in front of the open oven door. The whole cooker could definitely do with a clean. Gertie earned her living as a cleaner. She also liked things put away and not left out, collecting dust. But some areas of the house were overlooked, like the kitchen drawer that was difficult to close because it was full of things that 'might come in handy'. Connie decided that on her next day off she'd set to and scrub the filthy gas cooker until it was squeaky clean.

She knelt down in front of the open oven door. That James Mason film had never mentioned how uncomfortable it must have been for Susan Shaw to get her head in the oven. A bit hard on the knees! Wait a minute, Connie thought. Anyone with an ounce of sense would make themselves comfortable. Put their head on a pillow?

In two minutes, she was back from her bedroom with her pillow, which she threw down in front of the oven. Now she smiled to herself. At last, she could see the probable relevance of the film cameras not following every move that the Susan Shaw character, Maisie, had made. She looked at her watch. All this messing about getting everything ready took ages. If they'd shown it all, the film would have had to be much longer.

'There must be an easier way to go,' Connie murmured.

'No! Don't do it!'

Connie practically jumped out of her skin as Marlene, in her marabou-feathered dressing-gown and wedge-heeled slippers pushed her away from the cooker so hard that Connie fell onto her knees on the scullery floor.

Chapter Twenty-eight

'Ouch! That stings!' Connie, sitting in the armchair, tried to pull her leg away from the cotton wool being dabbed on her grazed and bleeding knee.

'Iodine's supposed to hurt. Don't be such a baby!' Marlene, kneeling on the rug in front of the range, applied more of the brown liquid to a fresh piece of cotton wool and started on her other leg. 'I really thought you were about to do away with yourself,' she said.

'Why would you even think that?' Connie asked, squeezing her eyes shut against the pain. Without waiting for an answer, she added, 'You should be a footballer with the tackle you gave me!'

'I mean it, Connie. You scared me. I thought you were so upset about Ace letting you down you couldn't stand it any more.'

'If I was thinking about doing anything as daft as ending it all, it wouldn't be by sticking my head in your mother's rancid oven! Have you looked inside it?'

'Well, no,' Marlene said. 'I can't cook, can I?' She used the back of her hand to push her blonde tresses off her face, got up and began gathering up the items she'd used to clean Connie's knees. With the fire tongs, she poked the used cotton wool through the bars of the range where it sizzled, burnt and disappeared. After tightening the top on the small iodine bottle, she went to the sideboard drawer and stuffed it inside. She asked again, 'What were you doing?'

'It was something that happened in a film and I—'

Marlene didn't let her finish, 'Oh, you and your films!' Her voice was scathing.

'You asked me,' said Connie. 'So I told you.' She got up, winced at the stiffness in her knees and said, 'I made a pot of tea, before you thought I'd decided to end it all. Do you want some?' She added, with more than a hint of sarcasm, 'Thanks for being so nice after nearly crippling me!'

Beneath the knitted cosy, the tea she'd made earlier was still hot, and as she poured it, she marvelled that Marlene had put an entirely different perspective on her experiment. The oven door was shut, the towel back on its hook and her pillow now on the scullery table. Marlene must have done all that, she thought. Poor Marlene. Did she really think Connie would throw away her life on Ace? Obviously she did. But she'd rushed to her aid to prevent her doing it, hadn't she?

With a cup and saucer in each hand she went back into the kitchen and slid Marlene's tea across the table to her, then sat opposite her cousin. She realized she could smell Evening in Paris perfume. 'What you doing home, anyway?' she asked.

'A night off. I was asleep and you woke me, banging about down here,' Marlene said.

'Is that my scent you've got on?' Connie asked.

Marlene's face coloured. 'It might be. You don't use it.'

'No, you're right. I don't even like it. It reminds me of cats' wee. You can have it. Then you won't need to go poking around in my bedroom for it, will you?'

Marlene began stirring her tea. Her eyes had narrowed. 'It's one of the most popular perfumes there is.'

'Don't keep on about it. I've said you can have it.'

Marlene eyed her suspiciously. 'You've never liked me. Why are you being nice to me?'

'Because I'm fed up with you trying to get one over on me all the time. You've been doing it since we were kids.

Did you have anything to do with Ace not turning up to meet me?' She flung the question at Marlene.

'You want the truth?'

Marlene was still stirring her tea. Connie leant across the table, took the teaspoon from her and clattered it onto the table. She sat back and waited for her to answer.

'No, I didn't. But I didn't remind him he was supposed to be with you either.'

Connie thought for a bit. 'But Jerome gave him my telephone message to meet me?'

Marlene nodded. 'But—'

Connie shook her head. 'But nothing! Don't you make excuses for him. I thought I was in love with him and I believed he loved me. But loving someone doesn't mean you should allow them to cause you pain all the time. Him and me, we're two very different people and I've come to the conclusion we want different things. I believed him when he said he wanted to marry me. But if we wed nothing will change. He'll go on building his empire with another club, number three, and then number four. I'll be showered with jewellery I don't want, and live a lonely life in a big house I don't care about, wondering where he is when his promise of coming home early is broken yet again.'

Marlene said, 'You've been wanting to say that to someone, haven't you?'

'Yes, and you'll do.'

'That night Ace forgot all about meeting you. He had too much to drink and—'

Connie put up her hand and Marlene stopped. 'I don't care about that. I do care that you'd think I'd let him destroy my life. He would destroy it, I know that now, if I let him. He breaks promises, like they're not important.'

She thought about the doctor he'd promised to send to Queenie after the botched abortion. The doctor who'd never materialized. Queenie had nearly bled to death giving birth. Had Ace sent round a doctor as he'd promised, perhaps all that anguish could have been averted. He was aware Queenie had no money for doctors. Connie could never really forgive him for that.

Marlene broke into her thoughts. 'I could tell you a few things,' she began. Then, 'And while we're telling truths I knew perfectly well what I was doing, and so did he, when I slid in beside him in the air-raid shelter.'

'Shut up! I don't care! We might look alike, you and I, but that's only some quirk of nature. We're very different people, Marlene. When we were young you used to torment me in any way you could. You didn't let me like you – you always needed to have the upper hand. You can't do that now. I've got a mind of my own.'

Connie thought about what was really important to her. What she wanted most of all was to stop the owners of the Criterion sacking Doyle for stealing when she was sure Gilbert Willard was behind the thefts. She was fed up with becoming distraught about Ace Gallagher, broken promises and weddings she didn't want.

There, she'd finally thought it through. She didn't want to marry him. She didn't want him. Connie gave a huge sigh of relief. She drank the rest of her tea and stood up. 'Stay there, I won't be a minute.' She walked determinedly down the passage into her bedroom and opened the top drawer where she'd put the perfume to stop it evaporating in the light. The box containing the gold bracelet, necklace and her engagement ring was tucked safely among her clothes. She'd sort all that out later, she decided, and closed the drawer.

The heavy, seductive scent of Evening in Paris went with her up the passage and back into the kitchen. She placed the small blue bottle on the table in front of Marlene. 'There you are, cousin dear,' she said. 'I promised you could have this perfume. I don't want it. It doesn't suit me. Neither does Ace Gallagher, who bought it for me, so you can have him as well.'

Chapter Twenty-nine

Connie hoped Queenie or Len could hear her banging on the door through the cacophony of noise inside the house. She smiled, relieved when the door opened and Queenie said, 'Blinkin' heck! You're an early bird. Gertie's not long left here for her cleaning stint at the Criterion.'

Connie put one finger in her ear, to try to deaden the sound of Jimmie Davis belting out 'You Are My Sunshine' as she stepped inside.

Queenie grinned and nudged her arm. 'They're nearly asleep. I'll turn off the wireless in a bit. With clean bums and full bellies Bette and Paulie should sleep for hours. I'll put the kettle on.'

Queenie pulled the belt of her ancient woollen dressing-gown tighter round her waist.

'You've lost weight!' Connie shouted, above the noise.

She couldn't help admiring her friend's svelte back view as she walked ahead of her into the kitchen. She took a deep breath of the homely smell of talcum powder and toast. Obviously Gertie had been fed before she'd left.

'Don't be so surprised. I've two goals, haven't I?' Queenie put a finger to her lips and pointed upstairs with her other hand. Connie realized she didn't want Len, who must still have been in bed, if definitely not asleep, to overhear. Though how anyone could make out a word they were saying to each other with Jimmie Davis at full blast was beyond Connie.

With cursory glances in both carry cots containing her children, Queenie sailed through the kitchen and into the scullery. 'Pull that door closed and we'll be able to hear ourselves speak.'

Connie did as she was told. 'What two goals?

Queenie lit the gas beneath the kettle. 'Have you forgotten my vow to make Len's eyes pop out of his head when he sees me in all my finery?' She struck a suggestive pose with her hands on her hips. 'Ta-da,' she said.

Connie laughed. This was what true love was all about, she thought, looking at Queenie in her tatty dressing-gown. A couple sharing, wanting to please each other, happy to be together. Her eyes glanced around the untidy scullery. A sink full of washing-up, a bucket with soaking nappies. There was definitely no excess of money in this house, no wildly expensive gold jewellery like she had in her drawer at home, but the place was filled to the brim with happiness and love.

'What's the second thing?' Connie removed her white cardigan, for the small room was hot. She pulled out a stool from beneath the table and perched on it.

Queenie tutted dramatically. 'You've forgotten, haven't you?' She stared at Connie, daring her to come out with the wrong answer. Then she began to hum, stuck out her arms, and whirled around as though she was dancing with a partner.

'You're bloody daft, you are, Queenie Gregory. If you mean those dance classes . . .'

'Course I mean dancing classes. You're not going to let me down, are you?' Queenie frowned.

Connie shook her head. 'I'd forgotten,' she said.

Queenie poured boiling water into the teapot. 'Good thing I reminded you, then, isn't it?' she said good-naturedly. 'You still haven't told me why you're calling so early.'

The sudden silence that occurred next was almost deafening. The scullery door opened and Len poked his head into the room.

'Oh, good, you've made tea.' He gave a big smile, stepped

inside and Connie saw his striped pyjama jacket was but-toned all wrong and his dark hair was a tight mass of shiny curls. 'Those two are spark out,' he said, nodding back towards the kitchen. His eyes fell on Connie. 'Hello, love,' he said. 'I'm glad to see you. I've got some ideas about how to catch that devil Willard out ... A bit early for you to come visiting, isn't it?'

'I suppose so,' said Connie. 'I want to hear your ideas.' She was excited.

'Yeah, well, if it's all right with you I'd like us to meet up tonight after the picture house has closed. Me, you, Doyle and my young projectionist, Gary.'

Connie nodded. 'Sounds good to me.' She wondered what the plan was but guessed he'd rather talk to them when they were all together. A thought struck her. He hadn't mentioned Gertie. 'What about Gertie?'

Both Queenie and Len looked a bit shamefaced. Queenie answered: 'You know what she's like. It'll be all round Gosport in five minutes. You need absolute secrecy about what you're up to because no one has any idea how long this will take.'

'You can't not say anything. She'll be terribly hurt,' Connie pointed out. 'She don't forget a thing and she'll remember there was already some talk of a theft.'

She took the mug of tea Queenie was holding out to her and mouthed, 'Thank you.'

'Don't you worry about Gertie.' Len nodded his thanks to his wife as she placed a mug in his hands. 'She'll understand perfectly. And she'll be the first to agree her fag smoke would be a dead giveaway. She needs her nicotine, doesn't she?'

Connie felt herself frowning. It was confusing, all this talk about cigarettes. 'I don't want Gertie to feel left out,' she insisted.

'She won't be,' said Len, 'and when this works, her house will be the meeting place.' He gave Connie a big smile. 'That'll make her feel important.'

'Honestly, Connie, I know what's on Len's mind. We've discussed it, me and him . . .' Queenie frowned. 'Not while Gertie was here in the house, obviously. And I think you and the others can pull it off. Can you meet them tonight?'

Connie didn't have to think twice. Gertie wouldn't worry about her being out later than usual: she'd think the film had overrun. Most likely she'd be in bed, anyway. 'I've already spoken to Doyle about Willard.'

'That's good,' said Len. 'How did he take it?'

'Stoically. He knows what a bounder Willard is.'

'Which is all the more reason Willard mustn't be allowed

to get away with his tricks. We'll meet upstairs in the projection room, after the picture house has been locked up for the night. If our so-called manager makes a late-night visit, he'll never suspect there's already people inside the place.'

'What about before he leaves? When it's locking-up time? Won't he wonder why the four of us are still hanging about?' Connie protested.

Len laughed. A lovely belly-laugh that rang through the scullery. Then he said. 'That bloke never stays until the end. He doesn't know what the national anthem is.' He drank some tea. 'Let's not talk any more now. We'll have plenty of time to share ideas tonight.' He put his mug on the draining-board and faced Connie. 'Now you can tell us why you're here so early.'

Connie didn't mind talking about Ace and Marlene in front of Len because she knew he and Queenie had no secrets. She'd got up early after one of the best night's sleep she'd had in ages and decided she needed to talk to her best friend about the happenings of last night, so here she was.

'I told Marlene I no longer want to marry Ace Gallagher.'

Before she'd finished her sentence, she saw the relief pass over Len's face, and Queenie gasped, 'Thank God you've come to your senses.'

Connie sat up straighter on the stool. 'Why are you both so pleased?'

Len pulled her to her feet and hugged her. 'I can't think of hearing a better thing to start my day. If you knew how worried Queenie and I have been about you getting tangled up with that man . . .'

Connie collapsed back onto the stool, 'Why have you never said anything before?'

'If we had, would you have listened?' he answered.

'Probably not,' Connie said. 'Marlene tried to tell me things.'

'I'll bet she did,' Queenie said. 'Anyway, how come you and her have suddenly got so pally?'

'Tell us what happened,' said Len, running his fingers through his hair. The curls fell back into exactly the same places. 'Come on, love.'

So, Connie explained everything while Len and Queenie listened. Connie sighed when she'd finished.

'At least you and her don't need to tread so lightly around each other now,' Len said. 'But she'll tell Ace what happened between you two and, much as I dislike the chap, I think you need to have a word with him yourself. You should be honest with him, Connie.'

Len was quite right. She owed it to Ace to tell him why

she'd changed her mind about marrying him. 'Why do you dislike him?' Ace and Len were two very different men. They knew each other but had never been friendly. Connie wanted to know why.

'All I'm saying, love, is that the man sails too close to the wind for my liking. I'm no tattle-tale. He'll tell you himself if he wants you to know anything. I'm just pleased you've come to this decision on your own.'

'And I'm so very happy,' said Queenie. She gave Connie a hug. 'You don't have to be at work until later today, do you?' Without waiting for an answer, she added, 'Why don't you spend a bit of time with me and the little ones? We could push the pram down to Walpole Park and watch the sailboats on the lake.'

Chapter Thirty

Tom heard them before he saw them. Bombers coming from beyond Portsdown Hill heading towards Portsmouth and the dockyard. Already on his way towards the shelter he saw the planes were in formation, blotting out the sky, like huge alien black birds. The sight turned his stomach to coils of worms.

And then the designated air-raid shelter was before him with people running helter-skelter to dodge the stray bullets from anti-aircraft guns. He held out his arm to steady a heavily pregnant woman afraid of overbalancing on the mossy steps. 'All right?' he asked.

'I am now,' she replied. 'Bless you.'

A cheer went up from the people about him, and Tom saw one of the planes spiralling downwards out of the sky, its droning engine now changed to a deathly whine. A cheer began in his throat but halted. The bomber would no doubt kill men and women when it ended its out-of-control journey.

Between them, Alan and he had shepherded as many, and more people, inside the shelter, as it could take. Tom breathed a sigh of relief as Alan mouthed, 'That's it,' and sat down on the narrow board seat near the entrance.

People had already spread themselves out, then had to move closer to each other as more and more needed space to sit.

Already the stink of too many bodies had filled the space with a sweaty heat. Some had brought sandwiches and were now unwrapping and doling them out to noisy children. Knitting needles were on the go. Amazingly, thought Tom, people looked accepting of their fate. But they knew this was what bombing was about so got on with it.

Tom, now watching the firework display through the doorway, caught sight of an old man leaning on a shop's windowsill. His stick had fallen from his grasp and he obviously couldn't walk properly without it. Clutching the sill, he unsteadily worked his way into the relative safety of the shop doorway, bending low.

The thud and crump of bombs could now be heard, and he could see fiery orange leaping every so often into the darkness of the sky.

Tom jumped to his feet and pushed outside through the slit of the door. Despite the smell of burning and cordite it was fresher there than the stink in the shelter. Even from a distance Tom could smell the old man's fear. 'C'mon, I've got you,' he said. He looked into the lined face, grinned, then took off his tin helmet and stuck it on the fellow's head. He hauled the man to his feet, amazed by how light he was. Once Tom had a good hold on the bony body he half carried, half dragged him across the road, stumbled down the steps and fell into the shelter, where Alan was waiting.

'Well done, mate,' Alan muttered.

A big woman put down her knitting and immediately took charge of the elderly man. Within moments he was supping tea from a flask, his face growing rosy with the shelter's heat. The woman had now joined in with the rest of the disharmonious voices belting out 'I'll Be Seeing You' to the accompaniment of a man with a mouth organ.

When the all-clear sounded, Tom knew he and Alan would spend hours sorting out folks whose houses were no longer standing, sending them off to emergency accommodation, helping householders look for lost pets or, worse, digging through rubble hoping to find someone, anyone, who'd refused to leave and had hoped to survive hiding beneath a table or the stairs. Tom sighed and thankfully accepted a flask top of hot tea. For a little while, at least, his world was all right.

'I knew that devil wouldn't turn up to work tonight,' said Doyle. 'The way he runs the picture house is a disgrace.'

'Well, it works out better for us that he doesn't care about the place. It'll make it easier when the big bosses find out how unreliable he is.' Connie had already told Doyle that he didn't have to walk her home but he said he wouldn't dream of letting her go alone and that his wife would understand. In fact, she'd give him a right telling-off, if he didn't see her home.

The air smelt of bitter cordite and burning, though the raid had been mercifully short tonight.

As usual when Moaning Minnie called, Len had exhibited the notice on the screen so that patrons could leave the picture house if they wished for the relative safety of the shelters. It always surprised Connie how many settled to watch to the end of the film. Afterwards, when the patrons had left, Connie and the other usherettes readied the Criterion for the morning cleaners. Then Doyle, Len, Gary and herself, after locking up, had retired to the projection room to discuss their plan.

'We're assuming he's the thief but supposing he isn't?' Doyle now said.

Connie stopped walking. 'You're being remarkably good-natured towards him, considering it's you he wants to get rid of.'

'I still don't really understand why it's me he's taken umbrage with.'

'I think he's jealous of you,' Connie said. She tucked her arm through his and they continued walking.

'Surely not. I'm an old man who's been working at the Criterion for years and loves his job,' he said.

'Exactly! Though you're certainly not old, you're experienced, and people like you. That makes him feel threatened,' Connie added.

'But he's the manager. And that's something I'd never want to be.'

Connie couldn't help herself. Again, she stopped walking. This time she frowned at him. 'Why ever not?' She'd jump at the chance.

'I love being a commissionaire. There's nothing like wearing all that gold braid, smiling at the patrons and welcoming them to our little picture house. I'm happy in my work, Connie. I don't mind checking up the money at night with you but I certainly don't want all the bother of ordering ice cream, paying wholesalers, and giving orders to the usherettes and cleaners.' He paused. 'Incidentally, Willard shouldn't, but he leaves all that to you, doesn't he?'

Connie shrugged. 'The staff don't seem to mind me telling them what to do and taking on extra duties. Probably because it's not something they want to do themselves.'

He smiled. 'Exactly,' he said. 'But I've never wanted that responsibility.'

'But you're happy to be in on this ruse to trap Willard.'

'Oh, yes,' said Doyle. 'And it makes me feel humble that you all want to help me.' He gave a little laugh. 'And I'll have no problems about staying late because my wife's taking the kids and the dog down to Cornwall to stay with her mother for a while. She'd like a break from the bombing here, she says. I'll be able to come and go as I please. How about you?'

'When Gertie's asleep, George Formby could be playing his ukulele in the same room and she'd never wake. She won't know whether I'm in the house or not,' answered Connie.

'What about Marlene? Won't she wonder where you are?'

'Marlene comes and goes like the wind at all hours of the day and night. We rarely bump into each other.'

'That's good, then,' he said.

Connie guessed he'd ask about Len's young projectionist.

'Young Gary lives with his gran and she never waits up for him. He'll be fine to stay.'

'And that just leaves Len, and as Queenie knows what's going on there'll be nothing to worry about where she's concerned,' Doyle said.

They'd reached Alma Street now. Connie and Doyle stopped on the corner. He looked at her conspiratorially. 'Do you think it will work?'

Connie reached up on tiptoe and gave him a quick, friendly kiss on the cheek. 'The horrible man won't know what's hit him,' she said, and began walking up the street, with a smile on her face.

Chapter Thirty-one

The black MG VA tourer, hood up, was parked outside Gertie's house. Connie's heart began thumping wildly inside her chest. She could see the outline of Ace sitting inside it. She guessed he was waiting for her, and that Marlene had expressed an opinion on their conversation of last night.

As she neared number fourteen the driver's door opened and Ace got out. 'Hello, love,' he said. He stood on the pavement in front of her, tall and good-looking, towering over her. She could smell the alcohol on his breath. 'Who was that man you walked home with?'

He hadn't recognized Doyle in the inky blackness. It had never occurred to her before that she resented his questioning. She decided not to answer him.

'We need to talk,' he added.

Connie didn't want a shouting match on the pavement

so she said, 'Come in.' She pulled the string through the letterbox and opened the front door. Already it seemed boundaries had been built between them. Normally, Ace would never have hesitated to let himself into Gertie's house.

He leant inside the car, and when he straightened, Connie saw he had the customary bags of food, offerings for Gertie.

Inside the house it was dark and still. She guessed, because of the late hour, that Gertie was asleep, Marlene too, possibly, either that or she was still out gallivanting after being at the club.

There was no fire in the range but the room was warm, and after putting on the electric light and closing the door between the kitchen and the rest of the house, so their voices wouldn't carry, she went through to the scullery and, out of habit, lit the gas beneath the kettle. When she stepped back into the kitchen, the brown carrier bags were on the table and Ace had made himself comfortable in the armchair beneath the window. Connie pulled out a kitchen chair and sat down. He spoke first.

'I need to apologize for the other night,' he said. 'Jerome gave me your telephone message, so please don't think he was at fault in any way.' Ace lifted his hand and ran it over his forehead, like he was thinking hard. He sighed. 'I've no other excuse, except I'd been drinking. I didn't take in what he was saying and, later, completely forgot I was to meet you.' He stared at her. 'I wish I could make up some less incriminating excuse but I haven't got one.'

Before she could say a word, he went on, 'You think everything is black and white, Connie. It's not. That's where we're different.'

Connie stared at him. His chestnut hair hung across his forehead in lank strands, like he'd spent a lot of time uselessly brushing it back. He looked tired, but so vulnerable. She resisted the temptation to go to him, to put her arms around him. It was very tempting . . .

Instead, she got up and went out into the scullery and, like clockwork, began making tea.

His words had struck a chord. Yes, they were different. And they wanted different things from life.

Connie placed the tea things on a tray and took it back into the kitchen. 'It doesn't matter that you forgot about me,' she said, putting the tray on the table. 'It hurt a lot at the time but it doesn't matter now.'

'Then why did you say those things to Marlene?'

'I thought she'd come into it somewhere,' Connie snapped. She took a deep breath. 'Ace, I know I was wrong to tell her, before you, that I don't want to marry you and I'm sorry for that. But it doesn't alter the fact that I'm tired of you hurting me. You can't help the way you're made and I can't help being hurt by different things you do. I just don't want it any more.'

'We were happy in Devon,' he said.

Why, oh, why did he have to bring that up? 'We were,' she agreed. 'I had you all to myself. No club there for you to run, no apparent worries. But once we got back, I hardly ever saw you. You didn't want me at the club.'

'That's not a place for you,' he said. 'Neither of my premises are.'

'See, there you go, making assumptions! I could probably help.'

He shook his head. 'I don't want or need your help.'

'Everyone needs help. You shut me out. I'm not some giddy woman, I practically run the Criterion.'

'A lot of what I do is illegal, black-market.'

Connie eyed the overflowing bags on the table. 'You think I hadn't guessed?'

'Jerome said I should be honest with you.'

'He's right. I'd have preferred you to talk to me, instead of other people making disparaging remarks about you.'

'Would it help if I confessed those stories are probably correct?'

Connie got up, set the cups in the saucers and began pouring the tea. 'Not now,' she answered. 'Because now it doesn't matter.' She pushed the milk bottle over the table towards him so he could help himself, then slid across the cup and saucer.

'So, if I'd done as Jerome suggested and told you all about my murky past, and present, you'd have accepted me as I am?'

'Probably not. Maybe I don't want to know the absolute truth because now we're back to you and me being two very different people. You say things that people want to hear because you need them to think well of you. Well, where was the doctor you'd said you'd send to Queenie? He didn't come and she nearly died. I don't suppose you gave that broken promise another thought. But it wounded me. How can I trust you, Ace? If you'd been more honest with me, it would have saved me a lot of hurt and sleepless nights.'

'I've never lied to you, Connie.'

'You don't think lying by omission is hurtful?'

'Oh, Connie,' he said. 'I forgot about the doctor. I do love you.'

'You shouldn't forget about promises that affect people's lives.' Her voice was hard but then it softened. 'It's not love you feel. You want me. Like adding me to a collection because I'm different. That's not love.'

He frowned. 'You knew what I was like when you first met me.'

'That's not strictly true,' she said. 'When Gertie took me in, I was all over the place. My mum had just died and I was dazzled by you. I'd never met anyone like you and I don't suppose I ever will again. To tell the truth, I don't want to. Then I won't get hurt again. I feel sorry for you because you love money so much, but all the money in the world won't love you back.'

He was staring at her. Her words had sunk home. 'All men want something more,' he said. Then he tried a smile to let her know he was all right with what she was saying. 'Does that mean blokes, rich or poor, are now off limits for you?'

'Perhaps for a while,' she said. His smile grew stronger. She felt herself melting inside. 'Drink your tea before it gets cold,' she said sharply.

Connie got up and, opening the hallway door, went to her bedroom. Pulling open the drawer, she took out the gold gifts he'd given her. Cocooned in the kitchen with the door closed once more, she put the box into his hands. 'I can't keep these,' she said.

'I don't want them back.'

She pressed the box into his palm. He frowned. 'Most girls take what they can and run,' he said.

Once his fingers had closed over it, she stepped away from him. 'I'm not most girls,' she said.

Ace drove down Forton Road, watching out for rubble and bricks that hadn't been cleared from the main road after the previous raid. The last thing he needed was any obstruction causing an accident to stop him getting back to the club and putting a drink inside him.

He wanted to cry but knew he wouldn't. The last time he'd cried had been when the Four Aces on the ferry had been razed to the ground by enemy bombs. Determination, not tears, had had the building up and running once again.

He actually admired Connie for her honesty. In the very early days of their relationship, he'd been overprotective of her and hostile towards anyone who showed interest in her. Look how he'd banished young Tommo Smith to Scotland because it had come to his notice that Tommo had passed the time of day with Connie in the pictures. It was pure jealousy on his part. He'd felt insecure about her, even then. He should have sat down with her one night, told her about himself, and asked her what she wanted from their relationship. Too late he'd found out she wasn't the type of girl to be bought off with expensive jewellery. He smiled.

No one had ever given him back his gifts! She had guts, did Connie.

But she spoke a lot of sense. She must have cared for him or it wouldn't have been possible for his careless, thoughtless actions to hurt her.

Jerome had been right all along, hadn't he? He and Connie were two very different people with vastly different lifestyles and ideals. Perhaps it was better for her to have made the break with him now, before she found out the real truth about his unsavoury past.

Ace knew then that he loved Connie. Really loved her. For the first time in his life he didn't want to control a woman or own her, like a possession. Connie had stolen his heart.

And whatever happened in the future he would always blame himself for not realizing it sooner.

Chapter Thirty-two

Gertie mixed the flour, bicarbonate of soda, salt and baking powder in her cream earthenware bowl. Then she picked up the large mug containing the small amount of syrup and the quarter-pint of milk she'd set to heat in a bowl of boiling water. The grey ash fell from her cigarette and landed on the kitchen table. With a quick flick of her hand, it was brushed to the lino. Pouring the milk and syrup mixture into the bowl she beat it until her wrist hurt. She'd already greased a loaf tin so she poured in the mixture, scraping out the last so none was wasted. Then she carried it out to the scullery.

'Half an hour and you should be ready,' she said, to the closed door of the hot oven, which now contained a syrup loaf for Connie.

Since coming back from Queenie's house, where she'd slept in the spare room after frightening herself nearly to death listening to Valentine Dyall's deep voice telling a horror story, she had yet to catch up with her niece. When she'd been in, Connie had been out. 'A bit of syrup loaf will cheer her up,' she said aloud to herself. 'Poor little love must be in a state.'

Marlene, stinking of Evening in Paris, had filled her mother in on her and Connie's difference of opinion. Gertie wasn't too sure where the bit about her having a filthy oven came in, though. Everyone knew most people spent too much time on cleaning ovens. Didn't the burnt and greasy bits dissolve and fall away the more the oven was used? Gertie stubbed out her Woodbine in the sink, then went back into the kitchen to find her cigarettes and light another. A fag helped her think.

'She said she wasn't going to marry Ace.' Marlene's words kept running around in her brain.

If what her daughter said was true, Gertie was pleased.

Not just because of his gangster friends. Oh, yes, she'd heard about them. That Billy Hill was notorious. One of the biggest criminals in London, a vicious man. It was probably him behind all the black-market stuff Ace managed to get hold of. Not that she'd say a word against Ace. He looked after his own, he did. And hadn't he always treated her right while lodging with her? Rent money regular as clockwork, and he'd gone on paying her when his flat over the Four Aces was habitable.

Even now he left a few tins, fags, groceries and perishables aside for her. She hoped that, just because he wasn't going to be in Connie's life any longer, he wouldn't forget all about his old landlady.

All the same, Connie wasn't really the sort of girl to suit him. And she'd tell her that when eventually she came home. And if Connie was miserable about it, well, a nice slice of syrup loaf would soon put her right.

'Sitting in the dark swilling that stuff isn't going to do any good.' Jerome switched on the electric lamp and wearily sat down at the wrought-iron table alongside Ace. The Gosport club had closed hours ago, and his back and knee were giving him gyp.

'You've got that bloody wintergreen stuff smeared all over you again, haven't you?' Ace's words were slurred. After staring unseeingly up at Jerome, he allowed his head to fall back onto his folded arms.

'I'm surprised you can smell anything with the stink of whisky all over you,' Jerome said. 'Just remember you're drinking away our profits.'

'Come down to gloat that you were right all the time, old

man?' Ace made an effort and struggled to sit up. His arm nudged against the bottle and Jerome put out a hand to save it falling from the table.

'I just need to make sure of a few things,' Jerome said, setting the bottle upright again.

Ace made a grab at it but Jerome moved it further away, out of his reach.

'You asking me if it's all over between me and Miss Goody Two Shoes?'

Ace pushed his empty glass towards Jerome and said, 'Fill it up for me, please.' He emphasized the last word.

Jerome sighed deeply but poured a couple of inches of golden liquid into the glass. Ace stretched out his arm towards it, but Jerome put his hand over the glass.

'Stop playing games,' said Ace.

'I want to know how drunk, how riled up you were, and whether you let slip anything to Connie that might come back and bite us on our arses. I advised you long ago to be as honest with the girl as you needed to be before she started believing too many other stories.'

'You mean did I get angry enough to want to slap her about, or to shout my mouth off about what really goes on in both clubs or does she still believe in fairy tales?'

Jerome was staring intently at him.

'Look, old man, the reason she doesn't want to marry me is because I've hurt her.' He gave a sarcastic laugh. 'I'm thoughtless and I hurt her! And she doesn't want to be hurt by me any more.' He stared at Jerome across the table. 'She really loved me, she cared, and I let her down. That's all there is to it.'

Jerome pushed the glass towards him and watched as, hand shaking, Ace picked up the drink. Finally, he said, 'You've been very lax about your duties to both Connie and the club just lately.'

'She knows as much, or rather as little, as she ever did. I didn't shout the odds about anything unsavoury.' Ace put his arms back on the table and lowered his head.

'A woman scorned can be a tiresome thing.' Jerome pushed himself up from the table. Ace was a fool to himself. He'd lost the chance to make people believe, by marrying Connie, that he was beyond reproach. She'd have made him happy, been a steadying influence in his life.

Jerome allowed his fingers to ruffle Ace's chestnut hair. 'Oh, son,' he whispered.

He switched off the lamp, rose painfully and went upstairs to bed.

'Quiet night, so far,' said Alan. 'The Germans are probably giving some other town hell.' Tom walked along Whitworth

Road beside his friend, looking for chinks of light in black-out curtains that might possibly guide enemy aircraft in their bombing missions. The torches they used had shields over the bulbs so the ARP team, too, obeyed rules. The torches, even with their feeble brightness, were a blessing, as were the white stripes painted on the trunks of trees, the edges of pavements and on unlit streetlamps. At first Tom had thought it was weird wandering the dark streets in the inky blackness. Sometimes he'd hear noises coming from houses. Disembodied voices, music from wirelesses, arguments, children crying or laughing. If it wasn't for the sounds Tom could have believed he was in a dream or a make-believe world. His gas mask and first-aid kit banged against his hip as he moved, bringing him suddenly back to reality.

'Listen!' Alan stopped walking and grabbed hold of Tom's arm.

Tom could hear the noise now. 'I thought back at Headquarters they said a raid wasn't expected tonight.'

'It's what happens. People get things wrong,' Alan answered. 'It's the enemy, all right. Can't you tell by the engines?'

Tom shook his head. 'But we've no time to evacuate people . . .'

'It could just be a stray,' Alan persisted.

And then there was the awful whistling noise, coming closer. 'Run!' shouted Alan. 'Get under cover!'

But it was too late to look for places to hide. The whistling sound grew closer, louder. Alan pulled Tom down onto the pavement. Knees, elbows, scraping the paving stones. Tom felt the grit scratching his forehead, his cheek.

Then there was an explosion, so close, that Tom thought his head and ears would burst with the force of the noise. A wind, fiercer than any he had experienced before, blew across his body. He felt sure it would take the clothes from his back or even the skin. He grabbed at his tin hat.

Then stillness. The relief he felt when Alan whispered, 'You all right, mate?' It made his eyes smart with tears.

'I've been better,' Tom said gruffly.

Alan laughed and, scrambling to his feet, put out a hand to help him up. 'That was fuckin' close,' he said.

Then doors were opening, men in pyjamas looking scared. People were yanking up bedroom windows criss-crossed with tapes and yelling out into the darkness, 'Is it a raid?'

'There's been no alarm!'

Alan was standing quite still, listening hard in spite of the myriad voices. Finally, he yelled, 'It was a stray. Don't panic.' Then, 'Leave it to us.'

The inhabitants, satisfied there was no need to rush to shelters, and used to night-time interruptions and distractions, dispersed, closing doors and windows.

Alan and Tom walked on down Whitworth Road, chatting to disturbed householders in dressing-gowns at their gates, putting their minds at rest and noting that mostly the dwellings were untouched, except for broken windows, rubbish strewn around gardens and shattered roof slates lying on the road.

Tom rubbed his eyes, only making them smart more, as dust and grit still spiralled in the air.

'It's got to have landed somewhere,' Alan said. 'But where?'

'No one's rushing around, shouting the odds,' Tom said. 'Maybe it's on the allotments.' The Whitworth Road allotments, its members well and truly proud of their Dig for Victory prowess, backed onto Daisy Lane, a school and its playing fields.

'I hope so,' Alan said, 'Less chance of maiming anyone there. Foxes, badgers, maybe . . .'

'There!' Tom said, pointing to the playing field. He could now make out the smoking crater made by the explosive. His heart was pounding as, over the wet grass, they approached fearfully . . .

Chapter Thirty-three

'No!' The cry burst from Alan's lips. He halted, grabbing Tom's blouson jacket to stop him walking any further.

Tom saw on the earth, the grass churned up by the bomb's velocity, a prone figure. Two arms, two legs, body intact. The bloodied man lay quite still. Alan reached him first and knelt down next to him.

'I do believe he's alive,' he said softly. Then his tone changed: 'Don't bloody stand there! Get help!'

For a split second Tom was turned to stone. He saw Alan opening his first-aid kit, and talking softly to the man, no doubt telling him he was safe now and— Instinct took over and Tom was running towards Whitworth Road and the nearest telephone box.

Before he returned to the playing field, he heard the strident sounds of an ambulance. The War Memorial Hospital was so close he could have gone there, but his telephone request had been answered in moments. Tom was more than a little relieved that caring for the injured man could be handed over to more experienced helpers. Already other ARP volunteers and a small crowd were in evidence. Tom managed to squeeze through them to get to Alan.

'Well done, mate,' Alan said. 'I think he's got a chance.'

They watched as the man, his tattered clothes stuck to his burnt and bloodied body, like a multi-coloured second skin, was loaded carefully into the ambulance.

'I wonder why he was alone out here,' Tom managed to say aloud.

'He wasn't,' the ambulance driver said. He smelt of fried food: the call must have interrupted him as he ate his supper. Tom gazed into his unshaven face as he continued, 'One of your lot had the unenviable task of shovelling up the dog's remains. Couldn't leave that for some kiddie to find.'

The driver climbed into the cab of the ambulance and, as the small crowd began dispersing, the vehicle made its way across the grass towards the main road.

'You two ought to get back to Headquarters,' said a stout man in blue, his hat adorned with a W. 'Get yourselves a cuppa. You deserve it.'

Tom had no idea who he was. In the dark he couldn't make out his badge, but his voice held authority.

'Good idea,' agreed Alan. 'We'll have those never-ending forms to fill in, as usual.' His voice was low. Everything had to be recorded – Tom was well aware of that.

He thought of how brave his friend was to have knelt by that mess of a broken man murmuring words of comfort. Would he have had the strength to do that? He wanted to say something to Alan about his courage instead of simply trudging wearily alongside him without speaking. But he hadn't the right words to say without sounding mawkish or gushing and he didn't want to embarrass either himself or Alan.

Tom looked back along the way he and Alan had walked. Despite the darkness he could just make out police and bystanders still hovering about the crater. It was always the same, he thought. People hung around after an event, however gruesome, to gossip and take stock of what had happened. Why should a warm summer night, like tonight, be any different?

'Listen!' Alan stopped walking. He stared at Tom. 'I don't believe it,' he added. 'It's another of the rogue German buggers! What are the chances?'

'I don't see how you can you tell it's not one of ours.'

'I told you, it's the sound the engine makes.' Then, 'Get down!' He yanked at Tom's arm, then shoved him. Tom felt himself being propelled along the pavement at a speed he didn't know existed only to fall alongside a metal horse-trough.

'Don't try to move,' he thought the woman's voice said. The unreal quality of her words made Tom think he was dreaming but then there was another voice, a man's. He could tell it was male by its gravelly undertones but the ringing in his ears made the sounds difficult to understand. The clanging was constant and didn't seem to vary in tone. It was very loud and was now drowning the woman's words.

'Don't move!' the deeper of the two voices advised.

Tom managed to open his eyes but the ringing tone hurt so much he immediately closed them. He tried again, raising his eyelids more slowly this time. There were indistinct shapes around him. He was in a bed. Not his bed. And as he tried to focus on the large shapes they began moving and the voices were lost in the noise in his head. The shapes turned ghostly and faded. He couldn't think. His brain didn't seem to be working properly. His head hurt, and the more he tried to understand, the more his head hurt, and then the ringing swallowed him.

The next time he opened his eyes it was to see another face staring closely into his.

'Doctor, he's coming round again.' The face had eyes that peered into his. Perhaps he should stare back but staring was too hard. He looked.

It was a kind face, a gentle voice. But now it was replaced by tired eyes, a skin that badly needed shaving and a mouth that opened and said, 'You were caught in a bomb blast but you're safe in hospital.'

Tom watched the mouth but he understood little of what the man was saying. Bomb, hospital, safe.

Whatever did it all mean?

'Tom, you're safe now.'

Tom. Tom? He was Tom. How did this man know his name? It hurt to think.

He slept.

He opened his eyes and saw a pretty young woman sitting at a table in the middle of the room. She had on a blue and white uniform. A white cap on dark curls. She was writing. He could hear the scratch of the pen's nib on paper. His mouth felt as if somebody had used sandpaper on his lips, throat and tongue.

His head hurt. He could smell disinfectant. The pale room

had beds in it containing people. It was a hospital! Yes, a hospital. But why was he here?

The young woman rose quickly and came to stand over him. As if she had read his mind, she poured water into a tumbler from a carafe on a locker by the side of his bed. Putting one arm beneath his shoulders she raised him just enough so he could drink from the glass. The water went everywhere but it didn't seem to worry her. He drank greedily until she moved the glass away. 'That's enough for now, Tom.'

'Why am I here?' His voice sounded like it belonged to somebody else.

'You've had a nasty bang on the head but you're safe now. Go back to sleep.'

When Tom woke up again Shirley was sitting by his bed, holding his hand, and he could smell her lily-of-the-valley perfume. He felt suddenly, ridiculously, happy.

'Awake at last, are we?' she said. He noticed she'd been crying. She had that shapeless dress on again and she was wearing her hat with the ridiculous feather. A well of tenderness rose inside him, mixing with the happiness.

'How d'you feel?' she asked.

'Thirsty . . . and hungry,' he said. 'How did you know I was here?'

'When you didn't come home, I telephoned the ARP headquarters – your telephone's been installed by the way, so I hope you won't mind but when the doctors assured me you'd recover I made meself useful. Taking telephone messages from people wanting to learn to dance. I told 'em all the classes won't start until you're on your feet again. Did I do right? It seemed wrong to let all you'd worked for so hard go down the drain.'

Tom was finding it difficult to take in what she was saying. Of course, he was making a living teaching people to dance. So far very successfully. What a lovely woman Shirley was, looking after business in his absence. 'Shirl, you're a treasure,' he said. 'But how did you find me?'

'You put me down as next-of-kin on your ARP enrolment forms. You've forgotten, silly boy!'

He squeezed her hand. 'Thank you,' he said. He wanted to say more but he didn't know how. He felt too emotional for the words to come out. So he asked, 'Am I all right?'

'You're lovely, you are,' she gushed. 'You lost your tin hat! You got stitches in your head but they'll take them out later—'

He didn't let her finish. Instead, he raised his fingers to his head. Stubble. Bandages.

'Leave it alone! They had to shave off some of your lovely

blond hair but it'll grow back, so they said. Other than that, Twinkle-toes, you're fine.'

'They' must mean the doctors, he thought. Such a small price to pay to be alive, he thought gratefully. 'Thank you,' he said again, just for the joy of being able to say it.

Shirley had got up and was now busying herself pouring water from the carafe into a glass. 'Can you hold it?' She handed it to him after he struggled up to a sitting position to take it. Although it felt remarkably heavy for only a half-glass of water and his hand shook ridiculously, he could raise it to his lips. He drank noisily, then realized Shirley was talking again,

'Bessie, a nice lady, has been coming every day. She's been waiting for you to wake up but she had to go for her shift. She'll come back, she said.'

He remembered who Bessie was. How kind of her to bother with him. 'How long have I been here? Shirl, I don't remember what happened. Do you know?'

'One question at a time. You've been in here long enough to have me worried sick, and Bessie knows all the ins and outs of what you were up to. You were on duty down Whitworth Road, checking for lights and such.'

'I don't remember any of that,' Tom said.

'They said it's quite usual after a head injury,' Shirley said.

'You saved a man's life. He was out walking his dog and he got caught in the first bomb blast.'

'There was a second blast . . .'

Bits were coming back to him now. He remembered running to the telephone box while Alan administered first aid to that poor, poor man . . .

It wasn't an air raid. No sirens. No, just stragglers probably coming back from a raid somewhere else, jettisoning their loads, said Alan . . .

Tom looked around the ward. He expected to see Alan in another bed. 'Where's my mate, then?'

Shirley sat down, overflowing on the hospital chair. She picked up his hand again. Hers was warm, solid. 'He didn't make it, Tom.'

The silence that followed seemed so much longer than it actually was.

'But he was right next to me.'

Then he remembered the strange sharp shove he'd felt as he and Alan ran.

'You mean Alan's . . .'

'Yes.' Her voice was very small. 'But it would have been instant. He wouldn't have felt . . .'

Tom had taken in the meaning of her words. He understood. He felt as if someone had thrown him from the hospital bed and stamped all over him . . . and intended to go on stamping.

Shirley squeezed his hand. 'When Bessie comes back, she'll—'

'Alan saved my life,' he said quietly.

Chapter Thirty-four

'Mr Jerome, there's a young man looking for you.'

Jerome smiled at the cigarette girl standing in front of him. Pretty little thing, a new addition, showing legs up to her bottom, dressed in the short, glittery black and white maid's uniform the older men liked.

Automatically his eyes now swept the dance floor and the bar area below. The small orchestra was playing Glenn Miller music, couples were dancing and his beautiful boys and girls, the taxi dancers, were waiting at the bar for new partners.

Cigar smoke, the smell of stale beer and money rose up the wrought-iron stairs to greet him. He moved to disperse the pressure on his aching knee. It was imperative he kept an eye on Mr Gilbert Willard and his pile of chips as he lounged in his seat in the casino behind him.

'Find Ace, will you, Edna darling?' He tried to be as tactful to her as he could without letting his annoyance show. Jerome had no idea where Ace was. He'd been looking for him for most of the evening.

The little blonde said, 'The young man's asking for you by name.'

Jerome pushed his spectacles further up his nose. Once more his eyes scoured the bar area below. His words came in a rush as he saw him. 'Oh, my God, bring him here to me,' he said. He watched her pert backside as it moved sensually down the stairs, then fixed his gaze on the young man.

And he was young. Perhaps seventeen? Certainly a long way off his twenties, Jerome thought. But there was no mistaking that gloss of auburn hair, so like the chestnut locks of his father. And tall! Every bit as tall as Ace.

He watched as Edna spoke to him, saw him smile at her and treat her with courtesy. Saw his head rise as he stared up to the top of the stairs. Saw the sudden smile burst on his lips as their eyes connected. There was vulnerability in the young man's gaze, and something more: steel . . . and determination.

Belle had obviously done a good job of raising Ace's son. The classic double-breasted dark blue suit with the waistcoat beneath, topping a white shirt, showed off the vibrancy of his hair. Plain black shoes, certainly expensive. And on the bar counter in front of him a dark blue trilby. Already he was gathering looks from the Four Aces' female employees and a few from the men as well.

A pleasantry from the young man made Edna laugh. Then he picked up his hat and swiftly began ascending the stairs.

'Looking for your father?' asked Jerome. He didn't want to sound formal. In fact, he wanted to throw his arms around Leon just as he had when the young man was a small child and forever climbing all over him. However, Jerome was wise enough to know now wasn't the time to show such obvious affection.

'He's not at the Southsea club, hasn't been for a few days, so they said. I felt sure he'd be here but Edna said she couldn't find—'

Jerome interrupted him. 'He's supposed to be here. But your guess is as good as mine as to where he's hiding.' He smiled at Leon. 'I'm delighted to see you,' he said.

Leon held his gaze. 'And I you. Can we go somewhere quieter and talk?'

'I'd like that,' Jerome said, 'but I'm keeping watch on a customer who's well over his head in debt to us.'

'Isn't there someone you trust who can do that?'

'Yes, your father!' Jerome laughed. Then he nodded at a thick-set man standing near the grille of the cashier's den. When his unspoken question was returned with a brief inclination of the man's head, Jerome said, 'Follow me.'

He led Leon downstairs and through the club's large kitchen into the smaller premises he and Ace used. 'All right in here?' he asked.

Leon put his arm across Jerome's shoulders. Jerome caught a hint of sandalwood cologne.

'It's been a long time and I've missed you,' the lad said.

Jerome felt his voice tremble with emotion as he answered, 'I've missed you an' all, lad.' He pulled out a stool from beneath the kitchen table and lowered himself on to it. 'Sit yourself down.' He waved to other stools and chairs. 'And tell me why you're here. There's no bother at home, is there?'

Ace paid for the upkeep on a decent property in Kent. He also sent money regularly to Belle, Leon's mother. The boy had received a first-class education, also paid for by Ace, his upper-class accent proof of that. Jerome could see that Leon, dressed as he was, wanted for nothing materially.

'Not now,' admitted Leon. He'd pulled up a kitchen chair and sat opposite Jerome, who waited for him to carry on. 'I've had enough of living in the back of beyond and I want to get to know my father better. There've been ructions at home about it. I threatened to leave with or without Mother's consent and now I've got her blessing.'

Jerome stared hard at him. 'Have you got her blessing?'

'Yes, I have.'

Jerome smiled. Leon reminded him of Ace when he was younger. 'That's all right then,' he said. 'It would truly upset the applecart if she came down here in a fighting mood.' Belle was formidable when she lost her temper. 'Then the only person left to persuade is your father.'

'I could be a great help.'

'I'm not sure he'll see it that way. The only reason he's kept your mother in such fine style is because he's never wanted you within a mile of any of his businesses.'

'So, he's nowhere in sight and you're left to do half a dozen jobs at once?'

Quick on the uptake too, was Leon, thought Jerome.

It was then Jerome remembered he was keeping tabs on Gilbert Willard and his play. 'I must get back to the casino,' he said.

'I'll come too,' Leon insisted.

Willard was still playing and he had a sizeable amount of chips piled in front of him. Jerome stood with his back to the game and far enough away not to be overheard by anyone except Leon, who was glancing at the players and asked, 'Is it the young bloke?'

'You're very smart. He owes us a lot of money, comes in with cash enough to play but we've yet to see reparation for his debt.'

'And you're letting him get away with it?'

Razor sharp, this one, thought Jerome.

'So, you let him take you for mugs? Allow him to win a little, lose a little, as though his original debt doesn't exist?'

'That's pretty much the position at the moment, except for further interest piling up. To bar him means he could disappear and we'll never get our money.'

'In other words, he can't pay but he comes in with cash enough to play?'

'That's about it.' Jerome turned, gave the nod to the big man at the cashier's desk that he was back, and ran his eyes along the players at the tables.

'My dad's getting soft in his old age?' There was an edge to the lad's voice.

'Not necessarily. He's wary. There was some bother a little while back about a bloke, a customer, who took his own life. A club's good reputation's not to be trashed so easily.'

'And you're letting that man over there believe you've just come up the Solent in a bucket! Why, he's laughing at you and my father.' Jerome saw the disbelief and disgust in his eyes. Eyes that weren't the steel grey of his father's but amber, filled with intellect and overflowing with cunning.

Jerome smiled at him. Here was a young man who didn't need to be moulded into someone else. He was already perfect.

Chapter Thirty-five

Len handed Connie a blanket and a pillow. 'I suggest you get your head down for a couple of hours' sleep and I'll wake you when it's your turn to keep watch.'

Connie had already screwed the empty cup back onto the flask of hot tea and now she nodded at him. She huddled down on the carpet behind the thick velvet curtains that shut out most of the noise from the Criterion's foyer. Pulling the blanket up around her neck, she rested her head on the softness of the feather pillow and tried to sleep. She thought about what they were hoping to achieve.

The picture house was locked up for the night, the takings in their usual place in the tiny ticket kiosk.

For several nights now the four employees had taken turns, two at a time, in watching for the thief to come in and remove just some of the money. Gary and Doyle had hidden here last night. Tonight was Connie and Len's turn.

They knew they were invisible behind the glass doors hidden by the curtain but were aware that sound travelled fast in darkness so it was imperative that they were as quiet as possible.

Two people were needed for each nightshift. Doyle had reasoned that the thief, when apprehended, was less likely to be able to deny breaking into the picture house if two volunteers were lying in wait ready to back each other up.

Connie could smell in the carpet the tread of thousands of pairs of shoes. Stale tobacco hung in the air, along with trapped body odour. 'If we knew what time the thief was likely to come it would save a lot of hanging about,' Connie whispered.

'Well, we don't know that, do we?' Len answered softly. 'So, it's best the picture house is locked up as usual, and we stay hidden until it's time for the morning cleaners to come in.'

'It's not often you're wrong but you're right there,' said Connie.

Len chuckled. 'Cheeky beggar,' he said.

Connie laughed softly. 'This is certainly more exciting than the film we're showing at present.'

'I thought you liked *Road to Morocco*?'

'I get a bit fed up with Bob Hope, and I'd rather listen to Frank Sinatra sing than Bing Crosby,' she said.

Len answered, 'Never mind. *Old Mother Riley*'s on soon, so you'll have a laugh.' His next words surprised her. 'I've got an idea what Willard spends the stolen money on. His wages too, no doubt.'

'Have you really?' Connie couldn't believe it.

'Last night when Doyle and young Gary were hiding and waiting here, Gary said his uncle Jack had taken him into the Four Aces last weekend. His uncle likes a flutter on the roulette wheel, so he said. Gary swore he saw Gilbert Willard hunched over a card table.'

'No! Was Gary sure it was Willard?'

'Well, he's hardly going to make a mistake, is he?'

'I hope Gary's uncle didn't let Gary gamble!' Connie said. 'Gambling can be like drinking. It takes a person over, if they let it. Becomes an addiction.'

'Exactly, and that could be the reason why Willard habitually robs the takings.'

'I wonder if you're right,' Connie said. She closed her eyes. She needed to think about this new information. And she ought to try to doze at least – when it was her turn to keep watch she knew Len would sleep like a log.

So, too, did Doyle. She pitied his poor wife, Jilly, putting up with him night after night. He snored like an ack-ack gun and Connie had had to poke him in the back several times to make him stop. It certainly wouldn't do for the thief to be warned off by the noise from an artillery gun in the picture house, would it? she thought.

'Do you think we're wasting our time?' she asked.

'No, I don't.'

'But there's not been hide or hair of anyone coming in here so far, and creaming money off the top of the night's takings.'

'That's only because at present he probably doesn't need it,' Len said. 'If he is gambling, he might be winning.'

'I suppose you're right,' Connie said. 'But I still don't understand why he doesn't steal all the money . . .'

'I've thought about that a lot,' muttered Len. 'The takings are paid into the bank daily, in the mornings, aren't they?'

Connie nodded. Though, of course, Len couldn't see that in the dark.

'You see,' he said. 'A little off the top of the ticket money won't be missed as long as the bulk is paid in daily as normal. At the end of the tax year, when the owners of the picture house discover the takings are lower and don't match up with the ticket sales, that's when they'll worry. But it won't be discovered until next year's audit. Which gives the thief time to be well away from Gosport.'

'I see,' said Connie. 'Queenie picked a sharp one when she married you, didn't she?'

'I haven't finished yet,' he said. 'Now, if all the day's takings were swiped, there'd be nothing to put in the bank. No money banked means something's wrong. The owners will be down here immediately, wondering why. I'm certain Gilbert Willard is putting the finger on Doyle to hoodwink us. I'm also sure, despite his threats, Willard hasn't told the owners that money is going missing. If he had, there would be someone down from head office already looking into his accusations.'

'So, if we catch him red-handed, two of us, his protestations won't hold water.'

'Exactly,' said, Len.

'But catching him at it is one thing. We can't lock him in his office, can we, until the owners or the police get here?'

'We don't need to apprehend him. We inform head office of our findings. It's us they'll believe, not a fly-by-night like him.'

'So we surprise him and let him go? Supposing he leaves Gosport?'

'Not our problem. Number one, we've proved who the

thief is. Number two, the police will do their duty and catch him.' His eyes shone through the dull light. 'You really should get some sleep, Connie. Especially as I suspect you've had a few sleepless nights after breaking up with Ace. Are you sure it was what you wanted?'

Connie pushed herself up on one elbow. 'I'd rather not talk about it, Len, except to say I'm glad it's all over. He'd tell me lies or perhaps not the whole truth. It's a relief not to love him any more.'

'Then I'll not ask you anything else,' he said. 'But you should rest, you know.'

Connie closed her eyes again.

During the past week the four of them had waited at night in the picture house, taking it in turns to catch Willard. So far, their activities had been secret. Connie was pleased they'd decided to exclude Gertie from this part of the operation. Not only did she need her sleep but Gilbert Willard would only have to unlock the main door and smell her fresh cigarette smoke to know something was up.

She must have slept because the next thing she knew her shoulder was being shaken and Len's whisper was so close to her ear that she could feel the warmth of his breath.

'Sssh! Someone's come in!'

Connie raised her head from the pillow and listened. It

was dark no longer. The electric light from the foyer shone below the length of curtaining covering the glass doors. She heard the clatter of keys dropping onto a hard surface.

She stood up and leant against Len, who had pulled the curtain aside slightly, and was watching the scene unfolding in the payment kiosk. He moved so she, too, could watch. What she saw almost took her breath away. Their manager, Gilbert Willard, was calmly taking money from the blue bank bag and stuffing it into his trouser pocket.

'Move now before he puts everything back the way it was,' whispered Connie.

'Are you ready?'

'Quite ready,' said Connie. 'You apprehend him. I'll slip the bolt on the main door so he can't run out.'

Connie held the curtain while Len pulled back the glass door and moved quickly down the steps. He stood in front of the doorway of the small ticket kiosk so Willard was hemmed in and said, 'Caught you at last!'

At first the manager looked bewildered, as though he couldn't comprehend that he'd been caught red-handed. Then he said, 'What are you two doing here? I've just dropped in to check on the takings and make sure everything's safe.'

'By stuffing money in your pockets?' asked Connie. 'We've caught you in the act of stealing.'

'Don't be ridiculous. I've got a key!' Willard was floundering now, trying to excuse himself.

'So has Doyle but it's not been him taking money, has it?'

'I can explain.'

'Dare say you can,' said Len, 'but you'd only tell us lies.'

Willard looked scared now. Connie could almost smell his fear. Sweat had appeared on his forehead. 'What are you going to do?' he asked.

Then Len said something that surprised her. 'No, it's what you're going to do,' he said to Willard. 'I think you ought to put back every penny you've stolen and tender your resignation as manager of this picture house. If you do that, we won't tell the owners you've been systematically stealing from them. If, however, the money isn't forthcoming, the owners and the police will be involved. You've got seven days to think about it.'

Connie took a deep breath. This was a completely new turn of events. She was sure this hadn't been agreed with Doyle or Gary. Or herself for that matter.

Willard, knowing he was beaten, said, 'I can't possibly remember the exact small amounts I've taken.'

'Not asking you to,' said Len. 'But you've a good idea of the total and that's what I suggest you hand over. As long as the books tally at the end of the financial year, you'll be in the clear, and well away from Gosport, I hope.'

'But I can't possibly—'

'Connie, go into the office. Phone the police and the picture-house owners.'

'All right, all right . . .' Willard looked a defeated mess. He rubbed his hand across his sweat-slicked forehead. 'I agree.'

For a moment Connie thought he was about to cry, the way his young face crumpled. But he took a deep breath. 'One week?'

'One week,' agreed Len. 'One week and the total amount of the money you've stolen is to be handed either to me or to Connie here. Also, during that week we won't expect to see you working in the picture house because of your resignation.

Just remember, after seven days, if you've not complied, we call in the big guns, police and owners.'

Then Willard did something Connie thought highly unusual: he stuck out his hand for Len to shake. Connie remembered he had attended a very posh school. He was offering a gentleman's agreement. Len shook his hand.

Then Len stepped back to unbolt the entrance door. 'You can go now.'

Willard made a move towards it. Len pulled him back by his collar. 'Empty your pockets first,' he said.

'Sorry,' said Willard. Connie had to stifle a laugh as Willard pulled out handfuls of coins and set them on the ticket desk.

When he was ready to leave, Connie stood at the door. As the manager made to pass, she put out her hand and said, 'Keys?'

He nodded towards the kiosk where his keys to the Criterion still sat.

No one spoke as Gilbert Willard left.

Connie fluffed the curtains back to make sure no light escaped the newly locked door. 'I didn't know you were going to make a deal with him.'

'Neither did I until the words came out of my mouth,' Len said. 'What do you think?'

'That it's best not to get the police involved unless it's absolutely necessary. It could damage the picture house's reputation and I'm sure the owners would like to avoid that. The staff and patrons will definitely be happier he's not around,' she added, 'and we can manage quite well without him ... One week and we should have all the money returned?'

'A week,' echoed Len. Then he added, 'We said we'd let Gertie in on the secret. Do you want to?'

Connie anticipated his words. 'I don't know about you but all I want to do now is sleep. Let's not wake her tonight.

And I really think Doyle and Gary should know the outcome first, don't you?'

He nodded. 'The four of us should keep this to ourselves until the week is up.'

Connie said, 'Seven days. Then we tell Gertie and she can do her *News of the World* impression to all of the staff here at the Criterion.'

Chapter Thirty-six

A few days later Connie and Gertie were waiting outside Queenie's front door.

'Hello, my lovers,' said Queenie. 'Come inside and I'll put the kettle on.'

'My, you look a sight for sore eyes,' said Gertie. 'No kiddies?'

Connie thought her friend looked wonderful. She was wearing a yellow cotton sundress that she could see wasn't new, but with shoulder-straps showing off her lightly tanned skin. Its belt neatly encircled her tiny waist and her hair was newly bleached to perfection, almost exactly the same shade as Jean Harlow's.

'Thank you!' Queenie executed a mock curtsy to them both. 'Bette and Paulie are asleep in the garden in the shade.' She had walked through the house to the scullery and now she lit the gas beneath the kettle. 'How are you both?' she asked.

Connie took a deep breath of the comforting smell of talcum powder and baby milk that was now as familiar to her as Queenie's Californian Poppy perfume.

Gertie immediately pushed off her shoes. She'd been complaining about her bunions on the walk to Queenie's.

'You've no idea how happy everyone is at the Criterion because his lordship, Sir Gilbert Willard, appears to have taken a few days off.' She pulled out a chair from beneath the table and flopped onto it. 'Oh, that's better.'

Queenie glanced at Connie, who smiled and said, 'We don't care if he never comes back.' A conspiratorial wink was shared between the two of them.

'*Gentleman Jim* is the film showing today. Ooh, that Errol Flynn's lovely. I certainly wouldn't kick him out of bed in an air-raid,' said Gertie.

Queenie laughed. 'From what I've read about him in the papers he doesn't get kicked out of any beds.'

Gertie had bent down and was busy massaging a mis-shapen foot. Queenie looked at Connie and mouthed silently, 'Any news?' Connie shook her head. She knew Queenie was referring to Willard returning the money to her. He hadn't contacted Len either.

'I hope the manager never comes back,' said Gertie. 'We're managing fine, aren't we?' She looked pointedly at Connie.

'Well, your job's the same, Gertie. It's me and Doyle who are run off our feet, but everything's going smoothly, very smoothly indeed.'

Connie didn't want to appear smug and say she was happier now than she'd felt in ages, or that she enjoyed working much more than she ever had before. Being at the Criterion wasn't a job now, it was a labour of love. Whether it was because her mind was also free of Ace, she couldn't tell. Why, she'd even found time to cut out a few film stars' pictures from *Photoplay* and stick them in her scrapbook. That had made her feel closer to her mum. It had been good. All she knew was that she woke up in the mornings with a smile and slept well at nights. Except when the Germans decided to pay Gosport a visit in their planes, on their way to the Portsmouth dockyards, and leave calling cards in the shape of bombs.

'Did you hear the news this morning? Bloody liberty, I call it,' said Gertie.

She'd lit up a Woodbine and blew out a stream of smoke.

'Too busy with babies,' said Queenie.

Connie shook her head. She was dying to go out into the

garden to see Bette and Paulie, but thought she wouldn't be in anyone's good books if she woke them, so she decided to drink her tea first.

Gertie took another drag on her fag. 'The court in London says any money what the wife manages to save from her housekeeping belongs to her husband.'

'Really?' asked Queenie, pouring tea into cups. 'That don't seem fair.'

'Len's good to you, though, isn't he?' Gertie was peering at Queenie.

'I couldn't wish for a better bloke. I get his wage packet unopened. He says, "What's mine is yours and what's yours is your own!"'

'You're lucky. Not all men are like that.' Gertie poured milk into her cup and some into Connie's as well, whether she wanted it or not. Connie was going to say she was glad she didn't have a husband who didn't treat her well, but thought better of it. Instead, she said, 'I've been reading about that new drug called penicillin. It's curing infections and blood poisonings left, right and centre. It's wonderful, isn't it? I did think if doctors had known about it before, especially in the Great War, a lot of lives would have been saved.'

'A lot of lives could be saved if that Hitler didn't want to rule the world!'

Gertie was snappy and stirring the milk into her tea so ferociously Connie thought she'd break the cup. She took the teaspoon away from her. 'The war can't last for ever, love,' she said.

Everything went quiet in the scullery until Queenie said, 'Stay here, you two. I want your opinions on something.' Then she gulped back her tea and the cup rattled as she set it down on its saucer.

'Wonder what she's up to,' Gertie said. Connie could hear her friend running up the stairs. She listened to doors banging, drawers opening and closing in the bedroom, then footsteps hurrying down the stairs.

'Close your eyes, both of you,' Queenie insisted, hiding behind the scullery door. Connie knew she was making sure they weren't peeking. 'Don't open them until I say so. When Len asked me to marry him, I was already pregnant by that Yank. You'll remember how ill I was after the birth of the twins . . . We couldn't . . . er . . . you know . . . The hospital said to abstain. Anyway, it's taken me a while to get better and to get my figure back. We haven't got money to splash out on new outfits so I've been hoarding bits and pieces from second-hand shops and jumble sales. Connie knows about this. It's been my one ambition since we wed, to dress up just for Len and, well . . .' She faltered again. 'You know what I mean, don't you? Show Len just how much I love him. You can open your eyes now.'

Connie gasped. The blonde bombshell wearing a figure-hugging gold dress and high heels with peep-toes would have given Jean Harlow a run for her money any time.

Gertie was gaping. She closed her mouth, then opened it long enough to say, 'Cor! When Len sees you in that get-up, Queenie, you'll be getting more than an unopened pay packet!'

Tom sat up in bed in hospital, pillows high behind him, reading an Ellery Queen detective novel.

'Put that away. You can talk to me now.'

He hadn't noticed Bessie walking up to the bed. 'Lovely to see you,' he said. 'Family all right?' She nodded and put a brown-paper bag with three apples inside it on top of his locker. 'Thank you,' he said. 'You shouldn't. They do feed me in here.' Pleasantries over, she fetched a chair and sat down. 'I'm sorry I couldn't be there,' he went on, 'but how did the funeral go?'

'I think Alan would have preferred a knees-up,' Bessie answered. 'A lot of people came to see him off. His family were very brave. A good turn-out from our members. He was a lovely man.'

There was silence. Tom knew she, too, was thinking about Alan.

'Anyway,' she said, 'I hope when you get out of this place you'll think twice about coming back too soon after what happened.'

'You must be joking, Bessie. If they discharge me in the morning, I'll be ready for duty the same night. Alan Crosby didn't save my life so I could sit on my arse at home listening to the wireless.'

He was actually looking forward to checking equipment, patrolling the streets until midnight, helping people wandering about seeking assistance, even the never-ending form filling.

'All right! Don't get your dander up!' She pulled a face, making him laugh.

He ran his fingers through his hair – it was growing back now and he no longer had so many bandages around his head. 'They're leaving off the dressings tomorrow,' he said. 'Be chucking me out soon.'

Tom was anxious to start dancing again, too. Shirley had said there was a list as long as her arm of people who'd telephoned to either ask about the classes or to join them. He'd had enough of lying about in bed, reading newspapers and novels, his limbs stiffening up. That was no good for dancing: he had to practise, practise, then practise some more. He'd discovered a place in the hospital where he could try out a few steps – the patients' bathroom was quite spacious. Unhappily there were no locks on any of the doors and quite a few times he'd been caught, once when he was attempting a vigorous shuffle-ball change with improvised arm movements and an elderly woman was wheeled in for a bath. She'd thought the show had been just for her but the nurse hadn't been pleased.

It didn't stop him practising. Dancing helped to take his mind off the death of his friend. He was going to miss Alan.

He'd had a lot of time to think, being in bed most of the time. Life was short. Hitler was trying to make it shorter. He'd thought most of all about the girl in the picture house. Maybe he ought to look for her. He knew he should leave it to Fate but Alan's death had shown him that life and love must be grabbed with both hands and held on to before either could be cruelly snatched away.

Bessie was now telling him about the antics her youngest was up to with a puppy they'd rescued from some ruins. She was a good woman, he thought.

He saw the shadows beneath her eyes, heard the tiredness in her voice. Bessie had a family. She was a full-time ambulance driver and an ARP warden, yet she'd found time to pop in and see him. He felt humbled.

Tom was aware he could never tease her mercilessly the way Alan had. Neither would he dare to eat all the Nice biscuits she brought in. But he knew he was lucky to have her as a friend.

Chapter Thirty-seven

'Are you comfortable in your room upstairs, along the hall from me, Leon?'

Jerome folded last night's *Portsmouth Evening News* and left it on the table next to the loaf on the breadboard. The headline said, 'Man's Body Found At Gosport's Forton Creek'. Jerome was surprised he hadn't heard about it sooner, from the club's patrons. The dead man's name hadn't been revealed because the next of kin hadn't been informed.

Jerome smiled at the young man sitting opposite him on the stool in the kitchen. Cat was curled into his lap and purring loudly. On the floor a dish contained the remnants of sardines. Leon idly stroked the animal's glossy fur. The lad was taking an interest in the club's business. He'd become like a shadow to Jerome.

'It has everything I need for comfort,' he answered. 'I've

told Mother I'm happy and it's good getting to know my father.'

'And are you? Getting to know Ace?' Jerome felt good today. His back had eased and his dodgy knee, so far, wasn't giving him trouble. He'd liked Leon asking questions about the business, and sometimes his reflections on the way things were done in the club made Jerome feel good.

'He's agreed to me spending time at both his clubs. If you're asking me whether we've had any heart-to-heart chats the answer is no. He seems to prefer Marlene's company and boozing in the bar.'

'Give him time, lad. Marlene helps take his mind off other things. You've sort of knocked him off his throne. The women in here look as if they'd like to eat you up and the men are as jealous as hell.' He laughed. 'It's good for him to have a bit of competition.' Jerome also liked the way the lad didn't pull any punches. He said what he thought, no matter who it involved.

Leon was tickling Cat behind one ear. It was a favourite place to be petted. Jerome liked it that Cat had made a friend of Leon. The feline didn't go to many people. Men especially made it bolt. Jerome thought the poor thing had been treated badly before he had taken it in. Cat tolerated

Ace. With Leon it showed almost as much affection as it did Jerome.

The old man pushed his spectacles further up his nose, then set about collecting the breakfast plates, scraping the residue of bacon, egg and fried bread onto the top plate and carrying them to the draining-board.

'I saw you having a word with Gilbert Willard in the casino the other day.'

'Would you rather I didn't talk to the players?'

'Good God, no! There's plenty I'd like your father to say to him but no doubt he's leaving the dirty work to me.'

'That's what I guessed. Do you want to know what we spoke about?'

'I expect you'll tell me.'

'I said he should think himself fortunate to be sitting at the table. Other men who owed half as much as he did wouldn't usually show their faces in the Four Aces unless they'd come to settle up in full.'

'What did Ace say when you told him this?'

'He's never asked. I told you, his interests at present aren't running further than the bar and that girl.'

'Ace don't bare his soul like a lot of people do. If he didn't want you around you'd soon know it.' He paused. 'I like it that you're showing an interest.'

'I figured one day part of this business might be mine. I'd like there still to be a business when that time comes.'

Jerome looked towards the window. The sun was shining but already the trees were shedding their leaves.

'You are aware Mr Willard hasn't paid his bill but neither has he shown his face here for the last couple of nights?' Jerome's gaze shifted from the window to the newspaper on the kitchen table, then to Leon's face.

'So? His seat at the table will soon be taken up by another loser who does pay his dues.'

Jerome saw not one hint of compassion in the compelling amber eyes.

''Ere, that bloke they found dead in the mud near the ferry is Gilbert Willard!'

Gertie was full of it. She was waving a late edition of the *Portsmouth Evening News* as if she was brandishing a flag. 'There's a picture of his mum and dad in the doorway of their house in Alverstoke. Big posh house. You can't see his mum very well – she's got a handkerchief up to her face.' She passed the newspaper to Connie, who glanced at the page, then put it down on the floor in the staffroom, next to a pile of empty film cans Gary had left there. Connie's face was inscrutable.

Len stood next to the sink, his arms folded. He was looking tired. Queenie had told Connie the twins had teeth coming through and both were restless at night.

'Have you got the letter?' Len asked.

Connie pointed to the table where an envelope sat with a typewritten sheet of paper.

Gary came out of the lavatory, went to the sink, edging Len aside, and washed his hands with Lifebuoy soap. 'That's better!' He rinsed them, then used a striped tea-towel to dry them.

'Can we get on with this? My Jilly will be wondering where I am.' Doyle had his mackintosh on over his uniform. He threw an apologetic smile at Connie. She knew he was tired but she had invited Doyle, Len, Gary and Gertie to a private meeting before she had a chat with all the employees.

Connie picked up the typewritten page. 'This came by post this morning from a Mr Edward Burton, solicitor and representative for the owners of this picture house. . .'

'Oh, don't read it all out,' whined Gary. 'I had a quick look at it earlier and it's got so many long words I didn't really understand much of it.' He looked imploringly at Connie. 'Why don't you just tell us in plain English what's in it?'

Gertie, sitting at the far end of the table lighting a Woodbine, said, 'I think that might be better, love.'

Connie took a deep breath. 'If it's all right with you two, I will.'

She looked first at Doyle, who nodded, and then at Len, who ran his hands through his curly hair. 'Yes, Connie.'

'All right, then,' she said. She was nervous. Her heart was beating fast and her hands were shaking so much that the page of writing was fluttering up and down.

'First I'd like to say it's a big shock to find out our manager is dead. It was also a bolt out of the blue to discover he was stealing money from the takings here. Most of you know we were the ones who caught him red-handed.'

'Bit late in telling me, but I do know now,' said Gertie. 'Anyway, I could never have slept on that hard floor. I'd never have got up again . . .'

'Please get on with it,' Doyle said patiently.

Gertie glared at him.

Connie felt a trickle of sweat run down her forehead and brushed it away with her free hand. 'We advised Willard to pay back the money he'd stolen and gave him seven days to hand it in to either me or Doyle.' She looked at Doyle for reassurance and he nodded. 'If he didn't, we said we would tell the owners of the Criterion who would no doubt prosecute.' Connie took a deep breath. She really wasn't used to being the centre of attraction and she was finding it extremely difficult to talk. It ran through her mind that that was something she must get used to, and soon.

'Len thought we could put the money back without him getting into trouble, you see, and I agreed. A week came and went but nothing happened.

'Apparently, according to this letter, Gilbert Willard had returned all the money to head office, a cheque, along with a letter tendering his resignation and explaining how we had tried to preserve the Criterion's good name by dealing with his theft ourselves.' Connie gave a throaty cough.

Gertie blew out a cloud of cigarette smoke. 'Who'd have thought he'd get the money? I bet he borrowed it from his parents—'

This time it was Connie who interrupted her. 'Obviously Mr Burton hasn't gone into detail but he's commended us for our diligence. The management will be sending someone down to thank us personally, and as we're without a manager they've given me the job.' This last bit of information came out garbled.

There was a moment of silence while her words sank in. Then Doyle stood up and shouted, 'Yes! Oh, well done, Connie!' He began clapping his big hands together, which was closely followed by an ear-splitting whistle from Gary, who had two fingers in his mouth.

Gertie covered her ears with her hands but her grin was wide. Len jumped up from his seat, and when he reached Connie, he put his arms around her and squeezed her until she cried, 'Oh, I feel I might break!' Then she interrupted the noise around her, saying, 'Thank you for your good wishes. I'll serve you all, the usherettes and cleaners, as well as I can.'

Len sat down again.

'Shouldn't be too difficult,' burst in Gertie, twisting out her dog end in the ashtray. 'You been doing it for ages anyway.'

There was laughter but Connie held up a hand until they'd quietened. 'I'll leave this letter here so anyone can read it.' She looked down at the printed page with the flourish of a blue-ink signature at the bottom. 'Now, I don't want to put a dampener on things but . . .' she paused '. . . from this letter it's obvious Mr Burton is unaware Gilbert Willard is now dead.'

The sudden silence was almost palpable.

'Surely you don't think his death has anything to do with returning the money . . .' Gary's voice petered out.

'What are you saying?' asked Len. 'You think he borrowed the money, paid his dues, then committed suicide because he felt bad about everything?'

Connie blinked her eyes to dispel the tears that had been threatening. Len had put into words exactly what she was thinking. She was about to speak but Doyle, in his calm voice, said, 'The *Evening News* doesn't say how he died. We've had raids – he could have been killed by falling shrapnel. He could have been drunk, out walking, slipped in the water and drowned. Connie, love, I really don't think you should burden yourself with this.'

'We all know he was a bad lot,' Gertie put in. 'Good riddance, I say.'

Doyle spoke over her: 'There will no doubt be a post-mortem . . .' He paused, looking at Gary's questioning frown '. . . To find the cause of death,' he added, 'and the result of that will be reported in the *Evening News*. In the meantime, I think we should congratulate ourselves that this picture house will be run to perfection in the future.' He looked at each of them in turn. 'Now, if you don't mind, I've finished work for the night and I'm going home to my wife.'

The chair slid back on the thin carpet, and he got as far as the door when he turned and said, with a huge smile, 'You're going to do us fine, Connie.'

Ace poured a large shot of whisky into his glass. There were a few dancers on the floor, moving to his orchestra's rendition of 'I Don't Want To Set The World On Fire'. He could see his girls, bought with tickets, doing their best to entice their elderly male partners up to the casino with promises that might or might not bear fruit later.

Marlene had arrived, gliding through the front doors of the club, like a ship in full sail. Eyes swivelled towards her as she slid her fur wrap onto a bar stool, knowing no one would dare remove it because she was his number-one girl. She looked at him, waved, then spoke to the barman. Her wrist glittered with the bracelet he'd bought her.

He could also see his son, Leon, matching slow steps to Jerome's as they came down the stairs together. Ace lifted his glass to his lips. He wondered why he'd been so worried when Leon had turned up out of the blue. There'd been little contact between father and son while the boy had been growing up. He thought at first the fancy schools he'd paid for had turned him into some kind of nancy-boy who'd have been frightened to get his hands dirty. The schools had been Belle's idea, not his. To keep her happy, he'd forked out for a decent education.

He smiled to himself. There was more of him in his son than Belle knew. For hadn't the young man proved himself? Shown his father where his allegiance lay?

Ace cursed himself for not sorting out Gilbert Willard's gambling debt earlier. If he'd attended to business instead of wallowing in drink and self-pity about his love-life, there'd have been no need for Leon to slip out of the back door of the club and follow Willard that night.

Willard had walked across the road near the ferry gardens. The tide had been low in Forton Creek, with Leon following his prey along the muddy bank, the shortest route back to that hovel the man was living in. Only he never reached it, did he?

Ace had watched Leon call to Willard. Watched the two of them angrily remonstrate before Willard turned his back on his son to continue on his way. He saw Leon pick up the wooden spar and hit him over the head, just once. The man had crumpled at the knees and slid down into the mud.

Ace had soon been back at the Four Aces, sitting at his usual table, swallowing whisky like it was going out of fashion, trying to erase the stink of the mud and the sight of his son killing a man. Willard was dead, he was sure of that. He'd sat and drank until Marlene and Jerome urged him to go to bed.

He'd fallen asleep alone in his room, wondering what sixth sense had sent him skulking after his son. Was it because Leon continually watched Willard at the gaming tables? Was it because Leon thought he, Ace, was allowing Willard, who owed him money, to walk over him? Was it because the young man needed to prove himself in some way to his father?

Ace might never discover the answer. One thing he did know was that he wouldn't speak of what he had seen that night to a single soul. Leon was looking after his father's interests. What more could Ace ask of his own flesh and blood?

Now he felt Marlene's arms slide around his neck. Her kiss was warm on his cheek.

'Sit down,' he said.

'I will in a moment.' She laughed. 'I'll find out what drinks Leon and Jerome want and play barmaid.'

Her silken dress was skin tight about her supple body. She smelt of heady perfume and, for a moment, he was reminded of Connie.

'You've started drinking early tonight.' The statement came from Jerome as he pulled out a metal chair opposite Ace.

'And you've started complaining already, old man,' Ace said, with a grin. He watched as Leon helped Jerome onto the chair. 'You sitting with us, son?' he asked Leon.

After giving Marlene a smile, Leon said, 'No, I'll go back up to the gaming tables. See you later.'

As he walked away, Marlene said. 'He's a credit to you, Ace.'

'I know,' Ace replied.

Chapter Thirty-eight

'It's no good trying to make her celebrate her new job if she don't want no fuss.' Gertie struck a match and put her hand around the flame to stop it setting fire to the elderly woman's hair in front of her. She lit her Woodbine, took a deep, satisfying drag, blew out the Swan Vestas and threw it down. 'Connie can be quite a madam when she wants.'

Gertie's head was covered with a turban made from a silk square and it had slipped back across her hair to reveal dangerous-looking metal curlers. 'And you can stop pushing!' She looked away from Queenie and snarled at the woman in the moth-eaten fur coat shoving into her from behind. The woman glared and threw her eyes heavenwards as if she had no idea what Gertie meant. 'This jumble sale don't start until two o'clock an' there's fifteen more minutes to wait till they open the doors an' you ain't getting in front of me!' The woman smiled as if butter wouldn't melt in her mouth.

'I hope it don't rain,' said Edith, scratching her ear. 'We're too far away from the entrance of the Sloane Stanley Hall to get any shelter.'

'How much nearer the front do you want to be?' said Gertie. Her voice was a bit muffled because her fag hadn't left her mouth. 'We'd have been right outside, if you'd got to my house sooner. First in the queue, we'd have been!'

'We'll all get in,' said Queenie, patiently. 'Let's just hope there's some good stuff in there.'

Gertie used her forefinger to knock the ash from her cigarette, which dropped down the back of the elderly woman's coat. Edith's face crinkled into a conspiratorial grimace as Gertie merely shrugged her shoulders.

Gertie was worried about Connie.

All around her, women and children were noisily talking and laughing, all squashed up together, like baked beans in a tin, with bags tightly clutched, ready to crush their jumble-sale spoils inside. Gertie could smell remnants of perfume, sweat and last night's cooking.

'Connie's worrying that Willard topped himself because they caught him stealing,' Gertie said.

'She's daft, then, ain't she? Why would he do away with

himself after giving back the money? That don't make sense,' answered Edith. 'The *News* said, "The cause of death is yet to be determined."' Someone had pressed against her and her mushroom-shaped hat had slipped sideways. 'I hate being squashed up like this,' she said, trying to put her hat to rights. 'We'll find out soon enough how he died. It'll be in the paper. Didn't it say, "An investigation is under way"? Anyway, how's she doin' being a manager?'

'Like a duck to water,' said Queenie. 'It's not a new thing for her to take charge, is it? And my Len says the usherettes and cleaners think the sun shines out of her eyes.'

'Do you think she's missing that Ace from the club?' asked Edith.

'Yeah! She's missing him like she misses toothache,' snapped Gertie. 'She's been much happier since she broke up with him. Best thing she ever did.'

'Waaaah!'

'Oh, my God, someone should shut that kiddie up!' said Gertie. 'What have you done with your two, Queenie?'

'Len's looking after them,' Queenie said. 'My feet are killing me in these high heels.' She grimaced.

'You might find a better pair inside on a table for sixpence.' Gertie laughed. She nodded towards Edith. 'She could do with a new 'at an' all!'

Edith glared at her.

Gertie nudged Queenie with her elbow, after taking her remnant of dog end from her lips and throwing it to the paving stone where she trod it flat with her lace-up shoe. ''Ere, how did the dressing up go with your Len?' She saw the rosy glow spread from Queenie's neck, up over her face and spread into her platinum hair.

'Don't be so nosy!' Queenie snapped, but she was smiling.

'Gertie,' she whispered. Gertie could see her eyes were sparkling. Shining like glittering stars in a dark velvet sky, 'You can keep Errol Flynn and Clark Gable,' she said. 'My Len's a real man!'

Gertie let out a loud cackle and Queenie joined in.

The elderly woman in front turned round with a disapproving frown that made both of them laugh more.

When they'd quietened Gertie added, 'Queenie, don't forget to grab any hand-knitted items you can find. Edith's making blankets out of knitted squares. She unravels the woollen jumpers, winds the wool into balls and knits it up again.'

'You've already asked me to do that. I'm not simple. I won't forget,' Queenie said. Then, in a softer voice, 'Don't worry about Connie, she'll be all right. Her smiles will be a mile wide when we start that dancing class. I phoned up and this woman named Shirley wrote down our names on the list. The bloke that runs it has been in hospital. Shirley said to contact her in a few weeks.'

She got no further for the double wooden doors on the Sloane Stanley Hall opened wide to show a wizened, grey-haired lady sitting at a table with an enamel bowl in front of her, ready to receive the twopenny entrance fees.

The crowd, elbows swinging, surged forward.

Tom had bagged the battered armchair in the ARP post in Forton Road. A tin mug of strong tea was at his elbow. The wireless was playing Gene Krupa swing music, and the Gosport girl group, the Bluebirds, were performing 'Sing, Sing, Sing'.

In his hands he held the *Portsmouth Evening News* and one foot was unconsciously tapping in time to the music. Four other members were in the hut, sitting around a small bamboo table playing cards for matchsticks, laughing, chatting, mugs of tea on the floor beside them.

Tom was waiting for Bessie to arrive. Tonight she was partnered with him again and, although he hadn't told her so, he would be eternally grateful for the way she'd helped him find the courage to get back out on the streets again. He'd been so scared that first night, expecting any moment to hear the wail of the air-raid siren and terrified he'd find himself unable to cope in an emergency. She'd walked alongside him, checking houses and premises for lights showing, and all the while she'd talked about her family, the puppy, and made him feel he wasn't some kind of oddity because he was terrified of the dark, and hearing stray bombers behind every cloud. When their shift was finished and they were back in the hut, all she'd said was 'There, wasn't so bad was it?' Then she'd produced a packet of shortcake biscuits and handed them to him. 'Get them down you.'

And now Alfie Benson pushed open the door to the hut. He was whistling happily but stopped once he'd stepped inside. 'It's great that music, isn't it?' His long face was beaming. 'I love Gene Krupa.' Tall and stringy, he reminded Tom of a runner bean with legs. Alfie, like himself, had wanted to join the navy but had been turned down because of his hearing difficulties. He said he hadn't even known he'd had problems with it until his medical examination. Tom liked him because he had a ready smile. And he was enormously solicitous with the elderly and the help they needed in leaving their homes and getting into the shelters. The only other fly in the ointment of life for twenty-year-old Alfie was his girlfriend, Phoebe. Tom had met them together once in the town. Phoebe had long blonde hair that she wore up in a Victory roll and at eighteen had a figure that turned heads on the street.

'I wish I could jive,' said Alfie. 'My Phoebe's good at it, but whenever we go down the Connaught Hall, she leaves me standing like a bally wallflower while she gets chucked about by some Yank. Them Americans can knock spots off us when it comes to jive dancing, can't they?'

'Go dancing a lot, do you?' Tom wondered.

'Fair bit,' Alfie said. 'I love foxtrots, waltzes, the Paul Jones and all those dances where everyone gets up on the floor and you change partners and get mixed up and people fall about laughing, but when it comes to jiving and swing, no one can do that like the Yanks.'

Tom smiled. 'They didn't invent jiving.'

Alfie pulled up a stool and sat opposite him. His forehead creased with disbelief. 'What do you mean?'

Tom could see he'd caught Alfie's interest. He'd never mentioned he taught dancing except to Bessie, and he'd have said nothing to her if hadn't known she'd met up with Shirley at the hospital and had got gossiping.

When he'd applied to work as an ARP warden, he'd explained that the navy didn't want him but he intended to help fight Hitler in any way he could. He'd signed on as a part-timer in case he was lucky enough to expand his dancing classes to evenings as well as afternoons. For the most part he'd been too busy helping other people to talk much about himself.

Hearing Alfie moan that he couldn't keep up with his Phoebe had given Tom an idea: he'd teach more of the so-called modern dances that the younger set liked. To build up his classes he needed to appeal to all ages. 'Jive is European,' he said. 'Swing is Dixieland jazz.'

'How the hell d'you know that?' Alfie grinned at him.

Tom shrugged. 'Jive is faster than swing with more kicks and bounces, and swing is where you turn and twist your partner more.'

'Get away!' said Alfie, eyes wide open, like he didn't want to miss anything. 'You sound like you can do it. Can you?'

Tom started answering hesitantly, but then his passion for dancing took over. 'Do it? I can teach you how to keep Phoebe glued to your side in the Connaught Hall. You two could be the couple on the dance floor everyone else stops to watch!'

Tom saw he had Alfie's rapt attention, the card players' as well.

He gave a small cough, picked up his mug from the arm of the chair and drank the dregs noisily.

''Ere!' called Harry Simms. 'I bet you're that dancing-class geezer what everyone's talking about. Up at Nicholson Hall? My Annie says you're bloody good!'

'Guilty as charged!' said Tom. Actually, he felt proud that he was known and talked about. All those lessons his mum had worked so hard to pay for had borne fruit.

'You playin' cards or what?' Clem Seddons asked Harry Simms.

Tom stared into Alfie's adoring face. 'The classes are restarting soon, now I'm up and about again. Come along with Phoebe, your first class on me,' he said.

'You're on!' said Alfie. Then, 'You finished with that paper? I want to see if there's any more on the bloke they found drowned in the mud round the back here.' He inclined his head supposedly to encompass Forton Creek that dribbled its way from the Gosport ferry and round to the bottom end of Parham Road, near the ARP hut.

'He didn't top himself,' Clem shouted. 'Paper says he died of a head injury. Well, he didn't do that to himself, did he?'

'Jesus!' said Alfie. 'My brother played cards with him down the Four Aces!'

His next words were drowned out as a bicycle was flung against the wooden wall of the hut and the door swept open to admit Bessie, holding in one hand her cycle light, and in the other her first-aid knapsack.

'Evening,' she cried, kicking the door closed behind her. 'Had the phone call yet?'

Tom knew that if a raid was imminent the volunteers were sometimes informed by head office before Moaning Minnie started wailing.

'It's a clear night,' said Bessie, 'and my corns are telling me something's going to happen. We've had it far too easy these past nights.'

As if Bessie had willed it, the phone rang, Clem picked it up.

'Right,' he said. 'Thank you ... Action stations.' He replaced the receiver. On cue Moaning Minnie began her wailing. Early or late, like now, there were no set hours for the planes to arrive.

Tom was outside in moments, just as the bombs started falling.

Chapter Thirty-nine

Bessie and Tom had been sent to patrol the town area. They hurried from the ARP post, checking on the way in to the heart of Gosport that blackout curtains were drawn on all premises, and helping disorganized people towards public shelters. Dodging falling shrapnel, Tom saw the sky was turning orange.

'It's Portsmouth they're trying to hit. Gosport's just in the way,' Bessie said. Already her face beneath her tin helmet was streaked with black smuts. The air about them was thick with the awful stink of burning wood, sulphur and sawdust. When the suspicious ARP team banged on doors, some householders shouted back they had heeded the siren and were going to earth in their own Morrison or Anderson appliances.

It was often necessary to enter partially bombed-out

houses in case rescue teams or ambulances needed to be fetched. That was the worst part, thought Tom. You never knew what you were dealing with or might find.

'It's going to be a long night,' he said to Bessie.

The sky was on fire. Smoke filled his lungs and every so often he heard the peculiar whistle of bombs coming nearer and nearer. Then he would pull Bessie close so they could press themselves tightly against the nearest solid wall until the moment was gone and allowed them to walk on again. Every time they sheltered Tom was frightened the building he was huddled against would crumble and fall on them both.

'It's a really bad night,' Bessie agreed.

Tom's head was filled with the sound of ambulance bells and rattling fire engines. Teams of firemen were trying frantically to direct hose-pipes onto burning buildings. Parts of his life unwound in his head like a reel of film.

Waiting, as a youngster, outside the King's Theatre in Southsea, ever hopeful of being chosen for the chorus line. His mother coming home from skivvying, preparing tea with hands misshapen by harsh soaps and bleaches, yet later pressing money into his palms for dancing lessons. Foxtrotting in the Four Aces wearing his two-tone shoes similar to the ones his idol Ace Gallagher wore. The feel of the fat bodies of the elderly women he'd danced with for money. The intense cold of the loch he'd dived into to rescue his friend. And always the girl in the picture house, her earnest green eyes and the magic that occurred when their fingers had touched.

As Tom and Bessie rounded the corner near Gosport ferry, they saw the fire billowing red and gold, and the black smoke pouring heavenwards from the Four Aces.

'This looks bad!' cried Bessie.

Two fire engines were pumping away at the rear of the building, the trickle of water seeming insubstantial amid the wealth of flames. Tom spotted the W on a hat worn by a fellow ARP volunteer. 'Anyone still in there?' he shouted. In normal circumstances by this hour the club would be closed. Ace, Jerome, the cleaners – they'd be inside, probably.

The volunteer shrugged. 'Dunno, mate,' he said.

The whole of the front of the building had caved inwards. Fingers of blackened wooden beams pointed skywards and dank dark puddles of water lay where the fire engines had previously put out flames. The roof had collapsed and the front door was no more. Inside he could make out the rounded shell of the bar where he had stood waiting for some woman, any woman, ticket in hand, to buy him for a dance.

Tom's torch picked out rubble and broken bottles. The sharp wind off the sea that had probably fanned the flames to burn the front of the club was now the same wind cooling the wet and smouldering embers. Surely no one could have survived in this, he thought.

'Anyone here?' called Bessie. She'd brought spades from the fire engine. Her torch was tucked into her belt. 'There's a cellar, isn't there?'

He'd forgotten the cellar where Ace concealed his black-market spoils. He nodded.

'Let's try shouting and listening,' said Bessie.

'Sounds good,' Tom answered.

'Hello! Anyone here? Hello! Hello!'

Bessie put up her hand to silence Tom and he sank to his knees, listening hard, against the damp rubble that reeked of burnt furnishings and decay.

Tom thought he heard a faint sound. 'Did you hear that?' he asked. He could tell immediately that Bessie had. Her eyes were shining.

'Someone's trapped below,' she said, falling to her knees and hauling broken joists away from where he stood. 'Hang on, we're coming!' she shouted.

Then, with a spade, she began hacking into the muck at Tom's feet. He set about clearing the area, working with her.

339

Every so often the sound of breaking glass and the ground shaking told Tom there was no let-up in the bombing. Occasionally he peered up into the sky at the searchlights wavering, trying to catch the outlines of the German planes. The returning fire from the ack-ack guns resembled fireworks.

The noise was ceaseless.

He stopped heaving lumps of cement and flooring and stood upright to ease his aching back. Some heat still remained in the wood and waste materials he was handling.

'Don't stop! We can save them,' Bessie cried. Tom was now unsure whether he'd ever heard anything. Perhaps he'd imagined the faint cries.

'If there's another direct hit, we won't stand a chance,' he said.

'We can't stop now,' she cried. 'My conscience wouldn't let me.'

It was almost as if the Fates had heard her, Tom thought later.

An enormous flash occurred. Both he and Bessie were flung to the ground.

For a moment Tom was stunned. Bessie screamed.

His mind immediately returned to the figure of the burnt man lying on the playing field. Quickly he blinked away the image and looked about him to see Bessie on her knees with her arms wrapped around her head. Everything about him was shaking. He wondered if this was what it would be like when the end of the world came.

When everything about them stilled, he saw her hold on to a door propped against the remains of one of Ace's wrought-iron tables and begin slowly to heave herself upright. 'C'mon,' she said. 'Get digging!'

On his feet once more Tom bent and began clearing lumps of parquet flooring and masonry. Then his knuckles hit what he realized was a heavy circular glass table top. He wiped his hand across its surface, amazed it hadn't shattered.

'Oh!' His fingers had grazed against something soft, hairy, protruding from it.

In the dull light, even using his torch, it was difficult to see clearly. He put out his hand again. His fingers sensed warmth through the hair.

He was certain the heavy glass from the ornamental table was weighing down whatever was trapped beneath. But now the thing was moving. A sort of twisting action was taking place under the glass. Tom took a deep breath, put a hand both sides of the table-top and grunted as he swung it sideways.

'Miaow!'

'Arghh!' Tom cried.

There was never going to be a way he could have prepared himself for the leaping, snarling object that at last, unhindered by the round of glass that had kept it pinned beneath the rubble, hurled itself sideways and, like a bullet, shot across what was once the bar and dance hall, and out into the night.

'That was Jerome's cat!' Tom shouted

His heart was banging a tattoo against his ribs and he was breathing heavily. He put his hands to his head, rocking backwards and forwards on his heels to allow his body and brain to come to terms with what had just happened.

Just when he thought he had got himself under control he heard the sound of suppressed giggling. Bessie was standing behind him. She had her hand against her mouth trying to conceal her laughter.

'I suppose you think that's bloody funny!' Tom wasn't over the shock.

He was unsure whether he felt anger at her laughing at him or relief that it had simply been Jerome's black and white pet cat that had scared him.

'Well, yes!' Bessie said. She was trying to keep a straight face and finding it hard to keep from bursting into laughter again. Then Tom, too, saw the funny side and joined in.

'Sssh!' Bessie grabbed his arm. 'There is someone down there!'

The cry was weak but unmistakable. 'Help!'

'Hold on! We'll get you out!' Tom shouted back, unsure whether he could be heard or not. Uncertain, too, whether he could actually reach them.

Again, he and Bessie battled against the rubble and bits of broken furniture that somehow had fallen beneath the surface of the floor. Tom pulled out a galvanized bucket and tossed it, clanging and clattering, across the surroundings.

It seemed to him that no sooner had he cleared a decent hole than immediately little items of rubbish fell into the space he had made.

Tins, jars, some intact, some broken, were now in his way. He saw it was food, a hoard of rations. Burst bags of flour, sugar . . .

'The cellar roof must have caved in,' Tom said. 'I'm going to see if I can clear away enough stuff to get down inside.' Already he was wriggling, wormlike, into the hole he had made.

'Don't be silly!' Bessie cried. 'Leave it to the rescue team.'

She sounded angry, and for one terrified moment he thought she might pull on his legs to stop him exploring further. If she did, there was every possibility the hole could collapse inwards and he'd be swallowed like the poor devil, whoever it was, below him.

'I can't wait for them,' he shouted. 'Someone could be badly hurt down here.' Bessie was the senior volunteer; but he knew she wouldn't argue with him.

Instead he heard her say, 'Have it your own way, then. But I don't want to lose you. I'm getting help.'

Heedless of the culinary treasure he was moving aside as he burrowed, and trying to ignore the dirt getting up his nose and clinging to his eyelashes, his heart rejoiced when he felt a draught of cool air on his face.

Tom called, 'Anyone there?'

He was rewarded by a weary 'Thank God!'

He recognized the voice immediately. 'Jerome?' Tom said a silent prayer that at last he had almost reached him. He still couldn't see light but the air was sweeter now.

'Jerome, can you help me get down to you?'

'Sorry, mate! You're too far above me. But if you keep on coming, I can help once you're clear.' Clear of what? Tom wondered.

Jerome must have caught in his throat some of the dust that was probably swirling below for he began to cough. Tom thought it sounded like a death rattle and hoped the old man wasn't going to die on him before he'd got down into the cellar, assuming he was able to, that was.

He was breathing better now. More air was filling his lungs. Stale it might be but it gave him the added strength to push away crushed packets of slick softness that slid beneath his fingernails and oiled his hands.

And then Jerome's familiar face was looking up at him. The old feller was standing, but only just, holding onto a wooden crate. His spectacles were dirty and crooked across his tired eyes. Tom saw one of the arms was broken.

'The lad's dead,' Jerome said. His voice, too, was broken.

Tom stared at him. He had no idea who 'the lad' was, but he could see the intense grief on Jerome's features. Down below, the head and upper body of a still form lying near another crate was covered with a sack.

'I'm sorry,' murmured Tom, because that was what Jerome surely expected.

The old man nodded. Then he let go of the wooden case and staggered beneath Tom, where he was suspended, head down, above broken shelving. He held up his arms and said, 'Let yourself drop and slide against me. It'll soften the fall.'

Tom hesitated. Jerome looked as if anything heavy falling against him would break his body. But he could either do as Jerome suggested or wait until help arrived, which could take for ever. If he could make it into the cellar in one piece, perhaps other people were in need of help.

He wriggled his arms free and, with a diver's stance, lurched forward.

As soon as his body touched Jerome's, they crumpled to the floor of the cellar.

'Shit!' The word flew from Tom's mouth. He lay for a moment on the cold stone, feeling his muscles and arms return to normality after his mammoth belly crawl. He realized Jerome was lying partly beneath him.

Jerome's voice filled the air. 'For a dancer, you're bloody heavy!'

Tom rolled away. His face was now inches from the old man's. He grinned. 'You all right?'

Jerome tried to smile. 'Just winded,' he said. Then he asked, 'You find my cat up there?'

'The bloody thing frightened the life out of me! Flew like the wind, it did.'

'Alive, then?'

'Course. Got nine lives, cats.'

Jerome said, 'More'n the lad had.' Sadness had returned to his voice.

Tom scrambled to his feet. He helped Jerome up, and again the packing case became Jerome's support.

'Ace is over there,' Jerome said. 'He's alive, just. And delirious.'

Tom reached for his torch, surprised it was still lodged in his belt. For the first time since landing in the cellar he was able to take in his surroundings. He knew Gosport was an ancient sea port, once home to smugglers and press gangs. The club had been built above a rat-run of tunnels, some of which Ace used as storage areas. The incessant bombing must have caused the tunnels to collapse. He and Jerome were enclosed in a small space filled with shelving and packing cases, but as his eyes strained to look for exits, he could see both ends of the cellar were filled with masonry, wood and detritus. Impossible for an old man to clear alone. Except he wasn't alone: he was sharing the space with a corpse and a man who was still alive but likely almost in a similar state.

Tom crawled over to the body. With trepidation he pulled back the sacking covering the upper part. He didn't know what he expected to find but it certainly wasn't this beautiful boy with hair the same startling colour as Ace's.

'Is he . . .'

'Ace's son? Yes,' Jerome said.

Tom felt for a pulse at the lad's neck. Already he knew he was dead – his body was too cold to be otherwise – but he needed to make sure. He looked across at Jerome and could make out the sheen of tears in his eyes.

'He took a knock on his head,' Jerome said. 'Not a mark to show for it.'

Tom knew nothing he could say would ease the man's pain.

His thoughts were cut short by the muffled wail of the siren announcing the all-clear. That, at least, was a blessing.

Without rising, he crawled to the second body lying on the stone floor.

Tom knelt beside Ace. His face was dirty but unmarked, his lower body hidden beneath what at first Tom thought was a wooden pallet but soon realized were oak girders, probably used to support the cellar's roof. A space had been cleared about him, no doubt by Jerome, to make him more comfortable. The extra dark patches soaked in the unmovable wood were Ace's blood.

'I couldn't drag him out,' Jerome said.

Tom heard the quiver in his voice. The old man was again near to tears. 'You did what you could and help will be here soon.' Tom was trying to keep Jerome's spirits up. There was no way he could lift, or should try to remove, the weight from Ace's lower body. He felt for Ace's pulse. It was steady. He looked peaceful, as if he was sleeping. With luck he'd live, Tom thought.

'Anyone else in the club?' he asked.

'No, just us, drinking and talking,' said Jerome. 'We came down here as soon as it got bad.'

Ace's voice startled him. 'You remember what that was like, don't you, Tommo?'

Tom's eyes flew back to Ace's face. The steel grey eyes were open and staring at him.

'How're you feeling, mate?' Tom managed, stifling his astonishment that Ace had spoken.

'Like shit!'

Tom smoothed back a lock of chestnut hair that had fallen across the club owner's forehead. 'Soon get you out of here,' he said.

'Can't see why you should. I've been a bugger to you . . .' His words faded and his eyes closed again.

Once again Tom felt his pulse. It still throbbed. 'Thank God,' he said.

Thoughts ran through his head. All this time he'd believed he hated Ace Gallagher for the way he had treated him. This broken man lying in front of him, with his dead son nearby, had practically ruined his life. Ace had lied to him, cheated him.

Then he thought of Alan Crosby, his friend who had saved his life and, in the process, had cut short his own. He realized how fortunate he was to be having a second chance at a life that was good, wholesome, and had no place in it for hate. He thought of Bessie, of listening to her chattering on about her family. Of Shirley, thumping away at the piano in Nicholson Hall. Her hat, which she refused to remove, and its ridiculous feather, bobbing around to the music. He thought of the dancing that he loved teaching, the steps he enjoyed sharing with his pupils. No, there was no room for hate in his life.

Not at all.

Tom got up and moved nearer to Jerome. He didn't say anything but he looked at the old man still holding on to the crate for support. He looked down at Jerome's crooked fingers, his blue-veined skin, then covered Jerome's hand with his own, willing warmth and hope into him.

Tom heard movements above. A man's voice called: 'Are you down there? Clear away from the hole. We're going to get you out.'

Tom mentally blessed the rescue team, and Bessie.

Jerome looked at him. 'Thanks, son,' he said.

Chapter Forty

'Aren't you happier now you know Gilbert Willard didn't do himself in?'

Connie stopped walking and faced Queenie. 'I'm not pleased he's dead. I hope they catch whoever did it as soon as possible. But if you mean, am I satisfied no one from the picture house is under suspicion, then, yes.'

Queenie, wearing a grey dress with shoulder pads and a belt that managed to make her tiny waist look even smaller, grinned at her. As usual she was drenched in Californian Poppy. The fragrance of the perfume, along with the sunshine, made Connie feel exceptionally happy. She put her arm through Queenie's and they carried on walking up Stoke Road towards the Nicholson Hall.

'I have absolutely no idea why I'm going dancing in the afternoon when I have to be at work early this evening,'

Connie said. She was aware she looked quite drab com-
pared to her friend, although she'd put on her dark green
button-through knee-length dress, its sleeves ending at her
elbows, its colour, Gertie said, matching her eyes. She'd worn
her black court shoes because they were comfortable. She
would be wearing them to work later.

'You're going to learn how to dance. It's a different thing
altogether. You don't want to go through life sitting out
every dance the orchestra plays just because the only one
you can do is the waltz, do you?'

'No, Queenie,' she said dutifully.

An arrow pierced her heart, remembering that long-ago
day at Southsea fairground and after, at the hotel ballroom
where Ace had taught her to waltz. She could hear his voice
inside her head now, counting the box steps, one, two, three.
Connie shook away those thoughts.

As if reading her mind, Queenie asked, 'Will you visit
Ace in hospital?'

'I don't think so,' said Connie, 'though I hear he's recov-
ering. Me and him are old news now. No doubt Marlene'll
be going into the War Memorial Hospital every day . . .'

'Always with an eye on the main chance, that girl. She
was so lucky she wasn't working at the club that night,
wasn't she?'

Connie shrugged. 'She kept her life but lost her job.'

'And you, soft as butter, take her on at the Criterion!'

Connie laughed, 'I had to, didn't I? She's Gertie's daughter, and if it wasn't for Gertie I'd never have started working at the picture house in the first place.'

'More fool you for taking the minx on!'

'Gertie's keeping an eye on her as a cleaner.'

'She'd be propositioning all the male patrons if you'd given her an usherette's job.'

'Oh, Queenie, she's not as bad as that.'

'She is! But, then, you refuse to see the real harm in anyone. Anyway, have you chosen a new head usherette, yet?'

Connie grinned at her. 'Sara Cantrell.'

'Oh, well done! She's been working at the picture house for a long time and deserves it. If you remember, she used to take over from me selling ice creams. One thing I'll never miss is standing beneath that spotlight.' Queenie squeezed Connie's arm, 'I'm really proud of you, you know,' she said.

Connie stared at her. 'Proud of me, why?'

'You've come a long way since you first started working at the Criterion. I never thought we'd ever see a woman manager. I mean, I know the last couple of men haven't been up to much and times are changing, with women taking on more responsibilities, but, Connie, I'm just so proud of you.'

'Stop embarrassing me,' she said. But Queenie's words had made her feel all warm inside. 'I'm going to make a few changes,' she said.

Queenie frowned, 'Such as?'

'Introduce a Saturday morning programme for the children. It'll bring in more money, and extra wages for the usherettes and cleaners.'

'What films can you show the little horrors? You can hardly put on *Gone With the Wind*.'

'I'll have a talk with your Len about suitable pictures but kids love cowboy films, and Randolph Scott has made loads. So have Roy Rogers and the first singing cowboy, Gene Autry.'

'What about Tom Mix?' suggested Queenie.

'Most of his films were silent. Only eight or nine were talkies,' said Connie. 'I think the kids would prefer westerns with dialogue,' she said. 'Oh, and the serial, *Flash Gordon*, with Buster Crabbe in it. Of course, I'll only be able to show U category films, suitable for children.'

Queenie was laughing.

'What's the matter with you?' Connie asked.

'It's you and your blinkin' knowledge of films,' answered Queenie.

'Never mind about my research on suitable pictures for

under-twelves. One thing I know absolutely nothing about is these blinking dance classes. Who's running them?'

'I don't know his name, but apparently he's brilliant. Got loads of classes starting up again after him being in hospital. He got caught in a bomb blast, apparently. When I phoned up, I spoke to a very nice woman called Shirley, who plays the piano for him, so she said.'

'If I don't like it, I'm not staying,' moaned Connie.

'Don't be such a misery!' Queenie pulled Connie to a halt opposite the White Hart pub. 'Anyway, we're here now.'

Connie looked across the road at the Nicholson Hall. Men and women were entering the side door, some young, some elderly.

'I'm really not sure about this . . .' But Connie allowed Queenie to push her in the direction of the open door.

'Don't you want to learn how to do jive dancing and the swing? Dancing like that's all the rage now.'

'What?' Connie said. 'I can barely do the waltz!'

'That Shirley said he's going to start with the waltz then work up to the harder dances . . .'

Connie found herself being propelled by Queenie through the doorway, where Queenie spoke briefly to a large woman wearing a ridiculous hat, then led her into a light and airy hall with chairs set around three walls. There was a stage, with a microphone in the centre and a piano at the side.

'So, this is where the magic happens, is it?' Connie settled herself on a chair directly in front of the stage. At the piano she could see the back of a tall, slim, fair-haired man who was flicking through sheet music. He seemed to be putting the pages in some sort of order. Connie thought, from the back, he reminded her of someone, but before she'd had time to think about that, he'd exited at the side of the stage, through a curtain.

'Do you think that's the bloke who's going to teach us?' Connie asked.

'I don't know, do I?' Queenie retorted. 'Who d'you think I am? The bleedin' Oracle?'

Connie scowled at her, then surveyed the large area of floor in front of her. It was polished parquet, a good dance surface, she supposed. She watched as the big woman she'd seen talking to Queenie swept in, smiled at everyone, then took her place at the piano. As she sat down on the stool, the large feather in her hat wobbled precariously. Connie was fascinated. So fascinated she hardly bothered to watch as the man returned from the far side of the stage and stood in front of the microphone.

'Welcome, everyone,' he said. 'I'm your dance tutor, Tom

Smith, and I hope you're going to enjoy my . . .' His eyes were roving around the seated people, and when they rested on Connie, he faltered. He stared at her, he smiled, and then, as if suddenly remembering he was supposed to be introducing himself to the class, he carried on speaking with only a hint of unsteadiness in his voice.

'It's him!' whispered Queenie, digging her elbow into Connie's side. 'The bloke who came looking for you in the picture house – the one you danced with at my wedding reception in the Swan!'

Connie was hardly aware of her friend's voice. She was too busy remembering that when he had touched her all that time ago she had felt drawn to him, like a moth to a flame. And now she watched him as he spoke to his audience. His confidence, his ability to make them smile, was evident.

She wondered what it would be like to run her fingers through that glorious blond hair, to draw them across the bare skin of his broad shoulders . . .

And then he was asking a question. 'I need a partner for a waltz. Who will accompany me?'

'Put your bleedin' hand up, Connie!' hissed Queenie, yanking her arm above her head.

And then she saw he was walking across the parquet

flooring towards her and asking, 'Please may I have the pleasure of this dance, Connie Baxter?'

Shirley at the piano was playing the introduction to 'I'll Be Seeing You'.

He hadn't waited for her answer, but as his hand touched hers to help her from the chair, she felt again the surge of electricity she'd remembered so well.

His lips brushed the side of her hair and Tom whispered, 'It's Fate, and I'm not letting you disappear this time, Connie.'

'Maybe I don't want to,' she said, breathing in his fresh sandalwood cologne. And all the while she was thinking, Life's not a bit like the pictures at all. Sometimes, it's even better!

Acknowledgements

Thank you, Juliet Burton. Thank you, as always, Jane Wood. Thank you, brilliant Florence Hare. Thank you, best copy-editor Hazel Orme. Thank you to my publicist Katya Ellis. I am indebted to all at Quercus who work so tirelessly for me. Thank you, dear readers, for your loyalty. I owe you so much.